BLUE STREETLIGHTS

BLUE STREETLIGHTS

An Edge of September Novel

Annie Jakes

For the girls—all of them.

CHAPTER 1

The closet reeked of booze, sweat, and Doritos. Fallon sniffed a fistful of her long, black hair and gagged.

Okay, so, not the closet.

Surrounded by darkness, she took a swig from the bottle in her hand and pressed her ear to the door. Music broke through the barrier along with dozens of voices, but the voice that had sent her barreling into the hallway closet at least half an hour ago had finally moved on.

That was the problem with these after-parties. It was always the same people: members of the band—her own and other's—groupies, friends of friends, and so on. And for some stupid reason, a lot of them interpreted a meaningless one-time makeout as making some kind of commitment.

Fallon's skin prickled as sweat slid down her back. She leaned into the door, and the cheap wood cooled her face. It had to be nearly three in the morning. Maybe she'd call an Uber instead of crashing here. As many nights as she'd spent on Calvin and Keith's couch, her own bed called to her tonight.

The handle jiggled above her head as the door opened, and Fallon spilled into the hallway. Calvin grinned down at her.

"Are you drunk?"

Fallon tried to bite his ankle, but he was too fast.

"You should've knocked." She flopped an arm across her face to block the harsh light.

"Who are you avoiding this time?"

"Don't know his name. Black hair. Tattoos."

"Let me guess. Is he closed-off and mysterious, too?" Calvin chuckled. "You're becoming predictable."

Fallon stuck her tongue out at the insult. She'd die before she let herself become predictable. Literally.

"If you're talking about Trevor, he left about ten minutes ago." Calvin gripped Fallon's hand and pulled her to sitting.

She took another drink of the now lukewarm liquid and regretted not snagging a fresh drink before slipping into the coat closet.

"You know"—Calvin slid down the wall and landed on the floor beside her—"you could just stop hooking up with randoms at parties. Then you wouldn't have to avoid them later."

"There are worse things than avoiding randoms at parties." She rested her head on his shoulder.

"Like what?"

"None of your business, empollón."

His bony shoulder shook with his laugh.

"I've known you for almost a year. You don't think I know when you're insulting me, even in Spanish? It's most of what comes out of your mouth when you're talking to Elliott."

"Because most of the time Elliott deserves it." Fallon shifted on the scratchy carpet. Her spandex shorts were perfect for fighting the heat and staying out of the way while she was drumming, but she'd kill for some baggy sweatpants now. "Where *is* Elliott? He usually stops by these things."

"Don't know. I think he was meeting up with someone tonight."

Probably some girl half his age. Their manager may have been good at his job, but he wasn't particularly pincerpled.

Prisnipled?

Prinpinseld?

Maybe she *was* a little tipsy. Fallon handed the remainder of her beer to Calvin who set it on the floor beside him.

He lowered his voice. "You ever heard of Robert Harrison?"

Her breath hitched.

"The booking manager for Twisted Fest? That's who Elliott was meeting?" There was only one reason a band manager would meet with the booking manager for the biggest battle of the bands festival of the summer. Adrenaline bolted through Fallon's veins. Playing Twisted Fest would mean Edge of September would play for thousands of people, including agents and producers.

If they landed a record deal, she could stay in California.

She shoved the thought away. That was tomorrow's problem.

"That's what Keith heard," Calvin answered. "Elliott is going to stop by practice tomorrow and fill us in."

Fallon considered texting Elliott right then and demanding answers but thought better of it. She could wait and catch up tomorrow with the boys. Instead, she removed her phone from its home in her left boot and scanned through her apps.

"Your couch isn't going to cut it tonight. I'm ordering a ride." She stood with some help from the dull green wall and was relieved to find the hallway wasn't spinning.

"You sure? You can have my room." Calvin reached a hand up, and Fallon yanked him from the floor. "Keith's family is having their annual Memorial Day brunch in the morning. You could come with. They have these crepe things that are unreal."

She shot him a look.

"You know my answer to that. I'll see you both at practice after."

Calvin shrugged, but his eyes were always too revealing. She'd hurt him. Her chest tightened. *He* was the one who'd asked her to do something he knew she would never do. How had she become the villain here?

It's better this way, she reminded herself again.

"It's not personal, Cal."

He scoffed. "To you, nothing is." He picked up her bottle from where he'd left it on the carpet. "You can't Uber alone. It's the middle of the night, and you've been drinking."

Fallon's neck heated. She'd only had two or three beers—plenty sober to get home.

"I can take care of myself."

"I'm finding you a ride."

"Oh, are you my father now? Someone may want to let Manuel Rivera know." She padded down the hall and into the small kitchen, Calvin at her heels.

The outdated kitchen was narrow, yet somehow cooler than the hall had been and nearly empty aside from a guy on the other end, washing his hands in the sink. What weirdo washed their hands at a party?

Ignoring him, Fallon stole a bottle of water from the fridge and downed half of it before Calvin caught up to her.

"Your father would agree with me. You need a ride."

"Someone needs a ride?" A smooth, British accent danced across the room. The guy from the sink approached them, drying his hands on a towel. "I was just leaving. I'd be happy to offer a lift."

Fallon's mouth went dry as she took in the guy before her. He had more than a few inches on her, as most people did since she was barely over five feet, and his messy, blonde hair added to that. Tan skin, though lighter than her natural bronze. Probably a surfer. His chiseled jaw was distracting, as was the rest of his well-toned self. Even in a hoodie and jeans, it was clear he worked out. But Fallon couldn't pull her eyes from his face. His mocha eyes glowed as he smiled at her—a magnetic smile that radiated kindness and authenticity. If the guy she'd been avoiding in the closet was her type, this guy was the very definition of her nightmare.

Good looks and sincerity were a terrifying combination.

"Fallon does." Calvin gestured to her. "She's only a few blocks away."

"You won't let me take an Uber, but you'll send me home with this stranger?" Fallon folded her arms across the flushed skin of her exposed stomach.

"How did you hear about this party?" Calvin asked him.

"My mate, Fitz Rayner, told me about it." He set the towel on the counter.

Fallon stiffened. She hadn't spoken to Fitz in over six months, since the night they'd called things off.

Well, the night *he'd* called things off.

Her blood heated, and she wondered how the kitchen had felt cooler only moments before. Surfer boy certainly wasn't helping.

"See?" Calvin clapped a hand on her shoulder. "He's not a stranger. He's Fitz's buddy."

"What if he's drunk? You'd be sending me to my death." Fallon was grasping at straws now, but there was no way she'd survive the five-minute ride home with this guy. He was gorgeous—and she knew just what to do with gorgeous men—but his very essence screamed "friendly conversation." Not her thing.

"I don't drink." Surfer Boy pulled a nearly empty water bottle from his back pocket as proof.

Calvin pegged her with a big, fat I-told-you-so look,

and that was that.

"Noah." Her ride stretched out a hand, and she sighed in defeat.

"Fallon." She shook his hand quickly, ignoring the buzzing across her skin.

She led the way from the kitchen and out the front door. She'd blown off saying goodbye to both Calvin and Keith, but Keith would be too wasted to remember and Calvin had pissed her off.

She was halfway down the steps of their condo when she realized she didn't know which car was Noah's. Dozens of cars lined the street on both sides. Noah passed her on the step and pointed to a small SUV parked a few houses down.

"Black Mazda's mine." He clicked his keys, and the headlights flashed.

A chilled ocean breeze met Fallon before she opened the door, and again she wished she had something to wear besides her drumming getup.

She slid into the sleek, leather passenger seat and scanned the car for red flags. Noah may have been a friend of Fitz's, but she was always careful. It was the real reason she'd conceded to riding with him. She knew Calvin was right about her taking an Uber alone at three in the morning in LA, even if she'd never admit it.

The car was spotless, no trash of any kind on the floor or seats. The dash looked freshly cleaned, and even the cup holders were free of crumbs and soda cans. Noah was either a serial killer or the cleanest guy she'd ever met.

As he buckled up, she turned to survey the backseat and froze when she spotted a car seat directly behind her.

This wasn't a baby seat. It was a booster, like a little kid would sit in. Noah couldn't be much older than her—twenty, maybe twenty-one at most. If he had a child this old, he would've still been in high school when they'd been born.

"You have a kid?" Fallon had never been one for subtlety.

Noah chuckled and drove away from the curb.

"I have a little sister. She's four. Sometimes she needs lifts, much like yourself." He winked in her direction.

Fallon shifted against the cold leather at her back.

"Well, thanks for letting me sit up front." She pointed to the right as they approached the end of the street, and Noah smoothly rounded the corner.

Ignoring the magnetic pull coming from Noah's side of the car, she crossed her arms and faced the window, hoping he would get the hint that the conversation could end there.

"Fallon, right?"

She grunted a response and pointed the next direction.

"Fun party tonight. Calvin seems like a good guy."

"He is." She meant it. She was lucky to have him and Keith as bandmates, even if she'd never let them get close enough to consider them friends.

She rubbed her arms, wishing away her goosebumps.

"You two are in the band together? With Keith?"

Fallon nodded.

"And you're friends with Fitz?"

"Something like that." Another shiver snaked through her.

"Strange we've never run into each other before now, innit? Must run in different circles." Noah glanced at her as they stopped at a red light. "Blast, Fallon, you're freezing." He stretched his arms above his head, hitting them against the roof of the car, and awkwardly removed his hoodie. "Here. This should help."

He pushed the hoodie toward her. She nearly turned it down, but something about the genuine concern in his face stopped her. She accepted it with a nod and pulled it over her sports bra. The plush material, still warm from Noah's body heat, immediately cured her chills.

She tried not to notice how nice it smelled—sweet, like vanilla or maybe caramel. Dumb, good-smelling boys.

Fallon leaned deeper into her seat as Noah adjusted the AC. His jaw alone could knock a girl out. He had high cheek bones and deep-set eyes. With his hoodie off, she could now see she'd been right about him being fit. He wasn't especially broad, but his back muscles were visible beneath his T-shirt. The veins in his forearms shifted as he returned his hands to the steering wheel, safely stationed at nine and three.

Something about a guy's forearms had always made her a little stupid.

"What? Did I go the wrong way?" He caught her staring and smiled in her direction again. It was a nice smile, even if it was too sincere.

"I was looking at your shirt. You listen to The Wonder Years?" She would've noticed the T-shirt immediately had she not been ogling the guy wearing it.

"They're one of my favorite bands. Soupy's voice is majestic. You should listen to his Aaron West and the Roaring Twenties stuff." Noah's eyes never left the road, but his entire face lit up.

An unwelcome flutter breezed through Fallon's stomach.

How was she into this guy? There was nothing dark or rebellious about him. In fact, he was everything she avoided—open, friendly, innocent. She was guessing on that last one, but she'd bet money Noah hadn't made a questionable decision in his life.

Calvin's words still stung from earlier. She might have a type, but she was anything but predictable. Why couldn't she have a little fun with Noah? Who said she couldn't reach outside her usual fling? Calvin?

Screw that.

"It's got more of an indie vibe than The Wonder Years," Noah continued, "but the vocals are worth it." He slid into an open spot a few yards from her complex. It was the best parking they would find in Glendale.

"You'll have to show me sometime." She smiled at him, letting a touch of mischief shine through to see what he'd do with it.

He met her eyes, and despite his ever-present smile, the intensity of his gaze shook her. Breathing was a memory, along with all coherent thoughts.

This boy was a whole different kind of trouble.

"I'd love to." His voice was low and rough. He held her stare for a lifetime before clearing his throat and glancing around the street, successfully bringing Fallon back to her senses.

"This is a nice flat. How long have you lived here?"

"Since I moved to LA."

Noah likely wanted more, but as far as Fallon was concerned, this conversation was crossing into personal. And she was still recovering from whatever had just happened between them.

"I'll walk you to your door." He cut the engine and popped the locks.

They wandered to the building entrance, and Fallon punched in the access code. The door beeped open, and Noah followed her through the lobby and into the elevator. Her fingers, mostly covered by the hoodie sleeves, tingled as she pressed the glowing "3" button, and her heart thudded in her chest.

Why did this feel like a date and not a potential makeout?

They emerged on the top floor and made their way down the hall to her studio apartment. Fallon reached for the key hiding in her boot and spun it between her fingers.

"Thank you for the ride. And your hoodie." She lifted a drawstring and ran it along her bottom lip.

"Glad I could help." Noah smiled again, but it was

different this time. Still honest but reserved.

He was *nervous.*

She could help with that.

She removed his hoodie, letting her hair cascade around her shoulders and praying it didn't smell as terrible as it had earlier. She handed the bundle of fabric back to Noah, who took it stiffly.

"I should be going." He paused. "It was a pleasure to meet you, Fallon."

Before she could change her mind, she closed her eyes, rose up onto her toes, and pushed her lips toward Noah's.

Only it wasn't the feel of his lips against hers that came next but the touch of his hands grasping her shoulders firmly but gently. Her eyes shot open to find Noah staring at her, eyes wide and head tilted back.

Her stomach dropped, and she stepped backward into her door. His hands fell away as she moved out of reach.

"Fallon, I—"

"Don't." She fumbled with her key.

"Please—" He reached toward her.

"Thanks for the ride." Her key found the lock, and she slipped through her door, closing it firmly behind her.

This was why she had a type. Guys who wanted her for nothing more than a good time weren't a threat. No personal connection. No attachment.

Nice boys were dangerous.

Fallon stumbled to her closet, ripped her gloves off their hook, and strapped them on. A few hours of kickboxing and she'd completely forget about the boy she'd left standing in the hallway.

Then she'd never think about Noah again.

CHAPTER 2

The buzzing wouldn't stop. Fallon reached blindly for a pillow and flung it at her boots laying discarded by her bathroom door.

The buzzing continued.

Groaning, she ripped her quilt off her body and lumbered across the apartment with one eye closed.

Her muscles were screaming. A full round of kickboxing had done them in, and now they were seizing from her movement. She gingerly picked up her boot from where she'd kicked it off, tipped it upside down, and let her phone clatter to the floor, still buzzing loudly.

She flipped it over and silenced the alarm she'd forgotten she'd set the night before. When she'd finally crashed long after four, she'd figured she'd never wake up in time for her weekly video call with her parents. She'd been right.

She rubbed her dry, itchy eyes and headed to the fridge for a bottle of water. Her muscles were already loosening—one of the benefits of being nineteen—but she'd be a little sore for most of the day.

She took another gulp of water, this time to wash down the ibuprofen she'd found in the cupboard.

She crossed the cool, checkerboard tile to the full-length mirror by her bed.

Shit.

Her call was in thirty minutes, and she looked like hell. Her ratted hair hung limply down her back. Her makeup, extra heavy from last night's gig, was smeared across her face, and her clothes, the same shorts and bra from the night before, smelled as bad as she looked: sweat, booze, and a hint of cologne from the hoodie she'd borrowed.

She'd managed to remove Surfer Boy from her memory for the most part. After all, he was no one to her, just some guy she'd used for a ride home. But something about him still nagged at her like a song she couldn't get out of her head.

At least she could feel confident they'd never see each other again. If they'd run in different circles this long, last night was a fluke. Nothing more.

Regardless, her parents couldn't see her like this. Manuel and Lisa Rivera were not the kind of parents who would approve of Fallon's vices, many of which she'd indulged in last night.

She made her way to the bathroom. A string of profanity cursing her aches and pains escaped her lips as she quickly showered and dressed in an oversized black T-shirt and neon pink leggings, knit socks pulled over the cuffs. She didn't wear much makeup outside of shows, but she threw on a blast of mascara and tinted lip balm.

When the clock struck noon, her clean hair was still wet but combed and trailing down her back. She retrieved her laptop and climbed onto her bed, sinking into her rich purple quilt. A pop-up announced a call. She took one last sip of water to calm her racing heart and answered.

Her parents' smiles appeared on the screen, but instead of the warmth she assumed most people would feel, apprehension coursed through her.

"Oh, my baby! Look how beautiful you are! You are more grown up every time I see you!" her mom gushed.

"Estas bella, mamá. Like always."

Lisa Rivera brushed off the compliment, but it was genuine. Her mom was a knockout.

As Fallon took in the image of her parents looking back at her, she thought—not for the first time—how much she somehow looked like both of them. She'd gotten her mother's almond eyes and petite frame, but her father's coloring. Her plump lips and dark hair were courtesy of the Rivera blood as well, but her mother's family, the Johnsons, had passed on their slim, pert nose.

"How was church?" Her weekly call with her parents was strategically scheduled for right after their services. Her father said that way they could speak with the Lord and then speak with their angel.

"Oh, Reinita, you would have loved it. The music today was some of the best I've ever heard it. Magnífica." Her father beamed at her, and Fallon swallowed the lump in her throat. Although her father's accent from his childhood in Mexico was watered down, his pet name for her, given by her Abuela Rivera before she died, still managed to twist her heart and make her question her choice to move so far away from her childhood home in Arizona.

"I wish I could have heard it."

Her parents beamed.

"How are things going with the band?" Her mother asked.

"We had a show last night."

"Somewhere safe, I hope." Her brows scrunched.

"Yes, mamá."

"Stay away from clubs. And bars."

"Of course." It had definitely been in a club.

"And don't stay out past midnight."

"Never." Always.

Fallon didn't especially love lying to her parents, but the truth was not an option. If they knew half the truth about her real life in California, they'd pull her out of LA faster than Keith could do a shot. And without their money, she would be on a one-way flight back to Arizona. She should have known better than to bring up the show in the first place.

"How are Calvin and Keith?" her father asked.

"Great. They say hi." Another bold faced lie, but she had to give them something.

"Tell them hi back!" Her mother's smile formed little creases at the corners of her eyes.

Fallon shivered, and her chest tightened further.

They worked through all the normal topics: her

father's work as a lawyer, her mother's quilting, the heat in Arizona, Fallon's disappointing lack of visits.

"We can do something special for Annora's birthday this fall." Her father smiled sadly. "We can go visit—"

"Things with the band are up in the air right now. I don't know that I'll be available that weekend." She'd make sure she wasn't.

Manuel sighed heavily before he spoke again.

"Reinita, we've been patient and supportive." He glanced at his wife who was staring into her lap. His eyes returned to Fallon. "But you know what today is. It's time to come home."

Fear flooded her body, and she pushed it away. She'd hoped they'd forgotten today was the day she'd been dreading since she'd moved to LA. She should have known better. It was probably circled in thick red marker on the calendar her mother kept above the desk at her real estate office.

"I know it's been a year, but I just need a few more months." She swallowed hard, forcing her voice to steady.

"The deal was one year—one year we would pay your way in Los Angeles. If the band wasn't supporting you by then, you promised to come home and go to school. This is not up for discussion. Your lease is up at the end of the week, and we are not renewing it."

"But—"

"I'm sorry, Reinita," Manuel cut her off. "Movers will be there first thing on Friday. Your flight leaves that afternoon."

Fallon's breath caught, and her veins completely iced over.

Movers were coming. Her ticket was purchased. It was done. Nothing she said was going to make a difference.

She'd known today marked the anniversary of her moving to LA. She'd left Arizona the week after graduation, and her parents had given her one year to make it as a drummer on their dollar. They'd paid for everything—her rent, her food, her clothes. She'd known she was out of time, but she'd also thought she'd be able to weasel a few more months out of them. Maybe another year.

They hadn't even given her the chance.

A calm settled through her body. She'd never let anyone make her decisions for her, even her parents. She may not know how she would stay in California, but she did know one thing.

All the shadows of her past—the pain, the shock, the grief—were waiting for her in Arizona, and there was no way in hell she was going back.

Twisted Fest. Calvin had told her Elliott had been talking with the booking manager of Twisted Fest last night. An idea weaved through her mind. It was risky, but it was something.

"Cancel it." Fallon lifted her chin and clenched her fists, pretending to have authority she knew didn't exist. "Cancel the flight. The movers."

"This isn't up for discussion—"

"Edge might be playing a huge festival this summer. We'll find out today if we got a spot. If we win, the prize money would be enough that I could stay out here." They didn't cut her off, so she pushed forward. "New deal. I stay in LA until after the festival. If we win, I stay for good."

"And if you don't?" Manuel countered.

"Then I come home. The festival is the first weekend in August. I'd be home in time for the start of the semester."

"Sounds like you just pushed back your deadline." He raised his brows. "What's in it for us?"

Ladies and gentlemen, her father—the lawyer.

She should have guessed there'd be a price. She had very little to bargain with, but there was one thing she knew her parents wanted more than anything, possibly more than her moving home. That she was even considering it would show how desperate she was. She'd have nothing left to gamble with, but if there was ever a time to go all in, this was it.

"If you pay for the summer," she blew out a breath, "then I'll go with you to visit Annora." Nausea that had nothing to do with her drinking the night before flooded her stomach. She breathed deeply and tried not to hurl.

Her parents exchanged glances again. So much communication between married couples was unspoken. She swore her parents could have entire conversations without a single word.

"Win or lose?" her father asked.

She nodded, unable to bring herself to repeat the words. Another wave of nausea tore through her.

"You said you *might* compete in this festival. What

if Edge of September doesn't get the spot?" Lisa finally spoke up. Her voice was kind, like she was hoping the answer wouldn't matter. That almost made it worse. They really were rooting for her success. They just wanted it on a deadline.

"Then I'll see you on Friday." Fallon swallowed hard. She knew the risk she was taking. The only reason she had to believe they might have the spot was knowing Elliott had met with Robert Harrison the night before. It was a stretch for sure, but her parents were considering letting her stay for a few more months. She could deal with the rest tomorrow.

She watched as her parents thought over her proposal, clearly not wanting to agree, but willing to do almost anything to get her to visit Annora. Her mother's eyebrows were scrunched together so hard there was a deep crease between them, and her father kept rubbing his hand over his scruff, eyes never leaving Fallon.

"Do we have a deal?" She finally asked when they hadn't responded in an unnecessarily long time.

"We can't sign another lease. The apartment complex only offers yearly contracts. No month-to-month. So...," Manuel glanced to Lisa once more before going on, "we have a deal if you can find somewhere to live. We'll cover all your expenses besides rent. That's on you." He folded his arms across his chest, leaving it up to her.

No rent. That was the most expensive part of living out here, and she had absolutely no money.

But she could find a way. Get a job. Find a place to

live. She'd survive.

"Deal." She squeezed her quilt in her fists.

"You're serious about this," her father said, part question, part not.

She nodded.

"Where will you live?"

"I'll figure it out."

He sighed again. "Alright, then. You're staying."

"I'm staying."

"If you change your mind," her mother's voice was gentle, "there's a plane ticket waiting for you."

"We're cheering for you," her father added, "but be safe."

"Of course, Dad." Her parents' first priority was her safety. Always.

A heavy silence fell between them, and Fallon felt her parents gearing up for another fight. She cut them off before they could get there.

"I really need to get going. It's going to be a busy week."

She pretended not to see the concern in her parents' eyes as they said their goodbyes. She snapped her laptop closed, flopped back onto her pillows, and flung her arms across her face.

She was staying in LA with no apartment, no money, and no job. She had five days left on her lease before she'd be homeless. She hadn't even started packing. She'd been so sure she'd be able to talk her parents into giving her more time.

She'd only halfway succeeded.

And then she'd been forced to bring Annora into it.

Twisted Fest or not, she was now committed to visiting.

Why couldn't her parents take a hint? Maybe there was a reason she hadn't been to Annora's grave in the three years, two months, and eleven days since she'd died.

Not died. When people died, it was usually a circumstance out of anyone's control. Illness. Accidents. Age.

Annora had been taken. Even years later, the memories of that horrific day and the ones that followed sliced through Fallon.

Annora had been the perfect daughter and sister. Smart, talented, clever. And Fallon's best friend. Even with three years between them, the sisters had been inseparable. People who didn't know better thought they were twins. It's how Fallon had known she was pretty. She must be if she looked like her sister. Annora was stunning.

Following in her father's footsteps, Annora was attending ASU to someday become a lawyer. She had goals. She was doing something with her life.

Then one night, Annora had gone to a club with some friends from school. A mass shooter had attacked just as she was leaving, hitting her and two of her friends.

None had lived.

The shooter—a disgruntled psychopath looking to make a statement—had been killed on the scene.

Annora Rivera had done nothing wrong. She hadn't even been drinking. She was better than underage drinking and partying. But in the end, it didn't matter. She was still gone.

Fallon had attended the funeral and gone straight home, skipping the graveside service. She would honor her sister and best friend, but she would not watch some stranger put her in the ground. She would remember Annora in her own way: by living every day to its fullest. No regrets, no tomorrows. She'd learned at only sixteen that it didn't matter how many "good" choices she made, any day could be the day she stopped living, and she wouldn't waste any of them.

Another wave of nausea crashed into her and sent her hurling over the side of her bed, ruining a sweatshirt she'd left balled up on the floor days ago. She wiped her mouth and drank from her water bottle. She shoved herself off her bed and crossed to the kitchen area of her studio loft, refusing to spend her Sunday replaying Annora's death.

With nearly two hours before band practice, normally she'd spend this time kickboxing, but most days she hadn't done a full workout at three in the morning. Her muscles had had their fill.

She removed a box of Fruity Pebbles from the first of her three cupboards and poured a bowl. The milk in her fridge smelled questionable, so she dumped it, found a giant spoon, and ate the cereal dry. From her perch on her barstool, she could survey her entire apartment, which wasn't difficult considering it was all one giant room. Her bed lived in the corner furthest from the door. Purple and gold pillows were scattered across the overstuffed mattress and homemade quilt reaching nearly to the tiled floor. Beside her bed was the gold-rimmed, full-length, standing mirror that was probably her favorite item in the apartment aside from the punching bag hanging opposite her bed. She'd picked up kickboxing after Annora's death as both a killer workout and a way to learn self-defense. It wouldn't do much against a gun, but she'd taught a guy or two a thing about consent.

The door on the other wall led to her bathroom—the most impressive part of the apartment and the reason she'd chosen it a year ago—with a walk-in shower and enough counter space to leave all her various tools and products in a constant, scattered mess.

She'd moved to LA three days after graduation. That had been the deal with her parents. High school diploma for a year of rent money. She wasn't even sure how much they paid for this place. But when they'd moved her out to the coast, they'd liked the safe neighborhood and upscale security measures.

Fallon's phone dinged, and she tapped the incoming notification, a photo from Calvin. If it was him inviting her to that damn brunch again, she'd take all the strings off his bass and hide them.

Three faces gleamed up at her from her screen. Calvin stood in the middle, scrunched between Keith, festively decked out in a T-shirt covered in hotdogs and American flags, and Eric, Calvin's boyfriend. Calvin had replaced his shredded jeans and black T-shirt from the night before with khaki shorts and a light blue polo shirt. Even his mousy brown hair had been nicely combed. She often wondered if Eric felt like he was dating two different people.

The three of them waved at her from under a tree in what she assumed was Keith's parents' backyard. She didn't know a lot about his family. Keith was one of a number of kids, all of whom lived locally. She'd been invited over more times than she could count but had yet to take them up on the offer.

It's better this way.

Ignoring the tightness in her throat, Fallon's finger breezed across her screen.

Fallon: *Anyone whip out the croquet yet?*

She shoved her phone into her bra, rinsed her empty bowl, and put it back in the cupboard with her one plate and cup. She'd considered getting more kitchenware, but it was only her, and she needed the cupboard space for snacks.

She padded across the cool tiles and landed on the edge of her bed before Calvin's response arrived.

Calvin: *Wouldn't you like to know*

Fallon didn't want to play this game today. She tossed her phone a few feet away on her bed and flopped onto the pillows behind her. When she drifted away, mocha eyes filled her vision.

She shook her head as if Noah's memory could be shaken off like water droplets. It wasn't like her to have a guy fogging her brain, but it also wasn't like her to go for a guy like Noah. Regardless, something about him had clawed its way into her mind, and that soft chuckle kept echoing through her head.

Unacceptable.

She jumped off her bed, laced up her boots, and headed out the door.

She'd seen some boxes downstairs the day before. If she was going to be moving out this weekend, she figured she better start packing, even if she had no idea where she was going to go.

CHAPTER 3

In the twelve months they'd been playing together, Edge of September had had two lead guitarists: Brian, who had gotten married and moved back east in the spring, and Drew, who'd only lasted about a week before he'd been called back home to Idaho to help a friend. Drew had texted a few times, but Fallon hadn't heard from Brian.

Since then, they'd made it work with just the three of them. Luckily, Keith was a talented guitarist in addition to his vocal skills. But as Fallon, Calvin, and Keith wrapped up band practice, there was an unspoken anxiety between them.

Elliott had messaged to let them know he'd be arriving soon with news about his meeting the night before—hopefully the news that they'd be playing Twisted Fest.

Fallon had been in knots all afternoon and had nearly texted Elliott early to demand the news. In the hours since she'd made the new deal with her parents, she'd realized just how stupid she'd been to hang her entire existence on the hope that they'd even be invited to play Twisted Fest. For all she knew, Elliott and Robert Harrison were long lost cousins and last night's meeting had been no more than a late-night family reunion.

"He should be here any second." Calvin adjusted his strap and tucked his bass safely into its case.

"What if we're wrong and we don't have a spot in Twisted Fest?" Keith flopped on the ratty couch directly across from where Fallon sat at her drums and tucked an arm behind his head of chestnut curls.

"Then we're no worse off than before." Calvin lowered himself onto the couch beside Keith and replaced his glasses on his nose.

Her heart raced faster. The band may not be any worse off, but she would be.

Elliott strode through the warehouse door and swaggered toward them. His leather jacket hugged his broad shoulders, and his thick, salt-and-pepper hair accentuated his scruffy, square jaw. Fallon wondered again how Keith and Calvin had never pieced together that their ex-guitarist Drew was his son. Elliott was Drew in twenty-five years. Strong jaw. Sexy smirk. Insanely handsome. Too bad Elliott was such a dick.

"Hey, hey! There's my favorite band." Elliott made his way to the bar beside the couch and perched on a stool. "You boys done for the day?"

Fallon didn't object to him referring to her as one of the boys. In fact, she preferred it. She'd caught him watching her with way too much interest after their first gig last summer and glared back with enough venom he'd never made a move. Now she was just one of the guys, or he ignored her completely. Either way, she won.

"Just finished." Keith slapped the arm of the couch. She climbed on, grateful for the invitation and escape from having to sit by Elliott at the bar.

"Well, I've got something to run by you. I spoke with Robert Harrison last night. You are all familiar with Robert, yeah?"

Fallon ignored the condescension she knew was aimed at her. Heaven help the stupid female.

"Booking manager for Twisted Fest. What did he say?" Calvin's irritation bled through his voice. She would have told him off herself, but right now she could barely breathe. Anxious butterflies were eating her from the inside out.

"Well, turns out he's got a few remaining spots for this summer's festival. He's looking to bring on a few local bands." Elliott folded his arms across his chest.

"We're playing Twisted Fest?" Fallon gripped Keith's shoulder to stabilize herself.

Elliott smiled smoothly. "You're playing Twisted Fest."

Cymbals crashed in Fallon's head. She was glad she was sitting as her body threatened to collapse beneath her.

They were playing Twisted Fest. She wasn't going home this week, and she was a step closer to staying in LA permanently.

Keith whooped out loud, curls falling into his eyes, and clapped Calvin on the shoulder. Calvin fist-pumped, eyes shut tight above his wide smile.

Her lungs screamed for air, and she remembered to breathe.

"Tonight, we celebrate." Keith turned to her. "Atlas?"

"I'm in."

Calvin nodded.

"There's more." Elliott shifted on the stool.

"What?" Keith asked, eyes narrowed.

"I'm also here to ask a favor." Elliott looped his thumbs through his belt loops.

"What favor?" Calvin leaned forward and rested his elbows on his knees, smile fading.

Elliott lifted a hand to the side of his mouth and called to where he'd left the door open on the far side of the warehouse. "Come on in!"

A shuffle sounded from outside, like someone had been sitting just beyond the opening. The sun beamed from behind the figure that now swaggered into their rehearsal space, shadowing his face, but Fallon didn't need to see his features to recognize him.

Fitz Rayner had arrived.

And damn if he hadn't gotten hotter.

His straight brown hair swept across his forehead skimming his thick brows as he walked out of the shadow and his face came into view. He showed no shame as his dark eyes skimmed over her, no doubt evaluating how she'd changed, just as she was assessing him now. Fine. Let him take her in. She knew what she had.

His crooked smirk told her he did too.

"Boots." A slight nod in her direction.

"Fitz." She grinned wickedly.

He held her stare before turning to the boys on the couch, a genuine smile replacing the loaded one he'd given her.

"Keith. Calvin." He embraced each of her bandmates in the way guys do—part hug, part handshake, part slap-on-the-back. Fitz nodded once at Elliott before sliding onto one of the other barstools.

"Clearly you all know each other"—Elliott glanced Fallon's direction again—"so I won't waste time introducing you. Fitz's band, Blue Streetlights, will also be playing Twisted Fest."

"And?" Keith motioned for Elliott to spill whatever it was he was getting at.

"We need a drummer." Fitz pulled a sucker from his pants pocket, removed its plastic wrapper, and stuck it in his mouth. "We want to bring Fallon on for the summer."

Adrenaline bolted through Fallon's body. She knew Elliott managed more bands than just Edge of September—including Blue Streetlights—but they'd never interacted professionally before. A few gigs and parties overlapped, maybe, but this was a first.

"Why?" She kept her eyes locked with his and hid the emotions racing through her.

"Maybe I miss you, Boots." Fitz shot her a wink. She blew him a kiss in return. If he wanted to play games, she'd play along—and win.

"Cut the crap. Why do you want Fallon?" Calvin asked. She scowled at him, and he had the decency to look sorry.

"Because we only want the best. You all know that's her. She plays punk like it's in her blood. If drummers like Fallon were easy to find, we wouldn't have spent the last two months looking for a new one." Fitz stared her down, all truth—the most honest she'd seen him since he'd walked in.

He wanted this.

"You are all familiar with Fallon's talent," Elliott cut in, "and I think you'll all agree she's a good fit."

"Except she's already in a band," Calvin mumbled.

"So, you want Blue Streetlights to kife our drummer while we're also trying to prep for Twisted Fest? And we're doing this from the kindness of our hearts? That's bullshit." Keith ground his teeth loud enough she could hear it from her perch on the couch.

"It's only for the summer. Blue Streetlights has another drummer in line, but they can't get here until fall. Edge of September can keep practicing and playing gigs. Fallon will play with both bands."

"*Fallon* hasn't agreed to anything yet," she spat at Elliott. He ignored her.

"Why not just give their spot in Twisted Fest to someone else? Sounds like their band is short a drummer." Keith motioned to Fitz who'd gone silent, but she knew he was taking in every single detail happening around him.

"The spot is for a punk band," Elliott stood. "Blue Streetlights is the best one I've got. It's in all our best interests for them to do well."

Fallon tried to process the information flying

between them, but her brain was still stuck in fight or flight mode. She had to stay in California, whatever it took. But if she played for Blue Streetlights, would that help or hurt her chances of staying?

Did she even *want* to play with them?

"We hold practice six afternoons a week. Mondays off." Keith eyed his friend. "Blue Streetlights would have to work around that."

"Easy," Fitz countered. "We practice in the mornings. Sundays and Mondays off."

Keith and Calvin looked at her. She raised her brows in question.

"Sounds like it's your call." Keith's face had relaxed, but his shoulders were still tight.

Calvin nodded his agreement.

But it wasn't as simple as they made it sound. Joining a second band for something as huge as Twisted Fest was no joke. No one in their right mind would take that on, even someone as desperate as her, especially if she had to find a way to survive in Los Angeles. She needed a job—one that actually paid. That would be difficult enough working around one band's schedule. Two would be impossible.

Fitz spun his sucker between his fingers, and she was suddenly all too aware of the drumstick she'd been twirling through her own. She placed it on the couch beside her.

"I need to think about it," she spoke directly to Fitz, ignoring Elliott hovering a few feet away.

"Fair enough."

Her gaze drifted to the red candy still twisting in his

long fingers.

"Sounds like you two can work this out." Elliott nodded to Keith and Fitz. "I'll be in touch."

Fallon strutted her way back to her drums to pack up for the day. Her kit would stay, but she always took her sticks home with her. She blocked out the sound of the boys catching up and Elliott excusing himself.

As she shoved her water bottle and drumsticks in her backpack, she became aware of the lack of conversation from behind her and the shadow over her shoulder. She caught a glimpse of Keith and Calvin packing up their instruments and coiling cords to her left. She rolled her shoulders and turned to face Fitz.

"Still playing the Pearls, huh?" He leaned against the edge of the couch where Fallon had been sitting only minutes before and folded his arms across his chest. The black fabric of his Henley pulled tight around his biceps—strong but lean. The sucker had disappeared.

She shrugged. "Not much has changed in six months."

"How have you been, Boots?" Fitz's smirk was cocky, but there was a sincerity in his eyes that made her skin prickle.

"I'm amazing." Other than being homeless, but that was none of his business. "What about you? Still living the dream?"

"Isn't that what we're all doing?" He huffed a laugh and motioned again to the space around them, the instruments, the music. "You okay with me being here?"

"Why wouldn't I be?"

"I haven't heard from you in months." Fitz pushed off the couch and stepped close enough to fill her lungs with his cologne. She cemented the smirk across her face and held her ground.

"Well, you only ever heard from me for one reason before that, and you put an end to such things." Her hands landed on her hips.

Fitz glanced at Keith a few feet away and lowered his voice, "Could we maybe go somewhere?"

"You want to start back up again, huh?"

"To talk."

"I'm busy." It wasn't really a lie. She did have stuff to do, like finding somewhere to live.

"Please."

Fallon flinched. Fitz was rarely this earnest, and she wasn't sure she'd ever heard him say "please".

She rolled her eyes.

"You can buy me lunch." She headed for the door. Fitz's gaze burned through her the entire way.

CHAPTER 4

Fitz rode a motorcycle, because of course he did. They weaved through traffic, Fallon's arms locked around his waist and his shirt brushing against her skin. He'd given her his helmet, but even through the visor, she could see the wind tear through his hair, though his back muscles remained tense.

He parked the bike in one smooth motion—everything Fitz did was smooth—and she followed him into the restaurant, an American-style diner with a jumble of retro decor scattered over the walls and workers in 1950's getups. He held the door for her, and as she passed, she felt his hand brush against the small of her back—cool and calloused, just like him. They ordered, and he carried their food to a high table by the window. Her feet dangled at least a foot above the floor.

Fitz sipped his soda and twisted the straw with his tongue. She rolled her eyes. He knew exactly what he was doing.

"So, this is how it's going to be?" She flicked her

chin at his cup. "A whole summer of you being passive aggressively sexy?"

"Is that even a thing?" He smiled, straw still playing with his bottom lip.

"It is. And you're doing it now." She picked a fry off his plate and shoved it in her mouth. "Why are we here?"

Fitz sighed and set his cup on the table.

"I want to ask you to drum for Blue Streetlights."

"You already asked me."

"That was a member of one band asking a member of another. This is you and me. No managers."

"And how is that different?"

"I'm asking you to do this as a personal favor."

Her blood cooled.

"Why?"

"Because you know how much this means to me." His eyes locked on her. No playfulness. No sexy taunting. This was a Fitz few ever saw. The real him. Vulnerable and raw.

"It's a big ask." She stole another fry.

"I'm aware." Fitz bit into his turkey wrap, chewed, and swallowed before continuing. "But we both know you can do it."

"I *can* do it."

"You just don't want to?" He lifted a single brow.

"I didn't say that."

"Is this about you and me?"

"Oh, come on." Fallon rolled her eyes. She leaned back into the cool plastic seat and wiped her greasy fingers on a napkin. "That was a lifetime ago, and it didn't mean anything."

It hadn't meant anything—to either of them. That's why it had worked.

For a few months last fall, they'd simply been each other's booty call.

They'd met after a gig they'd both played and instantly hit it off, which was a huge red flag in Fallon's book. But after their first night together, when most guys would have asked for a date or even round two, Fitz had put up a wall. He'd made it clear he didn't want a relationship, or anything even resembling it. He'd been shocked when she had completely agreed. From then on, they were friends with benefits—nothing more—until just after Thanksgiving when Fitz had called things off. He'd hinted that there was someone he'd caught actual feelings for, but he fell off the face of the earth after that. Not that Fallon minded. Actually, she preferred it. No strings, no attachment.

"Then why the hesitation?" He rested his forearms on the edge of the table. She kept her gaze on his face.

"I don't know that I want to take on a second band."

"It's not like you to run from a challenge."

"The timing's bad." She bit into her burger, dodging the bait he'd thrown at her. "I need to focus on Edge of September right now."

Fitz brushed his hands on a napkin. Mischief flared in his eyes.

"You do realize this could be good for Edge too, right?"

She barked a laugh. "Sharing their drummer? How?"

"If Blue Streetlights wins Twisted Fest, that puts you on the radar. People—important people—will want to hear your band, regardless of how you place. Your chances double."

Fallon's limbs tingled. She hadn't thought of that. If she could get the attention of producers or agents, it could mean big things for Edge of September. Maybe big enough to get a contract and keep her in California.

She'd have two chances to win and either would work in her favor.

"And of course," he continued, "you'd get an equal cut of the prize money."

But that was still a problem. If she practiced with Blue Streetlights during the morning and Edge of September in the afternoons, she couldn't get a job. No job meant no money, and she was counting down the hours until she had nowhere to live. The prize money would come too late.

She'd have to find someone who'd let her stay the summer for free. It was the only way.

Calvin and Keith were the obvious choice, but they'd drive her crazy within a week. Calvin would see it as a bonding thing, and he already struggled with boundaries, always trying to get too personal. Keith would just be bugged. Not to mention, they had no room for her.

Elliott had a spare bedroom but asking him if she could move in was practically inviting his very unwelcome attention—at least that's how he'd see it. He would have to be a last resort.

She studied Fitz as he finished off his wrap and

dipped a fry into the mountain of ketchup she'd created when they'd first sat down. She'd stayed at his apartment plenty of nights last fall. He definitely wouldn't take it as anything more than it was, and if he did want to hook up, then, hell, maybe she'd say yes.

Which meant they probably shouldn't live together.

But maybe he knew someone. Everyone who was anyone knew Fitz. There had to be at least one person who'd let her crash for six weeks.

"I might consider it." She wrapped her ankles around the legs of her chair. "But I need a favor in return."

"What kind of favor?" He raised one eyebrow.

"I need a place to live."

He stilled. "What happened to your apartment?"

"I'm moving out."

He studied her and leaned back in his seat.

"Are you asking to live with me?"

"Absolutely not."

"I'll try not to be offended by that." He smirked.

"Do you know a place or not?"

"And If I say no?" He held her stare.

"I'll ask Elliott. He's got a room."

Fitz's smirk dropped. His eyes darkened, and his shoulders stiffened. "You can't live with Elliott."

"Where then?" She shot back, her panic rising to the surface. "If you don't know anywhere and I can't ask Elliott, I'm out of options. I'll be back in Arizona by the end of the week." She didn't want to ask Elliott either, but Fitz sure as hell didn't get a say.

His eyes narrowed, and he studied her in silence. Finally, he returned to his drink.

"I think I can help."

"How?" She was about ten seconds from walking out the door, screwing Blue Streetlights in the process.

"With a Blue Streetlights bandmate."

Her body stiffened. "Not Josh."

Playing music with Josh Pratt, the Blue Streetlights bass player, would be amazing. A dream come true even. But living together was unthinkable. As much as she liked Josh, there was too much history there. It would be too painful.

"Not Pratt," Fitz answered. Her shoulders relaxed instantly. "Our singer, Cooper, has a spare room at his place. He'd probably let you stay. I can ask him."

"You want me to live with a bandmate?"

"Better than staying with Elliott."

"And he'll say yes?"

"For our drummer? Definitely."

It would solve her problem of finding a place to stay. And living with a stranger was a guaranteed way not to give anyone the wrong idea. Calvin could never understand and would see it as so much more than just a place to crash, and even Fitz was a bad idea. But she could stand a few months with this Cooper and walk away without looking back.

"Alright, I'll drum for Blue Streetlights—if I can stay in this guy's spare room." She shoved the last of her burger in her mouth. "And one more thing."

"A place to live isn't enough?"

"I'm not hauling my kit back and forth every day.

So unless you want to do it for me, Blue Streetlights is going to have to practice in the warehouse for a while."

"Done."

"This will be fun. You boys just might learn a thing or two about punk music." She plastered on her cockiest grin and snatched the last fry from Fitz's plate.

"Why didn't you just order fries?" he asked.

"Because *you* ordered fries."

"You haven't changed at all," he chuckled darkly. He stood and tucked his helmet under one arm.

"And you're a whole new man?"

He shrugged, but something in his eyes sparked. Fallon couldn't help but wonder what the last six months had held for Fitz Rayner.

CHAPTER 5

"I like that bass line." Keith flicked his chin at Calvin's fingers as they moved over his strings. "Keep it."

"Agreed." Calvin's final note rumbled through his amp.

Practice had gone better than Fallon had expected after a rough start. She'd spent her day off wondering the best way to break the news to the guys and eventually decided there wasn't one and had blurted it out first thing when she'd arrived.

The boys, as she'd expected, hadn't been thrilled about sharing their drummer with another band. Well, Calvin had been fine, but Keith's jaw had clenched so tight she thought he might break a tooth. Even so, he'd shrugged, and they'd moved on.

Until she'd told them they were also lending Blue Streetlights their rehearsal space.

That's when the yelling started.

"What the hell were you thinking?" Keith glared at her from where he stood behind the couch. She was grateful for the space between them. She wasn't afraid of him hurting her—Keith would never do that, and if he tried, she'd kick his ass—but standing close to people only accentuated how short she was. She didn't like them thinking their height advantage gave them any kind of upper hand.

"What the hell was I supposed to do? Haul my drums back and forth every day?"

"It does make the most sense." Calvin raised his brows at Keith, subtly mediating the exchange from the neutral zone by the bar.

"They are our competition at Twisted Fest. Who knows what bullshit they'll pull to beat us." Keith pointed a finger accusingly at her. "I'm surprised you are letting the enemy anywhere near your drums."

"They aren't the enemy. And for the next few months, they are my bandmates." She clenched her fists. "I trust Fitz."

"That's just swell, but not all of us have the same *relationship* you have with him."

"Eso es mentira. You two are friends."

"Friends? Is that what you two are? Because I don't remember you screwing your other friends."

"That's enough." Calvin stepped between them, deep lines creasing his brow.

Fallon's chest rose and fell with each angry breath. Keith's words were true, but it didn't change the fact that he was being a jackass.

"Fallon is right," Calvin continued. "If she's playing with them, they have to practice here." He eyed Keith.

"Whatever," Keith spat. He turned his back to them both and started setting up his amp.

And that was the end of it.

Since then, everything had felt normal. They'd run through some of their covers, and Keith had brought in some new stuff he wanted to get ready for Twisted Fest. They'd played through all of it.

It never got old—the sweat coating her skin, the beat and the rhythm flooding her body until only the pounding of her sticks could release the energy. Even after years of drumming, her muscles still burned by the end of the set. Fallon lived for it. It was the only way she could ever truly release the fire that constantly burned within her. No pain, anxiety, hurt, or fear could ever withstand the flames when it was just her and her drums.

There was a new drive to their playing now that they had Twisted Fest to get ready for. They went harder and longer than normal, but none of them seemed to mind.

"Let's run it one more time. Cement it," Keith said after nearly three hours.

The warehouse door swung open, stealing their focus. Fitz walked in, fingers tucked into the pockets of his black jeans. He sauntered to the couch and propped himself on the arm.

"Sorry to interrupt." He checked his watch. "Boots said you were normally done by now."

"And you wanted to help clean up?" Keith's voice sharpened, and Fallon nearly reminded him again that he and Fitz were friends.

"I told the guys to stop by. I figured you'd want to meet them if we're going to be using the space."

"You taking over already?" Calvin asked. She heard the tease in his voice, but Fitz missed it.

"Not at all. Take as much time as you want."

"Generous of you." Keith chuckled sarcastically. "Count it off, Fallon."

Fallon lifted her sticks above her head, but as the door squeaked open from the other end of the warehouse and a familiar face walked through, she stopped mid-count, flew from her seat, and rushed at the newcomer.

Josh barely had time to drop his bass before she leaped into his arms, wrapping her legs firmly around him as he spun her. His laughter soothed her, like a cool breeze on a hot night. Her own laugh echoed through the warehouse around her, quiet besides their long overdue reunion.

Josh set her gently to the floor but did not remove his hands from her waist as he leaned back to take her in. She did the same.

He looked exactly how she remembered him. His high-top fade complimented his heart-shaped face, and his flawless, deep brown skin contrasted his sparkling honey eyes beautifully. She knew he hated his height— only a few inches taller than she was—but that was dumb. Josh was perfect, and one of her favorite people ever.

"How's the best drummer in the world?" Josh smiled wider, and she couldn't stop herself from matching it.

"Better than ever." She grabbed his hand and dragged him to the couch. "You?"

"Freakin' fantastic. It's been way too long."

"Well, Fitz got you in the divorce." She sighed dramatically and pouted at Fitz, who'd moved from the couch and settled on a stool beside Keith at the bar.

"We stopped hooking up. I never said you two couldn't still be…" Fitz smirked, "whatever you two are."

Fallon didn't really have friends, but Josh was the closest thing she had to a brother. Their history was complicated at best and no one's business but theirs. He'd been the one who'd gotten her the spot in Edge of September, but after she and Fitz had gone through their non-breakup breakup, she hadn't seen Josh again. He was in Fitz's band, and they didn't run in the same circles.

"Let's blame him anyway," Josh whispered loud enough for everyone to hear.

"Agreed." She tucked her legs beneath her on the couch, band practice long forgotten. "I'm so excited to finally play with you."

"Dirty," Keith said under his breath, mood finally recovering. She flung one of her sticks at him, hitting him square in the chest. He grunted and tossed it back at her. She caught it with one hand.

"To play with *the band.*" She rolled her eyes. "But I'm sorry about Travis."

She hadn't really known the Blue Streetlights drummer, Travis, but she knew he and Josh had been close. His leaving the band was uncool to say the least.

"Life happens." Josh shrugged tightly, and she couldn't help but notice Fitz busying himself taking the wrapper off a sucker. "And we got quite the upgrade." Josh tugged on a strand of her hair, and she swatted him away. He caught her hand, weaved his fingers through hers, and rested their arms along the back of the couch.

"Hell, yeah, you did." She winked.

Fitz removed the sucker from his mouth. "Boots is the best there is. And she's coming back to her roots. Classic rock is great and all, but we all know punk is where she belongs." He caught Calvin's eyes through his lowered gaze.

"I think that's her call." Calvin's voice was clipped, rare for his laid-back, non-confrontational self.

"It is. I'm just excited to see her back in her element."

"I'm sitting right here, pendejos." Fallon scowled at both boys.

"Regardless," Josh cut through the tension, "we're stoked to have her join Blue Streetlights, even temporarily."

"Indeed." Fitz lifted his sucker in a mock toast before biting it between his teeth. She watched his mouth shift around the candy and cursed the heat that flickered in her.

"Is your singer coming?" Keith asked. "Or is Fitz pulling double duty?"

"Nah, we got a guy. Cooper. He's been with us almost six months now." Fitz answered. "Boots's new roommate."

"Roommate? You're moving?" Panic laced Calvin's words.

Fallon glared at Fitz. Calvin and Keith would have learned about the move eventually, but the last thing they needed today was more tension in the band. She pushed out a slow breath.

"My lease is up. Fitz told me this guy had a room available. It's temporary. No big deal."

"Have you even met him?" Calvin asked.

"No, but I assume he'll be here any minute. We can all meet him together, and then you can offer more unwanted advice on my life."

Calvin pouted.

"You've met him." Josh cut in.

"Not yet." She shifted on the couch, sliding deeper into the old cushions.

"He said he met you."

Her mind wandered through the interactions she'd had with Blue Streetlights in the last year. She was sure none of them included a singer named Cooper.

"Am I late?" A familiar British voice coasted across the room and coiled itself around Fallon's windpipe, strangling her where she sat beside Josh.

No way. No way was he here.

But he was. Noah, in all his hotness and friendliness, jogged to where they lounged and hopped on the stool beside Fitz. The two nodded a casual greeting before Noah turned to face her, that genuine smile lighting up his face.

"Nice to see you again, Fallon. Calvin. Keith." He nodded to each of them.

"Hey!" Calvin's eyes widened. "Look who it is! Noah, right?"

"See? You've all met before." Josh nudged her leg.

"Indeed. At a party a few nights ago. I gave Fallon a lift home afterward." Noah smiled directly at her, obviously feeling none of the tension that was currently squeezing her insides into pulp. Either he didn't feel the draw to her that she'd felt toward him, or he was doing a hell of a good job hiding it.

"You said his name was Cooper." She looked to Fitz and forced the butterflies into submission. She could deal with her mixed-up, unwelcome emotions later.

"It is. Noah Cooper."

"Well, what a lovely reunion. I'm going to pack up and get out of here." Keith stood from his stool and turned to Calvin. "Don't wait up."

Conversation continued around her, but Fallon couldn't focus on any of it.

Noah was going to be her new roommate?

There were probably twenty million guys in California. How was it possible the one guy she would be living with was the same guy she'd hit on—and been rejected by—only two days ago?

She didn't care that he didn't want to hook up. Whatever. There were plenty of other options out there. Noah was different, though. She wasn't generally attracted to guys like him, and she'd been left with only two options. Hit-him and quit him or stay the hell away.

Neither was now an option.

She could change her mind and tell Fitz the deal was off. But that left her back where she'd started— homeless in Los Angeles and four days away from a one-way flight to Phoenix.

She watched Noah from across the space. He laughed at something Calvin was saying. His sincerity was like a haze around him, almost visible. Her heart raced in her chest.

Her gaze darted to Fitz. He was studying her carefully.

Damn it. He was better at reading her than the others.

"Everything alright, Boots?"

"Fine." She forced a smile.

"So, when is Fallon moving?" Calvin raised his brows.

"As soon as she chooses." Noah looked at her. "Room's yours whenever you need it."

Fallon's stomach tightened. This was happening.

"Friday."

"Friday." Noah nodded once, and her body heated under his gaze.

She had to get away from him. She needed a minute to put her head on right and get herself thinking clearly. She yanked Josh from his place on the couch.

"Take me home." She grinned at him. "You can help me pack."

CHAPTER 6

Fallon glanced around the room again, praying it was somehow different this time.

No such luck.

Josh had driven them back to her place, and they now stood in her apartment beside a mountain of empty boxes and rolls of clear packing tape. She scanned the space for something she wouldn't mind Josh packing for her and came up short for the third time.

"Fallon?"

"What?"

"Where do you want me to start?" Josh asked again.

People being in her space—in her business—was all things terrible and unwelcome. But she'd been the one that had asked for help. A stupid decision made in a desperate attempt to get away from Noah Cooper.

Noah Cooper, her new roommate.

Fallon shook his face from her brain like an etch-a-sketch. She glanced toward the kitchen cabinets. It would have to do.

"Kitchen. We'll start there." She'd already started packing her clothes, and he wasn't going anywhere near her bathroom.

Josh followed her to the island and stacked his boxes on the tile floor. They both built a box and opened the nearest cabinet. Each one held only a few items.

This would go fast.

"So... you're moving in with Noah, huh?" Josh sat cross-legged a few feet away from her, packing what were probably expired boxes of granola bars. "How'd that happen?"

She removed a box of Froot Loops, leaned back against a cabinet door, and shoved her hand into the box.

"Not much to tell. I needed a room. He has one." Hopefully one that was far away from his own.

"Why are you moving if you don't have anywhere to go?" Josh flinched. "Sorry. That was rude. You know what I mean."

"My lease is up." She squirmed at Josh's prying. If he hadn't just given her a ride, and if he wasn't helping her pack right now, she'd kick him out. Instead, she shoved another fistful of Froot Loops into her mouth. A few sprinkled to the floor around her.

"He's a good guy, Noah."

"Seems like it." She reached for more cereal and watched Josh pack. "I figured if he wasn't you would've butted in about me living with him."

"I am butting in." Josh closed the box and grabbed the tape from the floor beside him. "But not to stop you. I actually think this could be good for him."

"Good for *him*?" She couldn't imagine a single way her moving in would help Noah.

"How much do you know about him?" Josh leaned against the cabinet beside her, propped up one leg, and rested his wrist on his knee.

"Singer in your band. Has a spare room. British." She ticked each item off on her fingers.

"Our band," he corrected.

"Right. Our band." She'd have to get used to that.

"Noah came here six months ago from England. His family moved here for his sister's medical treatment. Noah came with them, leaving everything behind, all so he could stay with his sister." Josh scanned her face. "He needs someone like you around."

She still wasn't sure what Josh was talking about, but she didn't want to know. He'd already told her more than she should know about Noah—especially if she was going to do everything in her power to keep him at a distance.

Which she was.

"So, how are your parents?" Josh grabbed another cardboard box from the stack and began filling it with more snacks.

Fallon tensed.

"Fine." She kept her voice clipped and hoped he'd get the hint.

"And you? You've never told me how you've been since—"

"I thought we agreed we wouldn't do this," she

interrupted.

"Do what?" His brows pulled tight.

"Have this conversation." She set the cereal down beside her.

"We never said that."

"I'm saying it now. We aren't doing this." She scooted away enough to look him in the eye. "I appreciate what you did for me, getting me in with Elliott and all, but I'm not going to talk about this. We are bandmates, and that's it. If you want to talk about the past, find someone else to do it with."

He studied her but didn't respond. She tried to read his expression. Most people would be hurt or angry if she'd said that to them, but Josh looked more pensive, like he was solving a riddle or trying to read something written in faded ink.

Finally he sighed and said, "Alright. We won't talk about it."

"And I'd appreciate it if you didn't mention anything to the band. They don't know about my past."

"Not a word," Josh promised. "Fitz and Noah know a bit about my own, but I've never given names, and they'll have no reason to connect anything to you if you don't give them one."

Fallon nodded once and returned to her spot beside him awkwardly.

"We good?" He knocked his knee against hers.

"We're good." She paused. "Thank you."

He squeezed her hand, and the tension between them evaporated.

"You stopped packing." She kicked the box of food a few feet away.

"Still a box ahead of you." Josh wiggled his eyebrows. It was a ridiculous challenge, but a challenge nonetheless.

"Bring it on."

They snatched up boxes and tape and were back to packing without another word.

Hours later, Fallon's entire kitchen, bathroom, and bedroom were tucked away in cardboard boxes—everything but her Froot Loops.

CHAPTER 7

Fallon arrived at the warehouse early and sighed in relief to find she was alone. She only had a few more days before she was living with a roommate, and she wasn't sure how much privacy came with that. She'd never even seen Noah's place. She'd savor the alone time while she could get it.

One look around the warehouse told her Blue Streetlights had stopped by the night before. On the far side of the space were two amps, a mic stand, and a pedal board that hadn't been there when she'd left the previous afternoon. A setup similar to Edge of September's, only mirrored, with her kit separating the two.

This would work.

Fallon circled the bar and climbed onto a stool to wait for the boys. She didn't have to wait more than a minute before the door behind her squeaked open. Footsteps echoed through the warehouse.

"Fallon! You're here early!" Noah jogged to the bar and jumped onto the seat beside hers. "How was packing yesterday?"

"I won." She grinned and ignored the subtle scent of vanilla that clung to him.

She tried to imagine what it would be like to live with Noah. She was picturing a life-size version of a gingerbread house—positivity and sweetness permeating every hallway and corner. But that didn't seem quite fair. She barely knew him, and the one evening she'd spent a whole ten minutes with him, she'd been drinking.

"I didn't realize packing was something one could win." The corners of his mouth turned up.

"I can win at anything."

Noah tilted his head to face her. "I'm actually glad to catch a moment before the others arrive. I want to talk with you about what happened after the party the other night. I didn't mean to offend—"

"You didn't." Fallon cut him off. Her eyebrows lifted, daring him to challenge her.

"Okay, well, I'm sorry nonetheless." He clasped his hands together and rested those beautiful forearms against the bar.

"Don't apologize."

"But I am sorry if I handled it poorly." Noah's forehead creased, and his eyes were locked on hers. His sincerity was unnerving.

"Apologize one more time, and I'll change the names of all the contacts in your phone to the names of 90's boy bands." She spun around to rest her back against the bar. "Speaking of that night, you never mentioned you were in the band with Fitz. Or that you sang."

"You didn't ask."

"Fair enough." She wasn't known for asking prying questions. Everyone else had gotten used to it. Noah would soon. "But you could have said something."

"I could say the same thing about you."

She shot him a questioning glance.

"I asked you about Fitz. You could've mentioned you two had a history."

Her shoulders tightened. "Fitz told you we had a history? What did he say?"

"Nothing, really." He sighed heavily. "Look. He actually sent me to the party that night to meet you. Casually. To see if I was cool with you being in the band. I asked how he knew you. I believe his exact words were that you 'were a kick-ass drummer and there was a history there.'" Noah lowered his hands. "That's why I didn't… reciprocate at your flat. I didn't want your decision about whether or not to join the band to be influenced by me. Not like that." He turned back to the bar. "Plus, I wasn't sure how Fitz fit into everything." His face shifted, and she watched his throat as he swallowed before she wrapped her mind around his words.

That's why he hadn't kissed her? Because of the band and some weird loyalty to Fitz? That was ridiculous. She'd never have based her decision on some random guy. And everything that had happened between her and Fitz had been purely physical. Fitz might be the one person in the world as detached as she was. He'd never care if she hooked up with Noah.

But Noah had refused to kiss her at the mere thought that anything between them could affect the band. His loyalty to Fitz and his own insane moral compass had stopped him.

Fallon's gaze darted to Noah, traveled up his muscular back and over his firm arms, traced his sharp jaw, smooth skin, full lips. Her mouth watered.

She was obviously attracted to him. She could tell him the truth here and now—that her "history" with Fitz was nothing, and he'd never care what she and Noah did now. But then what?

There was no way Noah was a friends-with-benefits kind of guy. He radiated commitment. And there would be no hiding from him in the coat closet if they were living together. No, a one-night stand was not an option either. Something had to keep this boy at arm's length.

Or further.

And if Fitz was that something, then so be it.

"It really is okay." She chose her words carefully, each had to pull just the right weight. "I didn't know that night that I was going to be joining Blue Streetlights." Not a lie, really. "If I had, I never would have hit on you, not with your connection to Fitz." Okay, that was a lie. "I don't want to come between you two."

"Exactly." He enunciated each syllable, sounding especially British. "I really am sorry I didn't say something." He nodded once then looked away, an expression she couldn't read written across his face. Then it was gone.

Fallon breathed deeply, and a weight lifted off her chest. Noah would keep his distance if he thought she was off-limits, she was sure of it.

Mission accomplished.

"So, Twisted Fest, huh?" His grin returned as though they'd been discussing anything else this whole time. "Have you ever been?"

"No." She shook her head, and her hair slid across her bare shoulders. "But I've heard it's incredible. Dozens of bands. All kinds of music. A guy I know played it a few years back. He said it's how he got signed."

Noah's smile faltered, but it recovered so fast she wondered if she'd imagined it.

"Fitz and Josh would be beyond thrilled."

"And you?" The question slipped out before she could catch it.

"Of course, I'd be chuffed as well." Noah hopped off his stool and worked his way through the obstacle course of instruments and accessories that littered the warehouse. He paused beside her drums, looked them over once, and turned back to where she still sat at the bar. "And what about you?"

His voice bounced off the cement walls of the warehouse, and his eyes burned with the same intensity she'd seen a glimpse of in the car the night they'd met. She swallowed, her mouth suddenly dry.

"I'm—" she started, but a squeaky door and a cheery voice interrupted.

"Sorry! We're here!" Josh clomped across the warehouse floor and wrapped himself around Fallon, nearly knocking her off her stool. She laughed and pushed him off, leaving an arm wrapped around his waist. His light-yellow T-shirt was soft against her skin, and she found that she enjoyed the warmth of him against her, like a familiar teddy bear.

"I got caught up at home, but Fitz was nice enough to wait for me." Josh motioned to Fitz who had followed him through the door.

She met Fitz's eyes, and he greeted her with a smooth grin. No sign of the vulnerability she'd glimpsed the other day.

Josh moved to where Noah was setting up, clapped him on the back, and together they got to work.

It was fascinating to see how Blue Streetlights functioned. The same basics and procedures as Edge of September but with a completely different dynamic. Edge's prep was all about taking care of your own shit. Everyone knew exactly what they needed to do to be ready to go, and they did it.

Blue Streetlights was more of a machine, each of the members somehow linked. Like the scenes in movies where two people are getting ready for work and one person toasts the Pop-Tarts just as the other person holds the plate. Somehow they just knew.

The boys didn't speak, but it was a comfortable silence. Even as the outsider, she could feel the cohesion.

Fallon lowered herself onto her throne and spun a drumstick in her fingers as she watched. She'd paired her customary black sports bra with denim cutoffs today, and the smooth seat was cool against the backs of her thighs.

The boys finished their setup, and all glanced at her, like she was the one in charge. She barked a laugh.

"You waiting for something to happen?"

"Just checking if you're ready." Josh's excitement was contagious, and she found herself matching his energy.

"I'm always ready."

"Lame," Fitz teased.

"It's not lame if it's true." She stuck out her tongue, and Fitz snapped his teeth.

"Are you two done? I was hoping we might actually play some music at some point." Josh adjusted his bass strap and tried to hide his smile. "I think Noah might die if we don't let him sing something soon."

"Wasting away as we speak." Noah's voice echoed through his mic.

"You've been coasting on classic rock for some time now, Boots. Still got what it takes to play punk?" Fitz's dark eyes burned into her, and goosebumps scattered over her bare skin.

"Guess you'll have to wait and see."

Fitz held her stare but didn't reply.

"Alright, knock it off." Josh snapped his fingers, and Fitz finally looked at him. "Let's start with a cover before we make Fallon jump into our original stuff. *Runaways?*"

Fallon counted off and jumped into the song, Fitz and Josh right with her. Fitz hadn't been completely joking when he'd teased her about playing punk. It had been a while.

And damn, she'd missed it.

Now, as the beat pulsed within her and the energy weaved its way through her veins, she remembered. Punk was where she'd always felt most at home.

Then Noah started singing.

And Fallon lost hold of her sticks.

One smacked into the wall behind her, and the other flew at Josh, hitting him right between the shoulders.

"Ow!" He arched his back at the force and stopped playing. He looked at her in confusion. "What the hell just happened?"

Fitz and Noah had stopped to stare at her too.

"Sorry. My bad." She scrambled to retrieve her stick from the floor.

"You okay?" Josh asked, one eyebrow still raised in her direction. He handed her the other drumstick.

Noah's voice had been…surprising. She'd expected a smooth voice, like how he spoke, accent rounding out the rough edges Americans lived for, but the voice blasting through the amp had been anything but. Noah's voice was haunting. Pure punk dripped from every word, gravel raking over well-chosen syllables and an edge to his velvety tone.

It was incredible.

"I think Boots was pleasantly surprised by our dear Cooper's voice," Fitz smirked.

Noah just watched her, but his ears tinged pink.

She narrowed her eyes at Fitz and counted off without a response. And they were back in it.

She thought back to the last time she'd heard Blue

Streetlights play. It had been last fall when she and Fitz were still hooking up, before Noah's arrival in the United States. Their last singer had been fine, but nothing that could hold up to Josh and Fitz or even their last drummer before he left.

With Noah, they were better than fine. Way better than fine.

The song finished out, and she brushed off Josh's praise. Fitz only nodded, like he knew exactly how at home she felt. She'd never tell him he was right. Noah didn't even turn in her direction. He kept his back toward her until Fitz called out the next song. He talked her through the progression, and off they went.

Fallon studied their sound, the punk classics but with their own spin. She played along, but she also knew today was more about listening. Feeling. Soaking it all in.

It was more than two hours later when Fitz finally called it, and she watched as the three bandmates deconstructed their setup as smoothly as they'd put it together.

CHAPTER 8

Flashbacks of the night they met bombarded Fallon as the cool leather of Noah's passenger seat pressed against her skin. Her clothes covered more than they had that night, but as it was summer in southern California, a tank top and shorts was still a must.

She'd been right when she'd guessed all her stuff would fit in Noah's car. He'd laid the back seat down, and the smallest box had to ride on her lap, but they'd managed everything in one load. Her furniture and the other half of her belongings—including her punching bag—were already on a truck back to Arizona.

Noah hadn't looked upset once—not when she'd told him they couldn't move her stuff until seven pm on a Friday since she'd spent the whole day in practice for one band or the other. Not when he'd realized Calvin and Keith weren't there, so he'd be her only help. Not even when her box of bras and panties busted open and spilled all over his trunk. Of course it was the underwear. It couldn't possibly have been anything else. He'd just pretended not to notice as she quickly gathered them up and resealed the box.

Fallon swallowed the awkwardness as they drove in silence to Noah's house. His parents owned the property, but he lived alone in the guesthouse. He'd said it was the best of both worlds. He could still eat their food, but he had total privacy, which he pronounced priv-acy, which was definitely not the most adorable thing in the world.

She wondered if she'd also be expected to join the family for meals. Hopefully not. That was an absolute no, and the last thing she needed was to get thrown out for turning down their hospitality.

"Nearly there." Noah's hands gripped the wheel, eyes locked on the road ahead.

"Do they have driver's ed in England?" she asked.

"They offer driving courses, but from what I can tell, the requirements are different than those in the States." The corner of his mouth turned up. "Why? Is my driving so terrible?"

"No. You'd be a driver's ed teacher's dream." She watched him spin the wheel smoothly, still fully focused on his surroundings. "Do you ever look away from the road?"

"I try not to."

"Even to change the music?"

"Even then."

"What if you sneeze?"

"I never sneeze."

Fallon snorted, and Noah's eyes sparkled, finally flicking to her for barely a second before they were back on the road.

They had only been driving for about ten minutes when he veered into a neighborhood. A nice neighborhood.

Like, *really* nice.

These were mansions. Multi-million-dollar homes lined the street on both sides, each with yards that were an insane size for SoCal. Towering trees blocked many of the homes from direct view, but the pieces she could spot from the road were unreal.

Noah slowed in front of a house almost completely hidden by trees. He turned into the driveway, and as they cleared the open gate, Fallon cursed under her breath.

The house wasn't a house. It couldn't be. Houses were not this size. This was a small castle. Okay, maybe it wasn't a castle, but in this area of Glendale, this much house on this much land was more than she ever could have expected.

The house looked old, but she was sure it was a style choice. Tudor, maybe? Wasn't that a thing?

Cream-colored stucco and dark brown beams adorned the front of the three-story structure, broken up by more than a dozen windows complete with old-fashioned shutters. The roof was split into sections, each coming to a point and sloped steeply like a cottage in the fairytales her abuela used to tell her as a child. Manicured hedges lined the walkways that led from the grand front door around the side of the house and out of view.

Fallon's parents were loaded, but this was a whole other level.

"What do your parents do again?" she asked but couldn't break her gaze from the property.

"My dad is the CFO of a large marketing firm in London." Noah continued past the house and toward a garage on the back side. "And until seventeen months ago, Mum was an adolescent psychologist."

She nodded, ignoring the oddly specific information and the questions that floated through her mind. They were roommates, not friends. She couldn't let herself care about his family.

Noah opened the garage door, inched his way into the space, and cut the engine. She unbuckled the seatbelt he had insisted she wear and walked to the back of the car where he was already unloading her belongings. He lifted a box and held it against his stomach.

"The guesthouse is around the side. We'll need to take a few trips."

She hauled up a box of her own and followed Noah out the side door of the garage and into the park of a yard, complete with a stream and a little bridge.

From there, she could spot the guesthouse. It had been hidden behind the mammoth building his parents lived in, but it was still an impressive size for two people. With matching stucco and shutters, it almost looked like the house version of the mommy-and-me outfits online. He had said "spare bedroom," so she could only assume it had two.

Noah approached the house, removed his keys from his pocket, and held the door open for her.

"First level is the sitting room and the kitchen." He

motioned to the space around them. A puffy sectional, coffee table, and enormous TV filled the open concept living area that attached directly to the kitchen with dark cabinets and an island. Everything was clearly high end, but it felt more comfortable than elegant. Fallon immediately liked it.

"Where should I put this?" She lifted the box in her hands.

"Wherever you'd like. But I can show you to the bedroom." He led her up the stairs. At the top were three doors, all on the same side of the single hallway. He stepped to the first door and opened it.

Fallon had expected something similar to Calvin or Keith's mismatched rooms, or even the masculine neutrals from the living room, but Noah's mom must have decorated. The room was beautiful. A queen-size bed was centered on the back wall with a light blue comforter draped over it and matching pillows stacked against a cream headboard. The nightstand matched the bed and held a lamp and a vintage clock. Other than the bed and the nightstand, the room was empty. Two doors lined the opposite wall.

"Two doors?" She asked Noah, who stood in the hallway, watching her.

"One is your closet. The other leads to the loo." His eyes widened. "Does it bother you that the only bathroom connects to your room? I thought you'd like it, but I'm now realizing you may not appreciate me having direct access to your room."

She rolled her eyes and dropped her box to the floor.

"Are you planning on murdering me in my sleep?"

He shook his head, face still serious.

"Then I think we'll be fine." She motioned to the box in his arms. "Are you going to bring that in?"

He set the box on the floor just outside the door and met her eyes with that burning intensity she prayed she'd eventually grow immune to.

"Let's be clear about something." His accent sharpened with his tone. "From this very moment, this is your room, and it will remain so for as long as you need it. That means only those you invite in are welcome. No one will bother you or invade your space. Even me." He set his jaw, and she had to swallow the tightness in her throat.

"Thank you." She waited until he disappeared down the stairs then moved the second box beside the first.

A private room. It was the best she could have hoped for, and she believed Noah that it would remain that way. Maybe she could just lock herself in here for a couple months and avoid him altogether.

She shook off the idea, tempting as it was, and headed back to the garage for another box.

She only made it a few steps out of the guesthouse before spotting Noah on the lawn, deep in conversation with a middle-aged woman. Her hair was the same blonde as Noah's, but her skin was paler, and he had a few inches on her. Even so, she still looked to be taller than Fallon. Her arms were folded, and based on the pinched lips and raised brows, she wasn't really thrilled with whatever Noah was saying.

The woman caught a glimpse of Fallon and immediately transformed. Her posture softened and a smile lit up her entire face—a smile she recognized immediately and was trying very hard not to think about constantly.

"You must be Fallon! Welcome to our home!" The woman rushed toward her.

"She's not really a hugger," Noah called from behind.

His mother stopped immediately, but her smile didn't falter.

"I'm so glad you are here. I'm Sarah Cooper." She stretched out her hand, and Fallon shook it. Sarah's grip was firm—a woman with a lot more to her than first glance would tell.

"Fallon Rivera. Thank you for letting me stay, Mrs. Cooper."

Noah's mom snorted. Actually snorted.

"Oh, Lord. Please call me Sarah. We're practically family now." She chuckled softly. Her accent was similar to Noah's but a little stronger. "And you are more than welcome. Stay as long as you'd like. In fact, if Noah hasn't mentioned it already, you are welcome in the main house too. Dinner's at six every night, and there's always breakfast foods in the morning. Or just come by for a chat."

Fallon didn't doubt for a second that this woman meant every word. Unfortunately, she didn't chat either.

"That sounds fun." She hoped the smile on her face looked half as genuine as the one Sarah was giving her.

"We should get the rest of her stuff, Mum." Noah inched toward the garage, his ears pink under the soft curl of his hair.

"Oh, of course. I just wanted to say hi." Sarah retreated to the main house, waving and smiling the entire way.

When his mom had disappeared completely, Noah let out his breath.

"I'm sorry about her. She's just very excited you are here."

"I see that." Her fingers fiddled with the strings hanging from her cutoff shorts. "Didn't seem all that happy about it before I got out here though."

"She wasn't upset about you being here." Noah resumed walking toward the garage. Fallon followed at his side, needing two steps for each one of his. "Quite the opposite actually. She's mad I haven't given you the entire guest house."

She nearly tripped over the perfectly manicured grass.

"She wants you to move out?"

"For you to have the house to yourself. There are guest rooms in the main house for me, she says." He stopped at his trunk. "Would you like that? For me to move into the main house?"

Yes.

She would love to have the guesthouse to herself. No Noah smiling and being all respectful and nice. It was a dream come true. But he had been so generous to even offer his guestroom to her, practically a stranger, and as badly as she wanted her privacy, a private room would have to be good enough. She couldn't kick him out of his own house. Even she wasn't that selfish.

"No. You don't need to move out." She hefted another box toward her new place.

Noah's house.

A flutter breezed through her at the thought, and she shoved it away. They were not a couple. She didn't want to be a couple. Commitment and attachment were the enemy, and a relationship with Noah would have buckets of those. Besides, he was under the impression she was off-limits—thanks to her. It was the only thing that made living with him safe. He'd never try to make a move or ask her out.

But as she watched Noah carry box after box to her doorway, she knew she'd need more than that. Knowing he'd sacrificed his evening to help her move, discovering that he'd been willing to give up the whole guesthouse for her, watching his muscles shift with each box he lifted—those forearms tightening as he gripped her belongings—she knew she'd need a thicker wall than just a fake ex. He would never hurt Fitz—that was clear—but that said nothing about her own heart.

He was a roommate, not a friend. She'd make that clear real fast.

CHAPTER 9

Noah was nowhere to be seen once all her boxes were in her room. He left the guesthouse with a "See you later" and hadn't been back since.

She was fine with it. In fact, it was all the better to be sure they weren't crossing paths. It gave her time to unpack and think through her plan for keeping him at a distance.

So far all she'd come up with was exactly that—keep him at a distance. Don't get personal, obviously. Don't spend any time together outside of band practice or the limited amount that was bound to happen when sharing a house. Though, from what his mom had said, Fallon was hoping he would spend meals with them in the big house. She definitely wasn't going to.

A light ache tugged at her heart. It had been a long time since she'd been to a family dinner, even if the family wasn't her own.

It's better this way.

She ripped the tape off the first box. Sweatpants, leggings, and T-shirts. She carried the box to the door

Noah had identified as the closet, opened it, and nearly dropped the box.

The closet in her old apartment had been amazing—a walk-in with plenty of shelves and rods to hang stuff. But nothing like this.

This closet was more like a small bedroom. A dresser stood against one of the walls and the other two had four shelves each reaching from floor to ceiling as well as a hanging rod. On the wall beside the door was a full-length mirror, and in the center sat a cushioned bench, likely a place to sit and put on shoes.

She could get used to this.

Hours passed as she carefully unloaded every box and bag. Everything she owned now lived in her new closet. Every set of leggings, sweatshirt, crop top, miniskirt, and bra was tucked, folded, or hanging in that magical space with room to spare. Even her collection of Doc Martins had a shelf of its own.

Maybe she'd go shopping this weekend. Her parents credit card still worked.

She belly-flopped onto the bed and was immediately lost in a pool of the softest bedding she'd ever felt. The mattress beneath her may as well have been a cloud. She wrapped her arms around a pillow and closed her eyes, allowing the day to wash over her.

✦ ✦ ✦

She hadn't meant to fall asleep, but that damn bed was a menace. She ripped her eyes open and searched for the clock on the nightstand.

1:07 AM.

Her stomach rumbled. She'd completely missed

any sort of dinner. She had no car and couldn't walk anywhere at this time of night. She grumbled and slid off the bed and into the dark hallway.

The few boxes she'd packed with food were stacked in the corner of the kitchen. She'd try to hunt down a box, or maybe Noah had food tucked away somewhere.

She snuck down the stairs, careful not to wake Noah, and wandered into the kitchen. He had left the TV on, now playing some reality show with a bunch of smiley people all wearing aprons and baking in what looked like a giant tent. She had no interest in baking; however, the TV gave the perfect amount of light for her to search for food without needing the overheads on.

A quick glance revealed there were twice as many cupboards as her old apartment. Hopefully that meant more food.

She opened the first and found bowls, cups, and plates. The second held spices and food she'd actually have to cook. But the third was a jackpot—an entire cupboard full of breakfast cereal.

Fallon doubled back to the bowls and poured herself a nearly overflowing portion of Reese's Puffs.

"Reese's, huh?" a voice called from behind her, causing her to drop her bowl. It clattered against the countertop, the noise way too loud in the otherwise quiet house. She spun around to find Noah's head poking up from where he'd been lounging on the couch. "A perfect choice for the middle of the night."

"I fell asleep and missed dinner." She lifted her bowl

in his direction. "Okay if I have some?"

"Have as much as you'd like." He laid his head back, his attention returning to his show. She could barely see him over the back of the couch, stretched across the cushions in plaid blue pajama pants.

And no shirt.

"Learning to bake?" Fallon threw some cereal in her mouth and watched as a man on the screen removed what looked like a chocolate cake from an oven.

"Indeed. No woman can resist a man who bakes." He was turned toward the TV, but she could hear the smile in his voice.

"Including your girlfriend?" She didn't know why she was asking, but maybe if she knew he was taken it would poison these stupid butterflies that had taken up residence in her gut.

"Don't have one. Besides, I only ever bake for one girl"—he leaned up on his arms—"and she's four." He winked at her.

So much for poisoning butterflies.

Noah glanced down at himself and bolted up as though he was just now realizing he was laying shirtless in their living space. He crossed his arms awkwardly and cleared his throat. "What about you? You dating anyone?"

"Nope." She ate more of her puffs.

"You and Fitz aren't...?" He trailed off.

"Nope." She swallowed. "Not anymore," she added quickly.

"Hmmm." Noah turned back to the TV and motioned to the guy with the cake. "He's my favorite.

He's got a passion for baking that makes all the difference in his recipes."

They watched another baker, an older woman, dump a whole plate of butter into a mixing bowl. Why someone would take the time to put the butter on a plate just to dump it in a bowl was beyond her, but it seemed important. She watched another baker mixing sugar into their own bowl of butter.

They were all British.

"Do you cook or bake?" Noah motioned to her bowl. "Besides your obvious abilities with breakfast cereals, I mean."

"Not at all." She leaned back against the kitchen island and popped more puffs into her mouth. "What are they making?"

"Most of them are working on their frosting right now. Their cakes are in the fridge."

"Their cake has to be cold?"

"Just cold enough not to fall apart or melt the frosting. It's for functionality, not a requirement," he explained, managing not to sound condescending. He rubbed his biceps, and Fallon didn't know if he was cold or feeling awkward about still being shirtless.

They watched as baker after baker constructed ridiculous towers with layers of cake and frosting and something they called "compote" that looked a lot like jam.

She was surprised at how comfortable she felt in Noah's house. She'd barely met him, and she'd only seen the house for the first time today, yet there was something relaxing and welcoming about both the guy and his home.

Noah broke the silence as though he'd been thinking the same thing.

"I'm glad you moved in. It will be nice to have a friend around the house."

Her chest tightened. It had only been a few hours, most of which she had spent sleeping. She shouldn't be this comfortable. He was already wearing her down and getting too cozy. He was exactly the kind of guy that would break her into pieces, who would hurt her the way she'd sworn no one ever would again.

"We aren't friends." She took her cereal back to her room and closed the door.

CHAPTER 10

Blue Streetlights always practiced in the morning. Josh and Fitz worked afternoons, and Noah had some kind of non-specified conflict most days around two o'clock. This worked out well since Calvin and Keith were busy in the mornings, but it meant Fallon spent most of the day at the warehouse practicing with one band or the other.

Noah had given her a ride that morning, not saying a word about her rude exit the night before. In fact, he acted like they hadn't talked at all.

Maybe he didn't remember. Maybe he had been asleep and was one of those people who could do things like watch TV and have conversations without knowing it. Probably not. It was more likely that her brush-off of his friendship hadn't affected him in the slightest. She wasn't sure if that pleased or irritated her.

They were the last to arrive and found Fitz and Josh already setting up. Much of their stuff was already set since they no longer had to take things down between practices, but the few things that had to be hooked up were nearly ready to go. Josh glanced up from where he was bent over a mess of cords connected to his amp.

"Hey, roomies! How was the first night in the new digs?" Josh's mocking smile was aimed straight for her. He knew moving in with Noah was killing her.

"No complaints here." She plopped onto her throne and stretched out her arms.

"Fallon snores," Noah answered.

A laugh burst from Josh.

"I do not." She shot a look at Noah, but her gaze drifted to where Fitz perched on a stool, guitar resting on his lap. His eyes hadn't left her since Josh had called her and Noah roomies. The darkness of his gaze brushed over her skin, and she swallowed hard. Heat rose up her neck until Fitz finally broke their connection.

Josh had returned to his bass, but Noah's eyes darted away like he too had been aware of the tension between them.

"Let's go." Josh strummed his pick across his strings, and a low rumble burst from the amp to her left.

Fitz took his place on the other side of Josh, and Noah gripped the mic stand a few feet in front of them both.

She braced herself. Even after nearly a week of rehearsing with Blue Streetlights, she still was taken aback each time she heard Noah's voice, like her feet were knocked out from under her.

It didn't mean anything. She just appreciated a good voice.

Or a super-hot, insanely sexy, deliciously gravelly voice.

Whatever.

Between Noah's voice and Fitz's stares, practice was getting intense.

By the end, her arms and abs were on fire. Playing classic rock required energy and stamina but nowhere near as much as punk. In the year she'd been playing for Edge of September, she'd lost some of it. If she hadn't been kickboxing regularly, she likely wouldn't have made it through practice.

Her phone chimed as the boys tucked away their instruments, and she removed it from her boot.

Calvin: *Atlas tonight to celebrate Twisted Fest. You in?*

Atlas was one of their favorite clubs, partly because of its playlists, but mostly because the bouncers didn't look too closely at her fake ID.

Fallon: *Meet you there.*

She reached to tuck her phone back in its home, but it went off again.

Calvin: *Invite the Blue Streetlights guys.*

Fallon groaned.

"What?" Josh lifted a brow in her direction.

"Calvin."

Josh chuckled and shook his head.

The last thing she wanted was Fitz's gaze or Noah's smile following her to the club. It was bad enough that they were at practice and back home. This was a chance to get away from both.

But it was her fault they were now mixed up with Edge of September, and she had no real reason to say no. Neither Fitz nor Noah mattered to her as anything more than a bandmate. Refusing to hang out with them said otherwise. And clubbing with Josh was always a good time.

Fallon: ***thumbs up emoji***

"Sounds like we're hitting Atlas tonight. You boys interested?" She sat sideways on the arm of the couch and propped her boots on the cushion.

"Oh, hell yes." Josh wrapped the last of the cords into a tight loop. "It's been way too long since you and I hung out." He swatted her arm and headed for the door.

"I'm in too." Fitz motioned to Josh. "Someone's got to keep an eye on him."

"What are you talking about?" Josh turned back to them. "I'm responsible."

"And I'm doing everything I can to fix that." Fitz faked a look of concern. Josh flipped him off before disappearing through the door.

"You coming?" She asked Noah. If not, she'd have to hitch a ride from somebody else.

Noah fiddled with his keys. "No, I—"

"Noah doesn't go out," Fitz cut in. "But I'll drive you if that's what you're worried about." He winked at her.

She stuck out her tongue. Pendejo.

"You coming home between practices?" Noah asked her.

She hopped from the couch and followed him to where he'd parked his car. Fitz's dark laughter echoed behind them.

As Fallon climbed into Noah's SUV, her phone went off again.

Fitz: *Pick you up at 10.*

CHAPTER 11

"Never have I ever gotten a tattoo."

Josh's voice carried above the roar of the club. Keith, Fitz, Calvin, and Fallon all drank. Eric pointedly did not.

"I thought you and Cal were going to get matching ones." Fallon called to him across the round table from where she sat between Fitz and Josh in the dimly lit club.

"We were, but *someone* can't decide what he wants." Eric stretched out his bare forearm. "So naked I remain."

"Who's naked?" Josh yelled across the table.

"My arm." Eric had been there, along with Calvin, Keith, and Josh when she and Fitz had arrived nearly three hours ago. They'd all danced until their feet hurt and then snagged a table. That's when the drinking games started. "Whose turn is it?"

"Mine." Fitz's hands clasped around a beer, his first tonight. He usually ordered a much stronger drink, but he'd driven and, therefore, would have to drive them

87

home. "Never have I ever moved to a different state."

Eric, Josh, and Fallon drank. Fallon had drunk almost every round. There was very little she hadn't done, and while something about that thrilled her, she didn't really want to get wasted tonight. She had a vision of herself sliding off the back of Fitz's motorcycle on the way home, and her second paloma was nearly gone.

"Let's do something else."

"Too much for you, Boots?" Fitz raised a brow at her. She watched his wrist swirl the liquid around in his bottle. *Why was that hot?*

"Never." She downed the rest of her drink and immediately cursed her competitive nature as the alcohol burned its way down her throat.

"I actually need to bow out too." Keith checked his phone and slid out of the booth. "I'll be right back."

Calvin's eyes caught hers, and there was no mistaking that look, the anxious creases aging his otherwise youthful face.

They were both aware of Keith's *habits*. But what used to be a little weed at parties had escalated to harder stuff a lot more often.

Fallon wasn't into all that. Alcohol amplified, but drugs altered. They were nothing but a great way to convince yourself you were having a fantastic time when in reality you were tripping in a public bathroom.

She and Calvin had never actually talked about Keith and what she was positive he was doing right this minute, but it was obvious they both knew. And she could read Calvin well enough to know he was more than a little worried about it.

"So, how's the new place really?" Josh sipped his beer, his gaze remaining on her.

"Fine."

"Oh, come on. Noah's not around. Spill."

Every eye around the table was on her.

"Nothing to spill. I haven't even seen Noah all that much." It was true. In the two days since she'd moved in, she'd barely crossed paths with him.

Fitz leaned back into the booth beside her, and the deep blue vinyl cushion rippled with the movement.

"Why did you move?" Eric rested an arm along the back of the bench behind Calvin.

"My lease was up."

"Why not just renew it? I thought you liked your place." Calvin's brow was still creased.

"Things change." She shrugged. She wouldn't talk about her parents with any one of these guys. She sure as hell wasn't going to do it with all of them together.

"Seriously? That's it?" Josh took another drink.

"You can't be surprised by this," Calvin said. "I don't even know why I asked. Fallon doesn't tell us anything."

"Not when you stick your nose where it doesn't belong," she cut in.

"Where it doesn't belong or where you don't want it?" Calvin's voice was foggy, smudged with bitterness and alcohol.

"It's the same." She forced a deep breath. Calvin was drunk and worried about Keith. This wasn't really about her, and the last thing she wanted was a blowup in front of Josh and Fitz.

"It's not."

"It isn't any of your business. If I had wanted you to know the details, I would have told you. Worry about your own shit." She flinched at her own harshness. Maybe she was letting the alcohol get to her a little too.

"Did you ever think that maybe friends worry about *each other's* shit? Or are you too focused on keeping everyone in their box?"

"What the hell does that mean?" Everyone else stayed silent, letting her and Calvin have it out. So much for not fighting in front of the band.

"You keep every bit of your life—every person, every desire, every bit of yourself—in separate boxes. Nothing touching. No one knows anything about you, and you aren't attached to anyone. No one sees the real Fallon, the whole you. You pack everyone away and give only what you absolutely have to to get whatever you need from everyone else. Need booze? Keith will hook you up. Need a place to stay? Noah's there. Need to get laid? Use Fitz."

"Watch it," Fitz growled.

Calvin went on, ignoring Fitz.

"Heaven forbid one of us tries to climb out of our box enough to actually care about you. I'd bet my bass you'd leave Edge of September in a second if you didn't need us to make it as a drummer."

His words landed like a slap to the face. Fallon's chest tightened and her hands ached for her punching bag. Or her drums. Really anything she could beat the shit out of. But she wouldn't break Calvin's stare, wouldn't admit that as much of an ass as he was being, he was right. She had put everyone in their own box. But he knew nothing. He thought he had her all figured out, and he didn't know the first thing about her.

She didn't *want* to live this way. She had learned the hard way that as badly as she wanted relationships and connection, the pain of not having them was nothing—*nothing*—compared to the pain of losing them.

Her chest rose and fell as blood pulsed in her ears. She knew what she had to do. She'd done it before when people got too attached, and she'd likely have to do it again.

She casually broke their gaze and shook the remaining tension from her hands. Fitz leaned forward, likely sensing the shift in her. Calvin sat completely still.

"You're right. Friends care about each other." She tossed her hair over her shoulder. "I guess we aren't friends."

Calvin's face fell as the brutality of her words sank in. Guilt clawed at her, but it was the only way he'd learn. He'd spent a year trying to pry his way into her life. It was time to shut the door and lock it for good.

Eric leaned in, likely ready to jump in to defend Calvin if she said any more. Even Josh had shifted like he might intervene.

But enough was enough. She had done all the damage she needed to, and with the anger simmering in her blood, she didn't want to be around anyone.

"You ready to go?" she asked Fitz.

Fitz's eyes darted to Calvin and back to her. He nodded.

Josh stood, allowing her and Fitz to slide out of the booth to where Keith now stood. His tight jaw and pursed lips told her he'd heard enough.

"What about the band?" His pupils were dilated.

"This isn't about the band. Edge of September is work. This is personal"—she glanced back to Calvin—"and clearly I've let things get too personal."

She turned to the door but stopped when Calvin stood and yelled after her. "What made you like this?"

Another rush of hurt flooded her body. She swallowed hard, refusing to let the tears come.

"Stay in your box," she snapped at him before glancing once more to be sure Fitz was following her and walking away.

***

Fitz didn't say a word the whole way home. Even when he dropped her off at Noah's, he simply nodded goodbye before pulling away on his bike.

Fallon stomped across the yard. Her guilt at hurting Calvin had subsided somewhere along the way, and now she was left with nothing but rage.

Who did Calvin think he was, calling her out like that? He didn't know a damn thing. He probably thought he was so *smart* and so *insightful,* saying all that shit about her putting people in boxes and only using them for her own benefit.

And that line about her only being in the band

because she couldn't make it on her own? What the hell was that about? She'd never been anything but devoted to Edge of September. She gave everything she had every practice, every gig. She'd staked her entire life in California on them getting signed at Twisted Fest this summer.

Calvin was an asshole.

She burst into the guesthouse and slammed the door behind her, not caring if she woke Noah.

But he wasn't asleep. Far from it.

She found him standing at the kitchen counter wearing baggy pajama pants and a loose white T-shirt, watching whatever was in the stand mixer. The rest of the counter was doused in flour. The mixer's motor hummed in the otherwise quiet house, and Noah flicked it off when he saw her.

"How was Atlas?"

"Fine."

His smile faded as he studied her face. "Are you okay?"

She ignored him and crossed to the cupboard for a glass.

He clearly wanted to ask more about her night and whatever had put her in her current mood, but he returned to his concoction in the mixer.

"I'm making cinnamon buns. I generally stick to desserts, but I thought these might make a nice treat for breakfast."

She grunted and filled her cup with water from the fridge door. She downed the whole thing and refilled it.

"Do you want to help?" Noah asked, eyes still on the mixer.

"Help you bake?"

"What else would I be talking about?" He lifted his eyes back to her, and his ridiculous expression almost brought a smile to her face. "Yes, bake."

"I don't bake." She placed her cup in the dishwasher and headed for the stairs but paused on the second step. "I'll help you eat them, though."

"I'm counting on it." He removed the bowl from the mixer and dumped the dough onto the flour-covered counter. She watched him work the dough into the flour for a minute or two before she climbed the stairs. There was something soothing about watching Noah bake. If it wasn't so late and if she wasn't so pissed, she might have stayed up just to watch him.

Instead, she closed her bedroom door, locked it, and flopped into bed.

CHAPTER 12

It was a battle of wills.

Fallon versus the laptop.

And the goddamn laptop was winning. Well, not the laptop, but all it represented

Her parents, really.

Sunday had snuck up on her. After the week she'd had, their video call was the last thing on her mind. She was pissed she had to have the call at all, but she'd gotten a text from her mom the night before.

Mom: *Can't wait to talk tomorrow and hear all about your new place!*

Translation: *You're still required to be on the Sunday call. Expect extreme judgement and obnoxious prying.*

They'd cut her off. Didn't that mean she could cut them off? She'd genuinely considered blowing off the call, but she knew how that would go. Since what happened to Annora, her parents were worriers. If she blew off their call, they'd assume the worst and be on the first flight to LA, especially knowing she might not have a home right now.

So, she sucked it up and got ready for the call. Noah had been gone all morning, likely spending Sunday with his family in the main house, so she decided she'd set up in the living area. If her parents happened to catch a glance at her fancy digs and see she wasn't lying dead in an alley or holed up in some meth house, maybe they'd lay off.

She sank onto the couch, her back to the kitchen, and tucked her legs beneath her. She opened her laptop, and the call came through almost immediately. Stomach swirling, Fallon answered.

"Reinita, it's so good to see you!" Her father's eyes wrinkled as his smile took over his face. "How are you?"

"Fine," she spat. She was still moody from the night before.

"Where are you? Did you find a new place?" Her mother squinted at the screen like she could Sherlock where her daughter was.

"I moved in with a friend. They had a spare room."

"You couldn't find another apartment?" her father asked. Her mother's eyes darted away. She had suddenly decided staring at the floor was more interesting than facing the daughter she'd abandoned.

"No, Dad. Not a lot of available apartments with only a few days' notice and no money. Weird, right?" She was being rude, but she didn't care. This was their fault. Her life was just fine before they'd decided to take everything from her. Now she was living with Noah and fighting with Calvin. She was not going to sit here and let them judge her for piecing her life back together as best she could.

"Don't be that way, Reinita. We are happy to pay for your home—here, in Arizona. There's a plane ticket for you whenever you're ready. Just say the word." Her father's forehead creased, and his deep brown eyes took on that super emotional quality that cut deeper than any words could.

"I'm not moving back. I'll stay here until I can get my own place, after Twisted Fest. That was the deal." End of conversation.

"So, the band is playing Twisted Fest?" Her mother's not so subtle change of subject interrupted what was surely going to be a lecture from her father on how growing up meant giving up on her dreams and becoming boring and predictable. He shut his mouth, and his lips thinned, like he was holding them together with too much force.

"We are. We've got a few weeks to prep, and then the festival lasts a couple days."

"Maybe we'll try to make it. We'd love to watch you play." Her father's face softened.

"No!" The word burst from her lips without warning, and Fallon tried unsuccessfully to cover her gut reaction. "I would hate for you to come all this way. It's going to be hot and crowded. Maybe if we win you can come to a gig this fall." Just the thought of her parents at the festival sent her stomach swirling again. They'd want to be introduced to everyone. They'd see a whole different side of her, a side she had no intention of them ever seeing.

They exchanged glances.

"You don't want—"

"Fallon? Are you home?" Noah appeared in the doorway.

Her stomach dropped.

"No. Go away," she yelled over her shoulder.

"My parents sent me to ask if you wanted—are you on a call?" He grimaced apologetically and tiptoed into the kitchen, like he could undo the damage by being quiet now.

"Is that Calvin?" Her mother's smile returned. "Oh, put him on! We want to meet him!"

Fallon's skin prickled. Her parents absolutely could not meet Noah.

"Is that your parents?" Noah whisper yelled. "Tell them I say hi!"

"It's not Calvin." Fallon answered her mom and turned the laptop so her parents couldn't see the guy now drizzling frosting over a plate of enormous cinnamon rolls behind her.

"Then who is it?" Manuel Rivera's stern eyes bore into her, even through the screen.

She groaned.

"That's Noah. He's in another band."

"Why is he in your house?"

She felt Noah freeze behind her.

"Because…" she took a deep breath and prepared for the worst. "It's his house."

"You're living with a boy?" Her mother's eyes grew wide, and her father's jaw was as tight as she'd ever seen it.

"I have my own room. He's barely around."

"No. No. No." Her father's face grew redder with each word. "You cannot live with a boy, especially not a musician."

Her muscles tensed.

"What do you mean 'especially not a musician'? What's wrong with musicians?"

"Your father isn't saying anything about musicians, dear"—Lisa shot her husband a dirty look—"but he's right. You cannot live alone with a boy. That's exactly how girls get preg—"

"It's not like that, Mom!" She could not believe she was having this conversation in front of Noah, who was still doing a damn lousy job trying to be invisible.

She switched to Spanish and prayed he wasn't bilingual.

"We are not together. I am just renting a room. That's all."

"That's how it starts." Lisa took her cue and switched to Spanish as well. "But before you know it…" She lifted her brows meaningfully.

"That's not going to happen."

"He's very good looking."

This had to end. Now.

"I've got to go. See you next week." She slammed the laptop closed. She'd deal with them later.

She set the laptop gently on the couch and faced the kitchen. Noah stood frozen, still holding a bag dripping globs of icing.

She stayed silent.

"I didn't mean to interrupt." Noah set the icing on the counter.

"And yet." She clenched her fists at her side.

"I'm sorry if I caused a problem." He held her stare. "Did you not tell your parents you were moving in with"—he swallowed—"here?"

"No. I didn't."

"Why?" He still didn't look away, but his face softened.

"Not all of us care to have our parents so involved in our lives. Or anyone else for that matter." She picked up her laptop and headed for the stairs. She paused as she passed the island where he still stood frozen in place. "So, if you could, please pass on the message for everyone to leave me the hell alone."

He didn't respond, but she could feel his eyes on her all the way up the stairs.

She headed straight for the shower. The hot water would cool her off.

But as she shampooed her hair and replayed the fight she'd just had with Noah, it was regret that filled her gut.

Had she really just chewed him out for walking into the house? *His* house?

She hung her head and let the water run down her back. She was pissed about her parents and upset about what happened with Calvin last night, and she'd taken it out on Noah, who had done nothing but save her ass this week.

She'd spent this whole week snapping at everyone—her parents, Calvin, Elliott, and now Noah.

She'd lived here for two days, and she'd been a bitch for all of it.

Calvin's words from the club thrummed in her mind. He wasn't wrong about her keeping everyone in her life at a distance. He didn't realize she did it on purpose.

But his jab about the band kept playing on repeat.

Would she sell Edge of September out if she could make it on her own?

She wanted to say no. She wished she could, but there was no point in lying to herself.

She would. If she had the chance to make it as a drummer without them, she'd leave Keith and Calvin behind without thinking twice.

That made her a shitty person.

She turned off the shower and squeezed the water from her hair. She grabbed her towel from the rack, and as she dried off, she started thinking through how she could apologize to Noah Cooper.

CHAPTER 13

"You're lagging." Keith didn't even look up as he flung criticism after criticism her way.

"I'm not lagging." Fallon glared at him. She refused to get riled. He was pushing her buttons on purpose. He and Calvin were both still pissed at her for the fight at Atlas last night.

"Well, the song is lagging, and you're rhythm. Figure it out." He reached for his water bottle on the floor beside him.

"Is this how it's going to be now?" She gripped her drumsticks in her fists. "We don't talk except for you to tell me everything I'm doing wrong?"

Keith shrugged.

"You said we weren't friends. This is how people who aren't friends behave." Calvin crossed his arms. It was the most she'd heard from him all practice.

"No, this is how pendejos behave. I don't get why you're so pissed about this. We were never friends, Cal. Nothing has changed."

"You really don't see anything wrong with that?"

His brow creased, and her gut flip-flopped at the eagerness in his eyes.

"I don't have friends. It works for me."

"Does it?" Calvin took a step toward her. "Because it seems lonely to me."

"I'm not lonely. I like not getting attached." Alarms were ringing in her head that this was all too personal, but she had to keep talking. She had to fix this. She'd meant to piss him off and push him away, but she hadn't thought it'd be this bad. The band couldn't function as it was, and they'd never win Twisted Fest if they weren't at their best. "I'm sorry."

Calvin stilled. Keith looked up from where he'd sat on a barstool.

"I didn't mean to hurt you. Either of you."

Calvin and Keith exchanged looks.

"Oh, come on. It's not that weird that I'm apologizing." She rolled her eyes.

"Except that it is," Keith said.

"You never apologize." Calvin blinked.

"Can we please just get back to practice?" She motioned to the sea of instruments around them. "We do have a gig in two weeks."

Elliott had kept their usual slot at the Garage. Even with Twisted Fest coming up, it was necessary to keep the fans and connections they already had. Disappearing would never do them good.

"Josh said Blue Streetlights is going to come, by the way." Calvin slipped his bass strap back into place on his shoulder.

"You talk to Josh?" She wasn't sure why that

bothered her, but something about it got under her skin.

"Sure. Not all the time, but he asked about it and I invited him. He said he and Fitz would be there to support their temporary drummer."

She didn't respond. So not only would Josh be there but Fitz too.

Her hands were suddenly clammy. She pushed the nerves aside. She played with these guys almost every day. She had no reason to be nervous, especially since she didn't give a shit what any of them thought of her.

Instead, she focused on the band around her, the band that had to win Twisted Fest. Losing just wasn't an option.

***

She hadn't been able to find Noah before Edge practice that afternoon and eventually decided he was likely in the main house. Since there was no way she was going in there, she'd had to wait on her apology.

When she got home, she settled into the couch and awaited his return.

However, when the sky darkened and she finished her eighth sitcom rerun, Fallon gave up. She changed into her pajamas and crawled into bed. It was early, but she was tired of waiting for Noah, and she was still drained from the night before.

She dozed for hours, unable to get soundly asleep. The bed was plenty comfortable, but her mind spun. At nearly midnight, she heard a noise beneath her.

The downstairs TV.

Noah.

She pushed off her covers but grabbed a blanket from the edge of the bed and wrapped it around her shoulders. She tiptoed down the stairs, careful not to make too much noise. She wasn't sure why she felt the need to be quiet, like if Noah heard her coming, he'd somehow disappear.

She nearly laughed at how backwards the situation was. She'd been avoiding Noah since she moved in, and now she was the one hunting him down, demanding face time.

She reached the bottom of the stairs, and Noah glanced at her from where he lay on the couch, same as he had been the first night she'd moved in. Except tonight he was fully clothed—pajama bottoms and a tank top. Noah invited her to sit with a wave of his hand but continued watching his show.

Fallon sat on the far end of the sectional from where he was and watched with him as the same people they'd been watching the other night carefully assembled cookies.

"Did you know," Noah asked, "it's pronounced 'mac-a-*ron*' not 'mac-a-*roon*' like most people think? Macaroons are different." His eyes stayed glued to the screen.

"I did not know that. Are they good?"

"You've never had one?" He finally looked at her.

She shook her head and pulled her blanket tighter around her.

"They're good."

"I believe you."

He returned to watching the show.

"Can we talk for just a sec?" It had been years since she'd done this—started a personal conversation. She was usually the one trying to get out of them. But an apology had to happen.

Noah nodded and sat up, resting his forearms against his knees. His eyes landed on her, and she found it hard to meet that intense gaze.

"I wanted to talk about this morning." She paused, and he jumped in before she could continue.

"I do too. I owe you an apology. I never should have interrupted or questioned you. It wasn't my place, and it was rude and judgmental. Can you please forgive me?" His brows drew together, and that sincerity he always exuded overflowed.

But wait. *He* was apologizing to *her*? Yes, he'd stuck his nose in her life, but she'd been straight up awful to him. He owed her nothing.

"You don't need to apologize. I actually wanted to apologize to you. I didn't mean what I said. I was defensive and stupid."

"Apology accepted." Noah slumped back into the couch and raked his fingers through his messy hair, somehow leaving it even more rumpled.

She blew out her breath.

"So…we're okay?" she asked. She'd never sounded so needy in her life. She tapped her fingers against the edge of the couch.

"We're great." Noah smiled at her, his true smile. She was surprised at how it soothed her. "Are you going to go back to avoiding me now?"

"I wasn't avoiding you," she lied.

"You were. But it's alright." He stood and walked to the cupboard, retrieving the box of Reese's Puffs. "Calvin said you like distance. I didn't want to overwhelm you."

He returned to the couch, shoved his hand into the box and removed it with a fist overflowing with breakfast cereal. He handed her the box.

"Calvin is a busybody. Don't listen to him."

"He cares about you." He shoveled a few puffs into his mouth.

"I know." She frowned and scooped out her own handful of puffs. She popped a few onto her tongue. "I wasn't avoiding you specifically. I avoid everyone."

"Enough said." Noah returned to watching his show. The baker was squeezing some kind of frosting between the little cookies. "Macarons" Noah had called them. They were all different colors and actually looked delicious.

"Is that lime?" She asked as a baker stacked green cookies on a platform.

"Pistachio. Lime would be gross." He scrunched his nose.

"Lime would be delicious." She refused to believe otherwise.

"Agree to disagree." He shrugged. "So, are we at least friends now?"

"You want to be friends?"

"Would that be so terrible?" Noah's teasing grin sent goosebumps skittering across her arms.

Friends. It was such a dangerous word, but this was what trying was all about, right? So maybe they could be something like friends. They could share Reese's Puffs and watch baking shows. Because as dangerous as he could be, he was also safe. She'd stretched the truth about her relationship with Fitz to keep Noah from getting too close, and as long as he still believed it to be true, he wasn't a threat. Besides, Noah had an expiration date. Once Twisted Fest was over, she'd probably never see him again.

"Alright." She handed him the box of cereal. "Friends."

They watched the rest of the episode. Noah clicked start on the next one, and the same bakers began mixing new ingredients in large metal bowls. She was asleep before they made it to the oven.

***

Noah was gone when she woke up. She sat up stiffly, and a fluffy blanket slid off her shoulders and onto the couch.

The front door squeaked open and closed again. Footsteps crossed the room and circled the kitchen island before stopping. She rubbed her eyes, and the sleep fog cleared.

Noah stood with his back to her, hips leaning against the island, reading something on his phone.

Fallon forced herself from the sectional and joined him. On the counter were two coffee cups, steam snaking through the small opening in the lids.

"Good morning, Sunshine." Noah said without looking up.

She grunted, snatched a cup, and took a big drink, willing the caffeine into her bloodstream. Only it wasn't the sweet, creamy taste of a mocha latte that hit her tongue. Instead, a scalding, bitter liquid filled her mouth. Instinct kicked in, and she dropped her jaw. The murky brown liquid spilled out onto the counter.

She slowly lifted her head to see Noah as the last of the disgusting drink dribbled down her chin. He still held his phone, but he was watching her. His eyes sparkled, and a smile played at the corners of his mouth.

"Hot?" he teased. He slipped his phone into the pocket of his jeans, then finally had the decency to toss her a hand towel.

"And gross." She wiped off her mouth and then the mess she'd made on the counter. "What is that?"

"Tea." He lifted the cup, took a confident drink, and hummed in satisfaction.

"How can you drink that?"

"I love it." He smiled and took another sip. He jerked his chin toward the untouched cup on the counter. "That one there is for you."

"No thanks." She waved it off and circled to the fridge in search of water.

"It's not tea. I don't know how you like your coffee, so I guessed." He picked up the cup and circled the other side of the island to meet her. "At least try it."

She took the coffee from his hand and sniffed it cautiously. It did smell good. And it was definitely coffee.

She brought it to her lips and tipped a few drops onto her tongue. Cinnamon and caramel. She took a bigger drink, and flavor exploded in her mouth. It was sweet and warm and smooth, with that unmistakable coffee essence beneath it.

"This is delicious," she gasped. "What is it?"

"Caramel vanilla macchiato with extra caramel sauce and extra whipped cream. I told them to make me whichever coffee had the most sugar."

"Well done." She took another drink and circled back around the island. "You're up early for someone who was still watching baking shows when I crashed last night."

"I don't sleep a lot." He shrugged. "Insomnia."

"You are up every night like that?" She took another gulp of coffee and lifted herself onto a barstool.

"Generally. Sometimes I watch TV. Sometimes I bake."

"You don't go out?"

"Go out where?"

"I don't know. Just out. Parties. Clubs. This *is* LA." If she didn't need sleep, or very little of it, Fallon would be out all the time.

"It's the middle of the night." He tilted his head to the side. "There's not much to do in the middle of the night."

"In Los Angeles, some of the best things happen in the middle of the night."

"I don't know." He shrugged. "Middle of the night adventures aren't really my thing." He paced to the other side of the island and leaned against the counter. She absolutely did not notice the way his thick hair fell across his forehead or the shift of his biceps as he propped himself up by his forearms, holding his tea in both hands.

"And having friends isn't really my thing. But look at me. I'm so great at it." She smiled mischievously at him, and he bit his bottom lip in response. She choked on her coffee.

Was Noah *playing* with her?

"You are wonderful at it. Best I've seen." He sipped from his cup. "I just don't go out much."

"Fitz mentioned that." When she'd invited them to Atlas, Fitz had known Noah wouldn't accept. Apparently, this was the norm.

"I find I'm content staying in."

"Because you don't know what you're missing."

"And how would you know? I'd wager you haven't spent much time staying in." Noah's chuckle rumbled in his chest.

"Staying in is a waste. Life is meant to be lived, and what better way than to go out and experience the world? If you stay home all the time, you miss out on everything."

"Not everything."

"Everything worth doing."

"I disagree. The best moments in my life have been the ones I've spent at home."

"Agree to disagree," she said, stealing his line from the night before. She pulled a strip off one of the leftover cinnamon rolls on the counter, and shoved it in her mouth, licking icing from her fingers.

"I do not."

"You do not what?" she asked through a mouth full

of gooey cinnamon goodness.

"I do not agree to disagree. I am right." His smile turned mischievous, and she thought she might fall off her chair.

"You aren't, but it's cute you think so."

"Then I propose a challenge. Call it a game. You show me how to live big in California. I'll do anything you want, no questions asked—"

"Deal," she cut in. He gave her an exasperated look, and she had to suck in her lips to stop herself from laughing.

"*But* for each outing I go on, you have to agree to do something at home. A dare for a dare." Noah arched his brows, a challenge in and of itself.

Her body heated. What he was asking of her was a lot. Too much, really. She was supposed to stay away from him. That was her plan. And what if Noah asked her to do something super personal? She was barely able to handle the conversation they'd had last night. She could always back out, but that really wasn't her.

But as she studied the face of her challenger, she knew that, somehow, she trusted him. He wouldn't push her too far. If Noah was anything, he was good to the bone.

And Fallon didn't back down from a challenge.

"How will we know who wins?" she asked.

"I have a feeling we'll know." His eyes sparkled.

"Deal. But last night was big for me. So, you have to go first." She offered her hand across the wide island, not even making it halfway.

Luckily, Noah was much taller, and his arm made

up the difference as he took her hand in his and shook it.

"This weekend?"

"This weekend."

CHAPTER 14

Fallon buttoned her cutoff denim shorts, pulled an oversized T-shirt over her head, and shoved her phone in her back pocket. It felt out of place, but this was a night her boots had to stay behind.

She'd spent the whole week deciding where to take Noah for his first night out. When she hadn't been at one band practice or another—or recovering from the exhaustion of rehearsing with two bands full time— she'd been combing Los Angeles for the perfect spot. It hadn't been tedious. She'd basically spent the week at clubs, drinking and dancing. She'd even made out with a cute blonde at the Boardroom a few nights ago.

Noah was always awake when she showed up in the middle of the night, often in the kitchen and covered in flour or chocolate.

However, even after four nights of looking, she still hadn't decided where to take him, until she'd gotten a text that morning. An invite she knew would be perfect.

She headed down the stairs, her sandals smacking

each step along the way, and was unsurprised to find Noah already waiting for her. He still wore the clothes he'd worn to practice earlier.

"You're going to have to change."

"Into what?" He looked down at his jeans and T-shirt that would be perfectly acceptable on any other occasion but that she knew would never be right for tonight.

"Swimming suit."

Ten minutes later, he'd switched to deep blue swim trunks, and the two of them were in his car headed west. He'd insisted on bringing towels, but she had refused to let him sneak out a bottle of sunscreen. It was almost midnight.

"Where exactly am I going?" Noah asked, eyes glued to the nearly empty streets of Glendale.

"Don't worry about it. I'll show you." She kicked her sandals off and rested her feet on the dash.

"That's very dangerous." His eyes darted to her feet a few times, and she didn't hold back her laugh.

"I thought tonight was about being adventurous."

"I think our idea of adventure is different."

She rolled her eyes. The guy had no idea how to cut loose. At this rate, she'd win the bet by the end of the night and never even have to complete one of his dares.

The palm trees flew by as they drove, and Noah's music played softly from the speakers. The Wonder Years. He'd been wearing one of their T-shirts the night they'd met. She'd listened to the stuff he'd recommended that night—Aaron and the Roaring

Twenties—but hadn't told him she'd been obsessed with it ever since.

She guided Noah out of LA and to the true heart of California. Sometimes they spoke and sometimes they didn't, but it was comfortable.

Noah was comfortable.

He parked the car, and as they climbed out, the sea breeze wrapped around her. A little bit of ocean clung to the air anywhere in California, but here at the source, it was like a crash of life straight to the lungs.

Noah met her by the trunk. Moonlight filled the sky, and voices carried from every direction.

"What is this?" He scanned the crowded beach.

"Beach Glow Party." She retrieved the glowstick necklaces she'd hidden in the car, cracked one, and strung it around Noah's neck. The pink blazed against his white T-shirt.

"I thought we were exploring Los Angeles."

"We are. But you have to get a feel for California as a whole before you can truly appreciate the city." She cracked her own glowstick necklace and wrapped it around her throat. "And nothing feels more like California than a glow party on the beach."

She gripped the bottom of her T-shirt and lifted it over her head, careful not to break her necklace in the process. She slid off her shorts and flung her clothes into the trunk beside the towels. Her sandals followed.

She turned back to the beach and found Noah staring, eyes glazed as he took her in, standing in the moonlight in nothing but her neon pink bikini. His eyes snagged on the lotus flower tattoo on her hip. She traced the tension in his throat as he swallowed. He blinked a few times, and his eyes returned to her face. She knew he'd find a knowing smile waiting for him there.

"Like what you see, England?" She winked.

"I just really like pink," he choked out. He stripped his own T-shirt off and tossed it beside hers in the trunk.

Fallon had seen Noah without a shirt before but curled up on the couch had not done him justice.

His tan continued past his shoulders, across his firm chest, and down his lightly toned abs. Everything was smooth and defined, and she couldn't pretend her fingers didn't itch to trace the contours.

"Do you come to these often?" His eyes scanned the beach again.

She shrugged. "I've been to two or three. They don't advertise. You have to know someone who knows about them."

"And you know someone?"

"I had a guy bring me on a date once." Her voice fizzled out as she realized what she was implying.

His eyes returned to her face.

"But this is not a date." It wasn't a question.

"No, it is not," she confirmed. As long as they were on the same page.

"Well, shall we?" His grin turned playful, and he reached for her hand, cupping it in his own.

As they wandered toward the water, the noise of the crowd rose, almost loud enough to overpower the crashing of the waves only yards away. Most people wore various forms of glowstick jewelry—necklaces, bracelets, anklets. One girl had them strung through her braids. The only other light came from giant blacklights scattered across the beach, lifted high in the air by metal poles, and of course, the moonlight reflecting off the water.

Everyone wore neon and white, and they glowed as they danced barefoot in the sand. Speakers stretched across the coast, blasting EDM. Games were set up to the side—mini golf, ring toss, and cornhole—all painted neon colors to glow in the dark. On the other side of the dance party were awnings with stools set up where people could get airbrushed tattoos.

Noah paused on the outskirts of the party, and Fallon tugged lightly on his hand.

"It's more fun if you join."

He raked his free hand through his hair and watched the people living life around him but said nothing.

She slackened her arms but didn't drop his hand. She stepped right in front of him, as close as she could without touching to be sure he could hear her without her yelling.

"What's wrong?"

"I've never done anything like this."

"Anything like what? Go to a party?"

He nodded.

"At least, not in a really long time."

"You were at Keith's party the night we met."

"And I hid in the kitchen until I had an excuse to leave." He looked meaningfully at her.

That explained the offer for a ride home.

"I never would have gone if Fitz hadn't told me I had to go to meet you," he continued. "I think he knew we'd be working together soon and wanted to see if the chemistry was there."

"And was it?" she asked. She knew the answer, but for some reason she needed to hear him say it.

"I'm here, aren't I?" His smile returned. "I knew the second I met you that I wanted to work together."

She was grateful for the ocean breeze blowing through her hair to cool her down.

"It's all a bit overwhelming, innit?" He scanned the beach again. "Is it safe to swim in the ocean at night?"

"Never killed me."

"That's not particularly reassuring."

"Exactly. I dare you, Noah Cooper, to go to a beach glow party." She smirked. "Unless you want to admit defeat before we've even started."

He returned his gaze to her, and the tightness in his posture disappeared as a smile spread across his cheeks.

She tugged on his arm once more, and this time he moved with her, matching her step for step until they were both practically running straight into the water.

The ocean crashed into their legs, and Fallon leaped into the waves beating against them. Sand rippled beneath her feet. Salt water caressed her skin and licked at her hair. The scent of the sea mixed with hints of cotton candy and margaritas floated out from the shore. Strangers surrounded them on all sides, and energy pulsed through the crowd, a rhythm she could have drummed to, an almost tangible feeling of truly living.

She glanced at Noah only a few feet from her and wondered if he could feel it too.

The water, skimming the edge of her bikini top, only barely kissed his stomach. Even so, he welcomed each oncoming wave, any one of which might sweep him away into the never-ending darkness. His eyes reflected the pink light of his glowstick necklace, and even from where she stood, toes sinking into the wet sand, she could see the joy radiating from him.

They spent hours doing everything and anything. They played games—Noah won at mini golf, but she crushed him in the ring toss—built a sandcastle complete with glowstick windows, and danced until their feet hurt.

She kept expecting Noah to tap out, but as the night wore on, he only seemed to gain more energy. She felt her own body flow with adrenaline. It was addicting.

Living was addicting.

Partying and playing and never letting a day go by where she didn't do exactly what she wanted to do. No regrets, no holding back. There was a flutter of delight as she realized the gift she was giving Noah, and she was glad she'd accepted his challenge. She couldn't imagine missing out on this, on everything, the way he always had. Life would be so empty.

When they finally worked their way over to the tattoo tent, Noah lowered himself onto the stool and hooked his ankles around the bars at the base. She had convinced him the night wouldn't be complete without an airbrush tattoo. He'd completely agreed on the condition that she get a matching one and that he got to pick it. She had told him to pick something cool—as cool as an airbrush tattoo could be.

He flipped through the binder of tattoo options, biting his lower lip in thought. He froze at a page near the middle, smiled widely, and pointed so only he and the tattooer could see.

"What is it?" Fallon gripped a lime margarita in her hand.

"You'll have to wait and find out."

She climbed onto the stool beside him and turned her back to her artist, giving her the best angle at her canvas. Cool hands stuck a stencil to her shoulder. A moment later, sticky paint misted over her skin and goosebumps erupted over her body. The artist let the tattoo dry before slowly peeling off the stencil, and Fallon moved for the next person in line.

Noah was already done and waiting for her just outside the tent, his right arm tucked awkwardly behind him. She downed the last of her margarita and tossed the plastic cup in a recycling bin.

"Did you do it?"

"Did you?" he asked.

She turned her back to him, pulling her hair to the side so he could see her new ink. Paint, really.

He burst into laughter, and she knew instantly she had a tattoo she'd be hiding for a few days. She grabbed his elbow and ripped his arm from behind him to see what monstrosity she was stuck with.

A neon pink dolphin glowed from his forearm, just

below his elbow. It reminded her of those Lisa Frank coloring books she'd had as a kid with the ridiculous animals with huge eyes in bright neon colors.

"I told you I like pink," he chuckled.

She stretched her neck as far around as she could and caught the edge of the same dolphin on her shoulder.

"Are you kidding me? Could you have picked a more ridiculous tattoo?" She kicked sand at him, and he laughed harder.

"I resent that. Dolphins are majestic."

"And super cheesy." She rolled her eyes but laughed anyway.

"Think of it as roommate bonding. This is your initiation."

Her gut twisted, and her laugh faded.

Bonding. That was not why they were here. She had brought him to the glow party to win the challenge. Bonding was not part of the deal.

Noah crammed his hands into his suit pockets and motioned with his head for her to follow him. She was careful to keep plenty of space between them as they got her a fresh margarita and crossed the beach. They landed at a cement block coated with sand. He helped her climb onto the tall ledge and then followed, sitting a few inches away.

From where they sat, they could see out over as much ocean as the blacklights could illuminate. They were far enough from the party they could again hear each other without having to yell, and Fallon was uncharacteristically grateful for the moment of calm, regardless of the unease she felt at spending any unnecessary time with Noah.

"Thank you for tonight," he said, continuing to look out over the water. "I'm afraid I've forgotten how to have meaningless fun."

The tension eased from her body. *Meaningless fun* was worlds better than *bonding*.

"That happens to be my specialty." She swung her foot to knock into his.

"I've noticed." He motioned to the party still raging on the beach. Over the next hour, the crowd thinned, but the music played on, and Fallon knew the party wouldn't end until dawn threatened to shut it down.

"You don't have to be so afraid of me, you know." Noah's voice broke the silence that had settled comfortably between them.

"I'm not afraid of you." In fact, if anything, it scared her just how safe she felt sitting in the dark on a beach beside him.

"Maybe not." He shrugged with his whole body. "But something's up. I see how you tense up or pull away when I get close."

She didn't respond. There was nothing to say that she could share with him.

It's better this way, she repeated in her head.

"Anyway," he went on, "I just wanted to let you know you don't need to worry."

He didn't say anything else on the subject but sat quietly, watching the crowd slowly diminish.

It was nearly four before he walked her back to the car. They spent the entire drive home discussing different baked treats, each of which Noah was surprisingly passionate about, and every time his face lit up, a shiver fluttered through her.

When they got home, he walked her to her bedroom before heading to his own and closing the door.

CHAPTER 15

When Annora had first been taken from her, Fallon had had a lot of nightmares. She'd dream she was at the club the night of the shooting, watching but unable to stop it. Or she'd dream that her parents had also been killed. And every so often she'd dream that it was her who'd been there that night instead of Annora.

These nightmares had faded over time and now only happened every few months.

Unfortunately, not long after Noah had left her at her door, she had crashed, and on the other side of consciousness awaited one of these terrors.

She knew she was dreaming; she always did. But no matter how she tried, she could never force herself to wake up. She just had to wait it out, knowing how it would end—watching her family, or herself, die.

Tonight, it was Fallon. She stood on the sidewalk, darkness around her except for a single streetlight shining high above. No sounds came from the club behind her. No one else was there.

From around the corner came a figure clad in

darkness. They stalked toward her, slowly but without hesitation.

Fallon had never seen the person who'd killed Annora and the others that terrible night, not even a picture.

But nightmares didn't need faces.

As the featureless silhouette drew nearer and nearer, she braced herself for what she knew came next.

But this time, she felt a tugging.

"Excuse me!" A child's voice echoed around her.

The person in her dream stopped, then disappeared completely followed by the streetlight, the club, and finally the entire curb.

"Excuse me!" the voice repeated.

Fallon pried open her eyes and found a small child tugging on her blanket near the foot of the bed. She bolted upright and forced her brain to wake up.

"Who are you?" The little girl had large blue eyes and soft blonde curls that cascaded over her shoulders. Rosy cheeks highlighted her fair skin and brought out the pink in her dress.

"I'm Fallon. Who are you?"

"My name is Amelia Cooper. I am four. Why are you in Noah's house?"

"I live here."

"Why?" She tilted her head to the side and a clump of curls slid over her shoulder.

"Because." Fallon glanced at the open bedroom door behind her. Wasn't someone looking for this kid?

"Does Noah know you live here?" The girl pursed

her lips and moved them from side to side.

"Yes, Noah lives in the other bedroom. I live in this one." Fallon pulled the blanket further up her chest, attempting to cover as much skin as possible. Suddenly her sports bra and shorts felt a tad casual.

"Oh, that's alright then." She shrugged and climbed onto the bed. She crossed her legs beneath her and propped her round face in her hands.

Apparently, they were friends now.

"I've never met someone named Fallon before. Have you ever met someone with my name?"

She tried to remember what the little girl had called herself. Amanda? Emily?

Amelia!

"Not in real life." Fallon scooted as far from the girl as she could without falling off the bed. "But I read about one in a book when I was a kid."

"There's an Amelia book?" Amelia's already giant eyes widened to the size of cymbals.

"Lots of them, all about the same girl. Her name was Amelia Bedelia."

Amelia gasped.

"That sounds AMAZ—"

"Amelia?" Noah appeared in her doorway, feet planted in the hall. "Amelia! You cannot go in here. Come out right now." His voice was stern, but not unkind.

Amelia hopped off the bed without a fight and dragged her feet across the carpet until she met her brother in the hall, head hung in shame.

"Go downstairs." He steered the girl's shoulders

toward the stairs, and she walked out of sight. He turned back to Fallon who was still frozen in her bed.

"I am so, so sorry. This will never happen again."

He reached for the door handle, still without setting foot in her room, and pulled it closed.

Whatever spell Amelia had cast on her was broken instantly, and Fallon bolted from her bed and straight for the shower. A quick rinse got the remaining salt water and sand out of her hair, and only minutes later, she found Noah sitting at the kitchen counter waiting for her.

He shot out of his chair when she entered.

"I'm so sorry. Amelia was looking for me, and I had run for coffee." He slid a cup in her direction across the counter. "It won't happen again."

She studied his face, the drawn brows, the pained eyes. She'd never seen someone so apologetic for something that was in no way their fault.

Although, last time someone had barged into her space, it had been him, and she'd bitten his head off. He was likely just protecting Amelia.

"It's fine. Really. She didn't know any better." She took a drink of the sugary sweet coffee he had brought her and moaned in pleasure. It really was the best coffee she'd ever had.

She crossed the kitchen, opened the cupboard, and found it empty. She'd managed to eat all their cereal.

"She said she was your sister?"

"Yeah." Noah sat back down. "She's usually with my mum and dad at the doctor at this time, but she had her appointment yesterday instead."

She moved to the fridge and found it nearly as empty—a few sips of milk, half a loaf of bread, and a door full of condiments. Noah ate most lunches and dinners with his parents, but she had been clearing out the little food that was in the guesthouse and ordering out for the rest.

"Is she alright?" Amelia hadn't seemed sick to Fallon.

"She's getting better." He smiled tightly and watched her unwrap a protein bar she found stashed in a cupboard.

She remembered Josh saying something about Noah's sister being sick, but she hadn't thought much of it.

She bit into the stale bar and nearly spit it back out. Noah watched her attempt to chew, not even trying to hide the amusement he was clearly finding in her battle with her breakfast.

"How is it?" He grinned.

"A little hard." She spoke through a mouth full of chocolate, nuts, and oats.

"Not surprising"—he linked his fingers and rested them on his lap—"considering I've lived here for six months, and I'm pretty sure those were here when I moved in."

She raced to the sink and spit the inedible mess out of her mouth.

"You knew that bar was ancient when I opened it. You didn't want to say anything?" She flipped on the faucet, stuck her head under, and gulped down mouthfuls of water.

"I thought it might be entertaining to watch you figure that out on your own." His grin widened. "It was."

She turned off the water and wiped her mouth on the sleeve of her *I-hit-like-a-girl* sweatshirt.

"Pendejo." She returned to her coffee.

"I'm sorry." He looked less sorry and more like he was trying not to laugh at her. "I actually need to run to the supermarket today. We need supplies for tonight. Why don't you come with me after practice, and we'll get some food for the house, too?"

"What's tonight?"

"I completed your dare last night. Now it's your turn." He checked his watch and moved from the counter toward the front door, pocketing his keys. "We have to go. We'll get breakfast on the way to practice."

Fallon's stomach rumbled loudly in response.

***

She did her best to focus through practices. Blue Streetlights ran smoothly, but when it was time for Edge of September, both her bandmates showed up late. Keith looked like hell when he finally got there, and while she didn't miss the concern on Calvin's face, her mind kept wandering to whatever Noah had planned for that evening.

"We have to finalize a set list," she repeated after they'd been arguing for nearly an hour. Keith had maintained his normal I-don't-give-a-shit demeanor, but Calvin was an anxious disaster.

"Maybe we shouldn't play any of our original

songs. People like covers," he said after what she had thought was a decent run of a song Keith had written that spring.

"No one who only plays covers has ever won. Ever." Keith eyed him from behind his unruly brown curls. "We have to play originals if we want a shot."

"Do we even have a shot? Some incredible bands have come out of Twisted Fest." Calvin sank onto a stool by the bar and rested his bass across his thighs.

"We're as good as any of them," Fallon reminded him. So was Blue Streetlights. She didn't bring that up, though. Today's practice had been tense at best, and bringing up her other band might push the guys too far.

"I know," Calvin sighed.

"But we don't stand a chance if we don't finalize a set list." She let her drumsticks hang by her sides but stayed on her throne. It was as comfortable as anywhere in the warehouse.

Calvin's phone beeped, and he pulled it from the pocket of his tan chinos. He swiped it open, read whatever had come in, and then looked up at her with wide eyes.

"What?"

"Why does Noah have a pink dolphin tattooed on his arm?" Calvin's brows quirked upward. Keith glanced at her.

The corners of her mouth turned up again, and she tried to keep a straight face.

"Sounds like a question you should ask Noah."

"I did," Calvin continued. "He said to ask you as

you had a matching one."

"Well, mine isn't on my arm, and the pink was his choice."

"You and Noah got matching dolphin tattoos?" Keith cut in. "Am I hearing that right?"

"Airbrush tattoos."

"Why?" Calvin's face was pure confusion.

"We went to a glow party last night, and I let him choose the tattoo. He chose a dolphin. I really think that says more about him than me." She shrugged, basking in the confusion of her bandmates.

"You went to a party? With Noah?" Calvin continued to stare at her. "Did the whole band go?"

"Nope."

"So, you two just went for fun?"

"Something like that." She shifted away from Calvin's stare that had grown increasingly uncomfortable as his questioning went on.

"Huh," Calvin huffed.

"How did you know about his dolphin anyway?" She quickly steered the conversation away from her bet with Noah. It was complicated at best, and Calvin did not need to be a part of it.

He flashed his phone at her, but she barely caught a glimpse of the photo.

"He sent a pic, and it was in the shot."

She hadn't realized Noah and Calvin had grown close enough to be texting, at least not regularly. Something about it bothered her, probably the overlap of worlds. Calvin was in her Edge of September world. He didn't belong in her Blue Streetlights world.

Too late.

Calvin tossed his phone into his backpack a few feet away.

"Now can we play?" Keith stood from the couch, and she lifted her sticks to count off.

CHAPTER 16

Noah was waiting for her when she left practice, and the two of them headed to the grocery store. As he filled his cart with three kinds of flour, four kinds of sugar, vanilla, butter, and more eggs than she could eat in her lifetime, she raided the cereal aisle, filling an entire cart with Cinnamon Toast Crunch, Fruity Pebbles, and all their crunchy, sugary friends—except Cap'n Crunch. That stuff was the breakfast cereal equivalent of running with scissors.

Noah offered to pay for all of it, but she'd insisted on using her parents' credit card. She was already living with him rent-free. He didn't need to cover her food too. In fact, she owed him, and she hated that feeling.

So, she bought Noah's cart too.

Their haul overflowed the guesthouse kitchen. Fallon needed two cupboards just for her cereal and another for the rest of her snacks—protein bars from this century, chips, jerky, and tortillas. Noah had gotten actual food like lunch meat and vegetables.

"Why did you buy real food? You always eat with your family." She shoved another bag of flour into the cupboard by the oven.

"I don't *always* eat with my family." He folded the last of the reusable grocery bags and stacked them under the sink.

"You have since I've been here."

"I find the guesthouse has been understocked recently."

Fallon stuck out her tongue.

"And now?" she asked.

"Now, it is restocked." Noah landed on a barstool. "Does Edge really only take one day off each week?"

"Unless we have a gig, yeah."

"That's intense."

"It's necessary if we are going to put up a fight at Twisted Fest with practices like today's shitshow." She sucked in her lips. She shouldn't be talking about this with Noah.

"What happened at band practice?" His forehead creased in concern.

"None of your business."

"I guess not." He shrugged.

"We're on for tonight, then?" She headed for the stairs, craving a nap after a late night and a long day.

"Tonight."

She wasn't particularly looking forward to whatever her challenge would be. Noah definitely had the better side of the bargain. Go out and have an awesome time one night and then chill at home—his favorite pastime—the next. She'd much rather be going out tonight, but that would mean losing the challenge.

And she never lost at anything.

She returned downstairs in pajamas shorts and a baggy Fall Out Boy T-shirt—the requested dress code— just before eleven and found Noah already waiting for her.

She'd gotten used to his various pajama bottoms and white T-shirts, but the black apron was new. She tried to hold back her laughter but failed miserably and almost fell down the stairs.

He scowled and folded his arms across his chest.

"Something you'd like to say?" His accent thickened.

She shook her head, getting her laughter under control.

"What are we doing?" She climbed up to a stool and watched him gather ingredients from around the kitchen.

"I dare you, Fallon Rivera, to make cookies with me."

The sound of her name on his lips sent shivers through her entire body, and it took a moment to process anything else that had come out of his mouth.

"Cookies? Seriously?"

"You don't like cookies?" He lifted one eyebrow, knowing damn well she liked anything with sugar in it.

"You said nights at home were some of the best in your life. I'd expected something a bit more…exciting than cookies." Drinking games. Poker. Even invasive, personal conversations, heaven forbid.

"I never said exciting." He added vanilla and chocolate chips to the mountain of ingredients on the island. "Besides, I have a feeling you haven't made cookies in a long time. Maybe ever."

His eyes found hers, and he waited for her answer to a question he hadn't technically asked.

But he wasn't wrong. She hadn't baked anything since she was a little girl when she and Annora would help her mother make holiday treats each year. That was so long ago Fallon could barely remember it.

"It has been a while."

Noah nodded once, then bent down behind the island. He emerged a moment later with a bundle of fabric in one hand. He shoved it toward her.

"What is that?" She eyed the black heap but didn't take it.

"I wore the requested uniform last night, glowstick necklace and all. You have to play by my rules tonight—unless you are already claiming defeat." He grinned wickedly.

She snatched the black wad from his hands. Straps and folds untangled until it was clear she was holding an apron, a match to the one Noah had tied around his own waist and neck.

"Need help putting it on?" He lifted the stand mixer from the corner of the kitchen and carried it to the island. His biceps and forearms tightened under the weight, pink dolphin tattoo sparkling in the kitchen lights.

"I think I can handle it." She turned her back to him and focused on tying apron strings—not on the guy behind her with the muscles and the apron and the dolphin tattoo that had somehow become unthinkably sexy.

The apron was too long for her. It hung past her pajama shorts and made her look like she wasn't wearing pants.

"Chocolate chip alright? I figured we'd go with a classic." He motioned for her to join him by the bowl, and she shuffled over to him, bare feet cool against the wood floor.

"Now the trick is"—he continued as he handed her a small measuring cup—"to have all your ingredients at room temperature. I pulled out the eggs and butter a while ago."

"Why?"

"I believe it has something to do with the texture." He dumped a stick of butter into the bowl. "I don't really know. I've just heard that's the rule, and it seems to work."

He filled her measuring cup with sugar. She dumped it in, and he instructed her to fill it with brown sugar three times and add those as well.

"I thought you called these 'biscuits' in England." She smashed the brown sugar into the measuring cup.

"Chocolate chip happens to be an exception. Even back home, these are cookies. Cookies are chewier. Biscuits have more of a 'snap' to them."

"We call that 'burned' here."

"Oh, please. You call aubergines 'eggplants' and ice lollies 'popsicles'. We are not the mad ones." He flicked on the mixer.

"What's so weird about popsicles?" She wouldn't argue the eggplant one. Eggplant was a stupid name for a purple vegetable that wasn't shaped like an egg.

"They aren't even made with pop!"

"Do you mean *soda*?" She didn't care at all what he called any of it, but she liked pushing Noah's buttons.

"You know exactly what I'm saying." The corners of his mouth twitched, and his eyes sparkled.

He walked her through the rest of the recipe. She followed each of his instructions as precisely as she could, partially because Noah had a way of giving instructions that was so *not* condescending it made her want to listen and partially because she wanted these cookies to be amazing so she could rub it in his face that she was the better baker—which wasn't true at all but would be fun as hell.

As she measured and he stirred, they talked. Music. Movies. Places they wanted to travel to someday. Fallon rarely told anyone, but she had always wanted to see the city in Mexico where her father grew up. She figured that flirted with the edge of "personal," which was still completely off-limits even if they were friends. But somehow, with Noah, it felt less personal. He didn't pry or ask questions or push her to say more.

He just listened.

And when she stopped talking, he moved on to another subject.

They fell into a rhythm, and a calm settled through her. She couldn't remember the last time she felt truly calm. It was foreign, like a memory you'd been told you had but couldn't actually recall. Fallon was usually a fire, blazing and burning hot, but tonight, something inside her had settled into glowing embers, still alive but steady.

Comfortable.

"Do you want more or fewer chocolate chips?" Noah held up the bag of chocolate chips.

"I'm surprised you have to ask." She quirked a brow.

He dumped in the entire bag.

He handed her a giant spoon to mix in the chips and squatted beside a drawer to find a cookie sheet.

"You've only lived here a week." The pans banged together as he removed one and placed it on the counter beside their mixing bowl. "It seems like longer."

"You've enjoyed it that much?" She plunged a finger into the bowl and scooped a chunk of dough into her mouth.

Noah elbowed her. "It simply feels like you've always been here."

"It kind of does." She braced her hands on the edge of the counter and hoisted herself up to sit on it. He handed her the cookie scoop, and she started scooping balls of dough and dropping them on the pan.

"I honestly didn't think you'd stay this long."

She paused.

"Do you want me to go?" Fear gripped her throat.

"No!" His hand grasped her knee, but he instantly removed it and tucked it behind him. Her skin tingled where he'd touched her. "What I mean is, I thought you'd want to leave. I thought you kind of hated me."

He picked up the tray of dough blobs, slid them into the oven, and set a timer.

"You thought I hated you?" She wiped her hands on a towel, grateful for something to focus on besides Noah.

"'Hated' is a strong word. I definitely thought you didn't like me. You didn't seem like you wanted me around, and after what happened that night after Calvin and Keith's party…" He rubbed the back of his neck.

"I told you that didn't matter."

"I know." He sighed and ran his hand through his hair. It landed wildly, skimming his temples and curling at his neck. "I just thought you would want out. I'm glad you didn't."

Her stomach fluttered, and she couldn't stop her focus from drifting to Noah. His mocha eyes traced her features, their intensity warming her face along their path. Her heart thudded in her chest, and she became aware of every inch of her skin against the countertop. Pinpricks trickled down her spine.

His mouth parted ever so slightly, and a breath escaped her lips as he took a step toward her.

Beeping sounded from the kitchen timer, and reality crashed around her.

Her mom and dad.

No apartment.

Twisted Fest.

Annora.

A river of ice burst through her veins. She couldn't get distracted by Noah—not by his apron, not by his pink dolphin tattoo, and definitely not by those enticing eyes. He was trouble—and not the good kind. Her instincts had been right the night she'd met him, and she couldn't forget that now.

Noah could never be a casual fling, and she could never be anything but.

That was the way it had to be.

"Fitz is coming to Edge's next gig," she blurted.

Noah froze, cleared his throat, and stepped away. He pushed a button on the timer, and the beeping stopped.

"What gig?" His voice was hoarse. He grabbed an oven mitt and pulled the cookies out.

"Our normal slot at The Garage. In two weeks. I don't care if you come, but Fitz will be there." She was being super obvious, but Fitz was her only defense, and she had to be sure there were no misunderstandings.

She slid off the counter and circled it to sit on the other side, putting the entire island between them.

Noah leaned against the counter by the oven. "We'll see. Clubs aren't my scene."

"Maybe that will be your dare that weekend." The tension around them was beginning to settle, but her heart was still hammering in her chest.

"Maybe."

"Can we eat them?" She nodded to the pan.

"They're a little hot." Noah's voice had returned to it's smooth, cheery normal. "But I'll get you one if you'd like."

She grinned, and he removed a spatula from a

drawer. He lifted a cookie from the pan, melted chocolate trailing behind, placed it on a paper towel, and slid it toward her. She broke off a piece and ate it.

Rich chocolate exploded in her mouth, but chewy, sweet vanilla swooped in and balanced it out perfectly. It was gooey and soft and all things a cookie should be.

It might have been the best cookie she'd ever had.

Melted chocolate coated her fingers, and she licked them clean. Noah turned his back to her and placed another tray of dough in the oven.

After he'd baked two more trays and she had eaten four cookies, they called it a night. As she headed to bed, she paused to watch Noah wash the mixing bowl in the sink. His hands moved methodically, like he'd done this thousands of times and it was all muscle memory.

This bet would be tougher to win than she'd expected. When he'd challenged her to an evening in, she hadn't thought he'd last one night out, but he'd stuck with her the whole way. And now, as she watched him replace the clean bowl on the mixer, she knew nights alone with Noah would be tougher than she'd thought they'd be.

She needed to up her game if she was going to win.

CHAPTER 17

The week could not have passed by any slower. Keith and Calvin had been late to every practice, and even when they were there, Keith was hungover, and Calvin was distracted. She'd bitten their heads off by the end of practice Thursday, and Calvin had cancelled practice altogether the next morning. At least it meant she'd get a break from both of them and an afternoon off.

Meanwhile, Blue Streetlights had become a welcome distraction. As Twisted Fest crept closer, Josh, Fitz, and Noah only got more motivated. Josh had shown up that day with two new original songs, and Fitz put her right to work learning them.

She didn't mind the extra work. Drumming was a release. It was one of the very few parts of her she didn't have to protect. She could give everything without pretending not to feel or care. And punk was addicting. It was pure energy and life in music form. She'd would be lying if she said she wasn't loving every moment behind her kit, even if she'd never give Fitz the satisfaction of admitting it.

Elliott arrived as they were packing up. He swaggered over to the guys and shook each of their hands. Fallon returned to her throne behind her drums, out of reach of Elliott. He nodded to her instead and leaned on a barstool.

"Three more weeks to Twisted Fest. Is Blue Streetlights ready?" His gray eyes jumped from bandmate to bandmate.

"We could win it tomorrow." Josh flopped onto the ratty couch. His confidence was charming and not altogether misplaced. Blue Streetlights sounded fantastic. They likely could win it tomorrow.

And Edge of September hadn't even practiced today.

Her gut clenched. Edge had to win Twisted Fest. She wanted Blue Streetlights to do well, and she would do all she could to make sure they did, but Edge was where her loyalty lay. If they lost and Blue Streetlights won, she would be counting on some producer to notice her and reach out. It was a long shot at best.

She'd talk to Calvin and Keith. They had to get their asses in line.

"I don't doubt it. And how's our newest member fitting in?" Elliott's question, despite being about her, was clearly aimed at anyone else.

Josh and Fitz spoke at the same time.

"Fallon's incredible."

"We're lucky to have her."

Elliott turned to Noah.

"Like a glove." Noah's eyes narrowed. "But maybe

you should ask her."

Elliott finally shifted to face Fallon. "And how do you feel it's going?"

"Couldn't be better." It was true, but even if she were hating every second of it, she'd never say a damn word to Elliott about it.

"Glad to hear it. And how are Keith and Calvin? I haven't heard from either of them since our visit a couple weeks ago." He lifted his brows, and she had to wonder if he somehow knew there was some tension in Edge of September. It didn't sit right with her.

"Perfect."

"Good." He clapped both hands on his thighs and stood. "Well, I'll be on my way. I'm headed to Sacramento for the weekend, but I got word this morning that Blue Streetlights has the 2:30 slot on Friday afternoon for Twisted Fest." He glanced back at her once more. "Edge of September will have the following slot at 3:30."

"That's a long time for Fallon to play without a break." Fitz shot her a glance from where he lounged on the couch beside Josh. She noticed Noah watching her from where he stood a few feet away.

"I tried to spread the bands out, but the crew wouldn't have it. They said it was a waste of time to take down her drums only to set them back up later. There will be thirty minutes between."

"It's fine," she cut in. She refused to let any of these men think of her as weak enough to warrant this conversation. "I can do a double set."

"Good girl."

Fallon tensed.

That arrogant, misogynistic bastard.

Noah's fists clenched at his sides, and his eyes went cold. Fitz leaned forward, likely prepared to dodge in front of her should she choose to give Elliott the beating he deserved.

"See you all next week!" Elliott called over his shoulder as he left, completely unaware of the tension in the room.

"He's a real asshole, isn't he?" Josh shook his head.

"Unfortunately, that asshole is contractually our manager for at least another year." Fitz tucked his guitar case away for the night and grabbed his motorcycle helmet from the bar. "See you all tomorrow."

He glanced at her and lifted a single brow in question, his way of checking on her. She nodded, and he left without another word.

"I'm out too." Josh leaped from the couch.

"You ready to go?" Noah asked. His face had softened again, and she wasn't sure if she was pissed or grateful for his kindness.

"Of course." She followed Josh and Noah out of the warehouse and locked the door behind her.

As she reached for the door handle, Josh's fingers brushed her elbow.

Could we possibly talk? I can give you a ride home." He smiled weakly.

"Sure." She glanced at Noah who nodded confirmation that he'd heard and drove away a moment later. She followed Josh to his car, the same

Ford Focus beater he'd driven back in Arizona.

"I can't believe you still drive this piece of shit." She adjusted the passenger seat.

"Why wouldn't I? This *piece of shit* is my baby." He shifted into first. "And she's got too many memories."

Exactly the reason Fallon would want to get rid of it.

"You needed to talk about something?"

"Next weekend. Blue Streetlights is coming to the Edge of September show at The Garage."

"I know. Fitz told me." The air conditioning was either off or broken, and her back was starting to sweat. She rolled down her window, and the breeze whipped her dark hair around her.

"So, I'll be there, obviously." Josh rolled down his window as well and raised his voice so she could hear him over the roar. "I was thinking of inviting someone else to come with us, but I wanted to check with you first."

"Why? It's open. Bring whoever the hell you want." She hadn't ever considered he might have friends outside the band. Calvin and Keith didn't hang out with anyone but each other.

Except…

Calvin and Eric had been dating a long time, and she figured Keith must have friends he got high with. Maybe they did have other friends, and she'd just never spent enough time with them to realize it.

Josh chuckled. "I'm still getting used to hearing you cuss. Language like that wouldn't have flown in your parents' house."

"There's a lot about me that wouldn't have flown in my parents' house."

"Fair enough." He turned onto her street and parked a few feet from the Cooper's driveway. She could see the garage closing. Noah must have barely beaten them back. "I only ask because the person I want to bring isn't exactly a friend."

"They're your enemy?" She wiggled her eyebrows.

"It's my girlfriend."

The air rushed from her lungs as the word barreled into her chest.

Girlfriend.

Josh had a girlfriend.

This shouldn't have been surprising. Josh was a catch, always had been, and a twenty-three-year-old guy was bound to be dating. Even so, she hadn't expected it. But she supposed just because she hadn't been able to move on didn't mean he couldn't.

She swallowed hard and grasped at a response, anything to kill the pitiful look he was giving her now.

"Of course you can invite her." She shrugged like there was nothing in the world she cared about less.

"You sure? I don't want it to be weird."

"It won't be." She gripped the door handle and practically fell out of his car. "Thanks for the ride."

She raced up the driveway as quickly as possible without it looking like she was actually running from him.

She crossed the thick lawn to the guesthouse and didn't see Noah as she staggered into her room and flung herself across her bed. A nap was definitely happening.

Except, as she pulled her blanket over her head, she didn't find sleep. Instead, her mind swirled with thoughts of Edge of September and Twisted Fest and her parents and Elliott and Blue Streetlights and Josh and his girlfriend.

She tried to clear her mind. Worrying was stupid and a terrible way to waste a life away.

She forced herself to focus on her dare for Noah that night. They needed to do something crazy if she had a chance of winning their challenge. As practice replayed in her mind, the perfect idea came to her.

It was *crazy*. In fact, she was already doubting if she should mention it at all. But if anything would get him to admit defeat, this was it, and tonight might be the one night they could pull it off. And even if he went through with it, well, Noah needed some crazy.

She removed her phone from her boot before she could change her mind.

Fallon: *We're going out.*

Noah didn't immediately respond, but a few hours later, as she sat at the kitchen island eating muffins that had appeared on the counter sometime overnight, her phone chimed.

Noah: *You've got another dare for me, then?*

God, even his texts sounded British.

Fallon: *Meet me at eleven.*

Noah: *Swim briefs again?*

Fallon: *Normal clothes. You need to blend in.*

Noah: *Blend in to what?*

Fallon: *You'll find out tonight.*

She considered telling him what they were doing, but she didn't want him to backout early and have it somehow not count as a win for her.

Or maybe a small part of her didn't want him to end their game.

But that was dumb. Of course, she wanted him to fold. It was why she'd accepted this stupid challenge in the first place. Somewhere deep inside her, she just couldn't pass up a chance to come out on top.

So, she let him decide what she meant by "blend in."

Fallon, on the other hand, slid into a black leather miniskirt and a red crop top that brought out her puffy lips. She couldn't help but notice how her dolphin tattoo, almost completely faded, peeked out under the draped shoulder. With her Doc Martins strapped to her feet, her phone safely tucked inside, she headed for Noah's room and knocked twice.

"Come in!" He shouted from behind the door.

She pushed the door open and found him sitting in a chair, slipping on a shoe. He'd gone with tan joggers and a light blue T-shirt. Perfect.

His eyes danced over her, and he stilled.

"I thought you said to blend in. There's not a soul on earth that won't notice you looking like that. You look like you're headed on a date. A hot one." He swallowed.

"First of all, all my dates are hot. Second, I told *you* to blend in. My clothes serve a different purpose."

He blinked a few times then motioned for her to lead the way. Soon they were in his car, headed into the heart of downtown Los Angeles.

"I assume you won't tell me where we're going yet?" Noah weaved through the streets of LA, still crowded even nearing midnight.

"Nope." She pointed for him to make another right.

They arrived at a high-rise building full of apartments way too pricy for Fallon. Noah parked on the street and fed the meter.

"What is this place?" He looked up at the towering glass monstrosity.

"Apartments. Nice ones." She headed for the entrance, Noah by her side, but paused just outside the door. "Listen. To get in, I'm going to need you to hang back while I talk to the doorman. As soon as you see me head to the elevator, walk straight there."

"What do you mean 'to get in'? Can I please know what we're doing?" He glanced around them anxiously. Her gut had been right that this guy was innocent. She almost felt bad.

Almost.

"To appreciate Los Angeles, you have to see it. And there's no better view than a high-rise apartment in the heart of the city."

"That's the dare? Take in the view?"

"Not quite." She stepped into the lobby.

It was well lit, bordering on too bright, for the hour and empty aside from a middle-aged man in a maroon suit and a funny hat sitting at a reception desk. Noah obeyed her instructions, hanging back by the door. Her heart raced, and sweat coated her palms, but adrenaline coursed through her as she approached the door attendant.

"Excuse me, sir." She tilted her head and blinked her eyes to make them look bigger. "I'm here for Elliott Cox, but I've forgotten the elevator code. Seems I had one too many drinks." She twirled a strand of hair around her finger and giggled.

The man looked her over once, stood from his chair, and walked to the elevator.

"I wish I could say you were the first"—he held out a badge and scanned it—"but this happens quite often." The elevator doors opened, and she slipped inside, Noah right behind her.

The man eyed Noah suspiciously.

"Don't mind my stepbrother," Fallon cooed. "He's going to sing for Elliott. He's going to be a star."

Noah waved, awkwardly playing along with a game he was only getting pieces of.

The door attendant nodded his understanding and returned to his desk as the elevator dinged closed.

"This is Elliott's home? Why are we here?" Noah practically yelled.

"We are going to break into Elliott's apartment."

CHAPTER 18

"Are you insane?" Noah's eyes widened and his fingers raked through his hair. "That's illegal!"

"Keep your voice down." She pushed the button for the 37th floor and leaned against the railing along the elevator wall. "We aren't stealing anything. We're just going to enjoy his view."

"That's still breaking and entering."

"The doorman let us up."

"Because you flirted with him!" He slumped against the railing opposite her.

"He assumed I was one of Elliott's girlfriends. His mistake."

"What if Elliott's home?"

"He's in Sacramento all weekend."

"What if the doorman knows that?"

"Then he never would have let us up. I was taking a chance. You should try it sometime."

Noah closed his eyes and leaned his head back against the elevator wall. She sighed heavily.

"You don't have to do this if you really don't want

to. We can ride this elevator right back down." She stepped across the racing elevator and stopped directly in front of him. She placed a finger on his chin and tilted his head to look at her. He opened his eyes. Leaning against the railing as he was, he was almost eye to eye with her. "It's your choice."

As much as she'd originally hoped he'd admit defeat, suddenly she desperately wanted him to agree. She ached for him to do this with her—this stupid, illegal, ridiculous dare.

His gaze traced her face, and he swallowed before nodding once.

"Let's do it."

The elevator dinged, and they emptied directly into a luxe apartment. Everything screamed wealth and elegance—the place of someone who wanted to show off.

An oversized sectional filled most of the space, aside from a guitar setup that looked pretty impressive at first glance. She assumed it was as high end as the rest of Elliott's apartment. A hallway to the left led to what she assumed were the bedrooms and bathrooms. To the right, the living room opened into a sleek kitchen. Whites, blacks, and grays were the only colors, and there were no personal items anywhere. The only art was a big-ass canvas painting of Los Angeles hanging on the living room wall, which seemed ridiculous considering his actual view was a thousand times more impressive.

Fallon had only been here once before. Elliott had invited the whole band over when they signed him on as their manager. She was pretty sure he had just wanted to wow them, but if impressing a bunch of broke twenty-somethings was what did it for Elliott, then whatever.

Noah moved lightly through the space, like Elliott might be able to hear them from Sacramento.

"You ready to see why we're here?" She took two cans of soda from Elliott's fridge, handed one to Noah, and led him across the kitchen to the sliding door on the back wall. She slid it open and stepped out onto the patio. Noah followed just behind her.

Even knowing what she'd see, her breath caught as she looked out over the city. The lights streamed in a scattered pattern as far as they could see in any direction. Nearby buildings blocked some of the overlook but somehow only added to the enormity of it all. The sky above was pitch black, not a star to be seen, which brought its own dark beauty.

She rested her palms on the railing and let her body relax against it. Noah did the same beside her. His face was as breathtaking as the view. The strong line of his jaw and his piercing stare as he looked out over the world mesmerized her just as they had the night they'd met and any other time she dared meet his gaze.

"What do you think? Worth breaking and entering?"

He broke away from the city to meet her eyes.

"Definitely." He smiled, and shivers erupted through her body. She turned back to the view, easing his intensity.

"I didn't think I'd get you up here."

"You almost didn't." He chuckled softly.

"What changed your mind?"

"You." He continued peering over the city, but she felt as though he was still somehow taking in every move she made down to each blink.

"Me?" she breathed.

"I trust you. That's what this challenge was about, right? Teaching each other a way of life otherwise unknown? It makes life exciting."

Her heart thudded in her chest. She'd never have thought of Noah as someone who looked for ways to make life exciting, but it was all she ever did. Maybe they had more in common than she'd realized.

"Do you often break into other people's homes?" he teased.

She bumped her shoulder into his hard enough he had to grip the railing to keep from tumbling sideways. It only made him laugh. They stepped back and sat in the chairs Elliott kept on the balcony.

"I do whatever I want. But no. This is a first for me. You have to admit, though, this view is worth it. I was not going to drag you to some half-ass view." She drank from her soda.

"Yes. One must be exposed to the whole-ass view to properly appreciate it."

Soda sprayed from her mouth, showering the cement floor of the balcony as she sputtered through a laugh.

"What?" He chuckled and drank from his can. The gleam in his eye shredded his attempt at faked innocence.

"I never thought something like that would come out of your mouth." She wiped her chin with the back of her hand.

"Because I'm British and proper?" He puffed out his chest.

"Because you're you."

"Maybe you don't know me as well as you think you do."

Los Angeles echoed around them—the traffic and people far below. Up this high, all the noise morphed and blended until no one sound stood out among the others, like California-tinted white noise. It wound through her and sent her adrenaline coursing.

"Did you always know you wanted to be a drummer?" Noah nodded to her fingers tapping out a rhythm on the small table between them. She hadn't even realized she'd been doing it.

"Not always." She stopped tapping. "But for a long time."

She'd been eleven. Her parents made both her and Annora take piano lessons as kids. Annora had been a natural. She was playing hymns within six months, and by the end of the year, she could weave melodies even their teacher had been impressed with. Meanwhile, Fallon could barely plunk out "Three Blind Mice." At the request—demand—of her parents, she stuck with it for two years until she could manage the basics.

One day, her father had been late picking them up, and she and Annora began exploring the music shop where their lessons took place. Her sister tested different guitars, basses, and even a ukelele, but Fallon had snuck through the sound system area and discovered a small room with a drum kit set up inside.

She could still remember the electricity tearing through her as she lowered herself onto the throne. Oak drumsticks peeked out from a black tote clinging to the side of one of the floor toms. They called to her. She slid the drumsticks from their home, and shivers skittered up her arms.

They'd purchased her first set of drums that day.

"How old were you when you learned to play?" Noah asked, bringing her back from the memory.

"I don't remember," she lied. She returned to the railing and looked out over the world, hoping he would take the hint.

He didn't, and a moment later, he was right beside her again, this time only inches away.

"I was fourteen when I started singing. I'm sure I'd sung as a child, but it wasn't until then that my voice had changed enough that my mum and dad put me in vocal lessons. By sixteen I'd joined the band. We played together for years until…" He paused.

"You don't have to tell me." It was none of her business, and she shouldn't care, even if she was a little curious.

"It's alright," he continued, misreading her dismissal. "I left the band to move here. We were just starting to take off, and I couldn't ask them to slow down or wait for me to get back to do something about it. But I also knew I couldn't stay behind, not with Amelia here in the States." He shrugged in a full body way that told her it wasn't as simple as he made it all sound.

She tried to picture herself in his shoes. She'd left her family to be here. He'd left his band to be with his family. It wasn't a choice she could ever see herself making.

"That's when you joined Blue Streetlights?" she asked, attempting to steer the conversation back to the band.

"My mum made me promise that if I came with them, it wouldn't be the end of my music. I met Josh not long after I arrived."

"Love at first sight, huh?" She batted her lashes at him.

"Something like that," he smiled. "How'd you end up with Edge of September? If you and Fitz are friends, why didn't you join Blue Streetlights?"

"I joined Edge long before I met Fitz."

"But you knew Josh before you moved here, didn't you?"

She stilled. "Did he tell you that?"

"He said you knew each other in Arizona." His brow scrunched. "Am I not supposed to know that? I'm sorry if I intruded."

"It's fine." She shook out her arms and wrapped her fingers around the railing. "Josh introduced me to Elliott. He set me up with Edge."

Noah stayed quiet a moment before sucking in a deep breath and blurting out, "Why don't you talk about your life? I know you hate prying questions, and you don't have to answer if you don't want to, but from everything I've seen and heard, you don't let anyone in. Everyone is kept at a distance. Why?"

She squeezed the railing on either side of her. He was trying to be a friend. Friends asked questions. He'd opened up to her about leaving his bandmates in England to move here. The least she could do was respond even if she refused to give details.

"Because tonight could be the last night of anyone's life. And if it's mine, I don't want any regrets. And if it's someone else—" She stopped.

"You don't want the pain," Noah finished.

She didn't have to tell him he was right, and he didn't ask for more. They drifted into comfortable silence. LA continued to breathe and flow beneath them, but on that balcony, life was still.

"We should probably get out of here." He smiled tightly and stepped back into the apartment.

She followed and found him standing in the middle of the living room, eyes darting across the space.

"What are you doing?"

He looked around once more before answering.

"Does Elliott always treat you like he did today?" His brows pulled together.

She shrugged. "El es un pendejo. I'm used to it."

He continued his stroll around the room.

"Maybe we leave a little gift before we go." He grinned at her, and the wickedness in that single grin was enough to make her knees buckle.

"Anything in mind?" she squeaked out.

He stopped in front of a cabinet beneath the television. He opened the doors and revealed an impressive movie collection.

"He still uses discs?" Noah's face was scrunched in confusion. "What year is it?"

"He's like forty. He still has a collection." She stepped beside Noah and skimmed over the titles. "They're in alphabetical order."

He paused and then, in one movement, swiped an entire row of movies off the shelf. Blu-ray cases crashed to the ground at their feet.

"Not anymore."

Fallon laughed at the ridiculousness of their prank but joined Noah in not-so-gently removing the cases from their perfectly organized homes.

"Wait." She crouched, emptying the bottom shelves. "We can't leave these here. If he gets home and knows someone's been here, he'll figure out it was us. I'm sure there's some kind of camera in the elevator or something."

"Blast, you're right." He hung his head. "I really wanted to do *something.*"

She scanned the mess of movies around them.

"We still could. We'll put them back completely out of order. Look at this place. It'll drive him crazy. But he'll probably blame one of the girls he brings home."

They replaced all of Elliott's movies on the shelves. She switched the discs between cases as Noah shoved others into sporadic locations, careful to tuck a few behind the rest where they couldn't easily be seen.

When they were finished, the collection looked exactly the same to Fallon, but nothing was in order. *Die Hard* was between *The Matrix* and *The Fast and the Furious* which she was pretty sure actually held *You've Got Mail.*

It was beyond stupid, easily the dumbest prank she'd ever pulled, but she hoped it would drive Elliott crazy.

They closed the cabinet and strutted out of Elliott's apartment like they owned the place.

CHAPTER 19

The next afternoon Fallon sat at her kit, arms burning and muscles aching from her shoulders clear down her back as she willed Keith to call it a day.

"That's it. Final set list." He rested his guitar against his thighs.

"You sure about ending on an original?" Calvin's voice rasped from singing backup.

"Definitely. It's our best and a total party jam. Crowd will love it. Judges will love it."

"So, is that it? We done here?" Fallon stood from her throne and stretched out her sore muscles.

Keith glanced at his watch. "Yeah, we're done." He lifted his guitar strap over his head and set it in its case.

"Actually, could I talk to you both before you leave?" Calvin secured his bass in its case and settled onto a stool by the bar. He gnawed on a thumbnail and his eyes looked anywhere besides her.

She circled her kit and crashed onto the couch. Keith climbed on the arm beside her. Calvin cleared his throat but said nothing.

"You gonna tell her, or should I?" Keith glanced at Calvin who looked more uncomfortable than ever on his stool.

"Tell me what?" Her eyes darted between her bandmates.

"I wasn't going to say anything until after Twisted Fest"—Calvin swallowed and tugged at his polo—"but I'm moving away at the end of the summer."

Her mouth went dry.

"You're what?"

"I'm moving to Oregon. In August."

"Why?"

"School. I've got finals in a couple weeks, and then I'm transferring up there."

"Wait. Finals? You're in school right now?" Her head spun. None of this made any sense.

"That's why I've been a little absent lately. I'm almost done with my associates at Glendale Community College." Calvin's forehead wrinkled, but the corners of his mouth turned up slightly.

"And Keith already knows? Why didn't you tell me?" She tried not to be hurt that he'd kept this from her.

"Are you serious?" His eyes widened. "You never let me tell you anything about my life. Either of us." He motioned to Keith who still sat propped on the couch arm, letting the two of them have it out like always. "If we so much as mention something non-band related, you run away—sometimes literally."

"You could have told me you were going to school."

"No, I couldn't." Calvin sighed.

"So, you waited until now to tell me you were moving?"

"You didn't tell me when you were moving either."

The pounding in her ears turned to silence, and the anger in her veins vaporized instantly. She knew he was referring to her moving in with Noah, but it was so much worse than that. She'd kept everything from them—the deal with her parents, the possibility of her moving back to Arizona. None of it was any of their business.

Except that it kind of was.

If she left, they'd be left without a drummer. She hadn't even considered how her leaving might affect them. They had a right to know.

She couldn't be upset with Calvin for doing the same thing she was, especially when she was the reason he'd held back.

"In that case, I guess I have some news as well." Fallon rubbed her aching arms. "Obviously, we are going to play Twisted Fest, and we'll give it all we have. But if the winner is announced and it's not us, then I'll be leaving Los Angeles."

Both of their faces dropped.

"Where are you going?" Calvin asked.

"Back to Arizona."

"Why?"

"It's a long story." She swallowed the ever-present hesitation at sharing anything personal. "I made a deal with my parents last year. I was actually supposed to go back a couple weeks ago."

Realization crossed Calvin's face. "That's why you moved in with Noah."

"I bought myself a few extra weeks, but I'm out of time. If we lose, I'm gone."

Calvin rubbed the back of his neck, and Keith nodded slowly.

"What does that mean for the band?" Calvin was the only one brave enough to ask.

"We'd hoped that if we won Twisted Fest before Calvin left, you and I could use the hype and the publicity to find another bassist and fast. But if you and Calvin both leave…" Keith shrugged. "I'm not much of a band on my own."

His elbows rested against his thighs, hands dangling casually.

"What are you saying?" Her words were rushed as panic took over her voice. "That would be the end of Edge of September?" Her fingers shook, and she squeezed her drumsticks tightly.

"I guess it all comes down to Twisted Fest." Keith walked to his guitar case and slung it over his shoulders. "If we win, Calvin can put off his move for a semester—long enough for us to record and find a new bassist."

He didn't have to speak the alternative. If they lost, Calvin would be gone, she'd take off, and Edge of September would officially be broken up.

Pain and loss gripped her chest. It shouldn't have. She'd known Twisted Fest might be her last Edge of September gig, but having her boys confirm it made it real—a truth she'd avoided for weeks but now had to face.

If they lost, it wouldn't just be the end of her time in the band. It would be the end of the band altogether.

It shouldn't have mattered to her. It made no difference in her life—she would be done either way—but that loss tugged at her until her chest ached.

"Guess we'll just have to win." Keith smiled tightly and slipped out the warehouse door.

Calvin was still on his stool, watching her. He rose and approached her without a word. He scanned her face, and her eyes stung at the tears she saw in his.

"It's okay, you know." His voice was steady despite the emotions he was obviously fighting to control.

"What is?"

"To love something."

***

Calvin dropped her off at the curb, and Fallon trekked her way around the main house, across the yard, and toward the guest house. The sunshine glazed her bronze skin, and she craved more. The California sun was like a drug on days like this, and she found herself looking for a reason to stay outside and a quiet moment to herself.

Very unlike her.

She climbed the small hill to where she knew a wicker loveseat overlooked the yard, but as she approached from behind the trees, she realized someone else had had a similar idea.

Noah was slouched on the loveseat, playing on his phone. He slapped the cushion next to him without looking up, and she lowered herself onto it. It wouldn't have been weird if there was a TV or if other people had been there, but sitting by him, so close they nearly touched, for no reason whatsoever, was sucking all the air from her body. The scent of vanilla drifted around her, and she wondered if her scent—jasmine and bergamot body spray—affected him the way his did her.

"Think Elliott has noticed his movies yet?" he chuckled.

"He deserved so much worse," was all she said.

Noah said nothing else but continued to play on his phone. She was grateful for the silence, another anomaly, but right now, she really wanted a moment to process all that had just come to light with the band.

She watched the sun move slowly across the sky. Noah had tucked his phone away after only a few minutes and also seemed to simply watch time pass. She felt more than heard her breathing sync with his. They watched time pass separately but together.

"Everything okay?" he asked when the sun began to sink.

Should I tell him I'll be moving if Edge loses? She only told Calvin and Keith because it changed things for them. It was their business.

It changed nothing for Noah. She'd move out and they'd go their separate ways after the festival regardless of who won. And knowing him, if he knew how badly she needed to win, he'd likely do something stupid like drop out. Maybe not, but he'd feel guilty.

"Everything is fine. Long day."

"It's your turn, by the way." He bumped her with

his shoulder but didn't pull it back. His forearm lay beside hers, barely brushing her skin. The touch sent goosebumps skittering down to her fingers.

She hummed her acknowledgement. Words were not forming as long as he was this close.

"I dare you to come to dinner with my family tomorrow."

She shot up, demanding her senses to process the challenge Noah had just flung at her.

"Are you insane?"

His mom had invited her to any and all meals the day she'd moved in, and Fallon had yet to take Sarah up on the offer. Noah was already way more involved in her life than she ever should have allowed. His family was out of the question.

"You dared me to commit a felony!" His face glowed with amusement.

"They never could have made that stick. It was trespassing at most."

"It's casual," he pushed. "Since we got to the States, my dad is obsessed with barbecuing. He does it probably three times a week. He told me to invite some friends this time. Josh is coming too. And it's outdoors. You won't even have to go in the house."

She groaned and flung herself back against the orange cushion.

He never would have broken into Elliott's apartment if he hadn't trusted her completely. She hadn't shown that kind of trust in anyone since Annora. There wasn't a damn thing she wouldn't have done if Annora had asked her.

Noah weaved his fingers through hers and squeezed gently. Electricity spread from their entwined fingers through her whole body. Her breathing stilled, and her limbs weakened. He meant it as a gesture of friendship, but there was nothing platonic about the magnetic pull drawing her toward him.

She tore her hand away, breaking the current.

"A barbeque?" Fallon confirmed as the fog cleared.

"Painless." Noah winked at her.

CHAPTER 20

The sky was still bright as they made their way through the yard to the big house Sunday evening. Padded outdoor seating scattered the patio, carefully spaced so visitors could have either private or communal conversations. Torches flickered around the yard, and the smell of grilled meat made Fallon's mouth water.

Sarah lounged in a chair near a middle-aged man standing over a grill with a metal spatula in his hand. She swirled yellow liquid in a glass with a lemon wedge on the rim.

"Fallon! I'm so glad you're joining us."

"Thank you for the invitation." She took a seat on the other side of the circle. Noah sat in the chair next to hers.

"So, you're Fallon." The man by the grill turned to her and wiped his hands on a small towel. A black apron that read 'BBQ Master' looped around his waist and neck, protecting dark jeans and a crisp light blue button-up that brought out the blue in his eyes. His silver hair was swept back neatly, and a charming smile lit his face. His accent matched Noah's.

"Whatever you're making smells incredible, Mr. Cooper."

"Please, call me Thomas." He returned to his grill. "We're going classic American. Hamburgers alright?"

"More than alright." She'd been living almost exclusively on breakfast cereal for weeks. Real food she didn't have to cook was a win.

"Noah, there's lemonade on the table." Sarah motioned to the other end of the patio. A cloth stretched over the edges of a long table, held down by a stack of plates, trays of burger toppings, a variety of soda cans, and a large pitcher of lemonade. Sarah's attention returned to Fallon. "My son says you're showing him some of the sights around here. What have you seen?"

Noah walked to the table for a drink, leaving her alone to answer. How much did he want his mother to know? He'd already told her more than Fallon would ever tell her own mother.

"We went to a glow party on the beach."

"A beach party! I bet you two had so much fun! I've been telling Noah since we moved here that he needs to get out and do things, but he doesn't listen to me."

Noah returned with a glass of lemonade in one hand and a can of Coke in the other.

"What are you telling her, Mum?" He handed Fallon the soda and sat back down.

"Just how happy I am someone has finally convinced you to go out once in a while."

"Noah going out? I'll believe it when I see it." Josh appeared from around the house, grinning ear to ear.

"It's true. I'm a changed man." Noah beamed.

Josh circled the patio and shook Thomas's hand.

"Good to see you again, sir."

"And you, Josh."

"And thank you for the invitation, Mrs. C." Josh plopped into the open seat beside Fallon.

"You know you are always welcome here. It's been too long."

"And for that I am truly sorry. When Noah called tonight, I dropped everything and rushed right over." He winked at Fallon.

Noah had just barely called him—the day after she'd agreed to dinner?

Noah stared into his lemonade.

Quick footsteps sounded from the house, amplifying until Amelia appeared in the doorway. Her blonde curls bounced around her face, and her piercing eyes scanned the faces of everyone on the patio until they landed on Fallon.

Having now met all the Coopers, Fallon realized that although both children had inherited their mother's blonde hair, only Amelia had her parents' sharp blue eyes, but they held a certain intensity that reminded her of Noah's mocha gaze.

Amelia resumed her running and stopped only a foot away from Fallon.

"I remember you. You are Fallon and you live with Noah and I can't go in your room." Her brows scrunched together.

Noah snorted, and Fallon smiled at Amelia.

"I remember you, too." She leaned forward to meet the girl eye-to-eye. "You are Amelia, and you are four."

Amelia smiled and nodded ecstatically.

"Amelia likes meeting new people," Sarah said, watching her daughter lovingly. "She doesn't often get the opportunity."

Noah leaned closer and whispered, "Amelia can't go too many places. They want her to minimize her exposure to germs and such."

"I have something to show you!" Amelia rushed into the house as quickly as she'd arrived.

"She's certainly taken a liking to you now, hasn't she?" Josh nudged Fallon's knee with his.

"I've barely even met her," she whispered back so only Josh could hear.

"Fallon made quite the impression on Amelia last week," Sarah said, "but I'll let her show you."

Amelia reappeared on the patio carrying something in her small arms. She scurried to Fallon and flung her arms out wide. At least ten books spilled onto the patio.

"Amelia Debelia!"

"Bedelia, love," Sarah corrected gently.

"Bedelia," Amelia repeated. Her cheeks tinged pink. "Mum took me to the bookstore, and we found lots of Amelia Bedelia books. I love them"—her eyes widened again—"SO. MUCH."

"We've already read each of them a thousand times." Noah gathered the books from where they'd landed on the cement and stacked them neatly beside his chair.

"I like the one where Amelia Bedelia has a cat." She stared up at Fallon, waiting for a response.

"Me too," Fallon blurted. She had no idea how to talk to kids. She didn't even remember the books other than the character's name.

Amelia nodded. Apparently, that was good enough for her. She bounded over to her mom and climbed into the seat beside her, smoothing her red checkered dress over her little legs. White shoes stuck out over the edge of the deep seat, one covering a yellow sock and the other a pink one.

"Burgers are ready!" Thomas announced.

Noah put together a small plate of food and handed it to Amelia, still sitting by her mother who was likewise accepting the plate Thomas had gotten for her.

Fallon followed Josh to the table.

"Should I have gotten a plate for you?" he teased her.

"Don't you dare. I will cut your shoelaces in half."

He laughed but handed her an empty plate all the same.

"Did you really get Noah to go out?" he asked as he assembled his burger. His voice had turned serious.

"A couple times. Why is everyone acting like that's so crazy?" She dumped some salt and vinegar chips on her plate and shoved one in her mouth.

"Noah doesn't go out. Ever."

"Why?"

"Ask him." Josh's gaze darted behind her, and Noah

appeared over her shoulder.

"Ask me what?" Noah's eyes sparkled in the light of the torches.

"Nothing." She scowled at Josh and walked away.

Dinner passed quickly, and Fallon was pleasantly surprised at how few prying questions the Coopers asked. In her experience—not that she had a ton—parents had a tendency to squeeze out every drop of personal information they could.

How old are you? Where are you from? Are you dating anyone? Tell us about your family.

And in that limited experience, they didn't react well when you told them to mind their own damn business.

But as the evening went on and the sun began to set behind the city, she realized the Coopers hadn't asked her anything about her life or shared anything too personal about theirs. They'd discussed music, places they'd traveled, and even Thomas's distaste for certain cheeses, but nothing that crossed any lines.

"Dessert?" Thomas asked just as the sun disappeared completely and only the torchlights flickered around them. Amelia dozed on her mother's lap but sat upright at the mention of sweets.

"Dessert?" her little voice echoed.

"Alright, alright. I'll go get it." Noah stepped toward the guesthouse but paused and turned back. "Fallon, some help?"

She shrugged and followed him to their house.

Their house.

She shook off the implication and went inside.

Noah opened the fridge and pulled out a tray of sugar cookies. They looked like they'd come from a bakery, each uniquely frosted to perfection, but she knew him well enough to know he'd made them entirely by hand.

"When did you have time to do this?"

"I baked them while you were asleep last night, and I decorated them this afternoon while you were at band practice." He set the plate on the counter. "Thanks for coming tonight. My parents were thrilled when I told them you'd be there."

"They've been really cool." She leaned against the counter.

"And Amelia adores you."

"I've barely met her."

"Seems that's all it takes." He shifted on his feet. "My sister had her first good test result yesterday. It's looking more and more likely she'll be able to go home by the end of the summer."

"That's fantastic." Fallon's heart warmed for the little girl. She wasn't entirely sure what Amelia had, but any news of her recovery was good news.

"It is," Noah breathed deeply. "So, I heard you and Josh earlier, talking about why I don't go out."

"We weren't—"

"No, it's fine. I just thought I'd answer without making you ask." He took a step toward her. "When my sister was diagnosed, I decided that I would no longer live my life for me, but for her. I became the perfect son and brother, or as close as I could be. If I couldn't heal her, I would make sure I did all I could not to take from her. If I never did anything dangerous, my parents could just focus on her needs, and that would have to be enough. I stopped going to parties. I stopped having adventures. I stopped living." He looked at her, eyes blazing. "As I say it now, it sounds stupid, but it was all I had to give."

"What about Blue Streetlights?"

"It was part of the arrangement of moving here. When I left England, I was leaving behind the beginning of a vocal career. My parents wanted me to stay, but I refused. They only agreed to bring me with the promise that I'd continue my music in the States."

She studied the pain in his face but said nothing.

"I never actually cared if Blue Streetlights got signed," he admitted. "I want it for Josh and Fitz, but it doesn't matter for me."

"Because you'll go back to England with your family."

It wasn't a question, but he nodded all the same. She chose not to identify the twist in her gut at the thought of Noah leaving the country.

Silence filled the space between them. She wondered if Noah had needed to admit all this to himself more than he'd needed to tell her, and suddenly it didn't seem like she was trespassing on something personal. Knowing how he'd carried this weight and chosen her to finally share it with, she felt...

Honored.

"Fallon?" Noah's voice softened, strong but gentle. "Can I ask you something?"

Her stomach tightened. Absolutely not. No questions. No prying. No personal connection.

But as Fallon studied his face, the lines and angles she'd come to know too intricately, she heard herself say, "Maybe."

"You said the other night that you keep people at a distance in case they leave." His forehead creased. "Who left you?"

Pain, raw and deep, coursed through her. Annora's face lit up her memory.

"No one left me." She forced a stinging breath. "My sister died."

"I'm so sorry." He reached for her hand and squeezed it gently.

"You didn't kill her." She knew the words were crass and rough, but she was sick of people acting like Annora's death wasn't exactly what it was. "Annora was taken in a mass shooting by some guy with a gun and a vendetta against the world." She swallowed the burning in her throat.

Noah remained silent. His thumb brushed the back of her hand.

"I decided then that I would never let a day go by that I didn't do exactly what I wanted. There are so many things Annora never got the chance to do. I want to do them all."

Annora had been bursting with spirit. Fallon could spend her entire life trying to live to the fullest, and she would still never come close to her sister. Annora had been life itself, a joy and passion Fallon could only replicate, never emanate.

Noah didn't release her hand. He captured her gaze with his, but this time Fallon didn't break away. She let their severity steal her breath and paralyze her.

"I've never told anyone about her." The words slipped out.

"Why me?" His voice was steady. His eyes fell to her lips, and warmth spread through her chest.

"I don't know." Fog muddled her thoughts. "I've never talked to anyone like I talk to you."

Only inches from her, she couldn't break his gaze, couldn't resist the pull of him. His fingers swept her hair behind her ear, and his thumb brushed her cheek.

The pull was magnetic, neither of them able to fight the undeniable. They weren't touching, but she was aware of every inch of him. Silent, but growing closer every second.

Until Noah pulled away with a sharp intake of breath.

"We should get back outside." He picked up the plate of cookies. "Amelia is probably waiting for these." He vanished out the door.

Fallon's feet didn't move. She stood frozen against the island, heart thudding.

She'd gone temporarily crazy. He'd nearly kissed her, and she nearly kissed him back. Her fingers brushed her lips where the imagined kiss lingered.

How had they both managed to lose control?

She should be furious with herself. She should be panicking and anxious about how she'd break his heart and avoid him for the rest of her life. But she couldn't feel any of those things. Instead, warmth radiated from her chest where her heart was racing. Desire burned across her skin, and longing bubbled up from within her.

She wanted Noah Cooper. Not just for a makeout or hookup or whatever. She wanted to *be with* him.

She forced herself not to think too far down that path. It couldn't happen. Even if she wanted to, she couldn't let him have that kind of control over her.

It's better this way. She repeated the words over and over until they sank in.

Nothing had changed. She didn't *do* relationships, even with someone as incredible as Noah. Her heart didn't get a say. Her heart was stupid—as all hearts were—putting wants and desires above what her brain knew was the right choice.

Hearts got broken.

CHAPTER 21

Fallon propped herself against the vinyl table in the greenroom at The Garage and spun her drumstick. She didn't get nervous anymore, but tonight was itching at her. As they waited for the green light to head to the stage, Calvin and Keith chatted on the couch. She caught pieces of their conversation but mostly blocked them out.

It had been five days since her dinner with the Cooper's and her moment of unbelievable stupidity with Noah in their kitchen, and even now, the memory sent waves of uneasiness through her. She'd woken up the next day with a massive regret hangover

Why the hell had she opened up to Noah like that? He was the last person she should be getting attached to. It was bad enough he was stupid hot and they lived together. Letting him in on a personal level was beyond moronic. She'd been avoiding him ever since. Other than their time at band practice, she'd barely seen him. She'd spent as much time as she could away from the house and had gone to bed early every night.

At least something had knocked him back into reality that night. She didn't want to imagine what might have happened if it hadn't. As much as she would have enjoyed it—and she had no doubt she would have—things would only be worse now.

She had to keep him away. Luckily, tonight's gig offered the perfect challenge for Noah. She'd dared him, in a text, to join Fitz and Josh at the Edge of September gig—a gig she'd be on stage for and, therefore, nowhere near him.

A knock came from the door, and Josh, Fitz, and Noah walked in. The space, already too small, was now stiflingly uncomfortable.

"Ready to go?" Josh crashed onto the couch beside Calvin.

Fitz leaned against the far wall, and Noah stood just inside the door, hands in his pockets.

"Yeah, the Garage is no big deal anymore," Calvin answered. "Hasn't Blue Streetlights played here?"

"Only once. Elliott usually books us across town at The Venue."

"Is that the place with the balcony that overlooks the stage?" Keith's eyes were glazed, which she hated, but he seemed mostly coherent.

"That's the one. Always has a great crowd." Fitz lifted his chin ever so slightly from where he still stood against the wall. His leather jacket had to be roasting him in this overcrowded room, but he didn't seem to care. His dark hair shifted and skimmed his temples. It was longer than it had been six months ago, but it suited him. Actually, it was a very similar length to Noah's messy blond hair, but where Noah's was a casual messy, Fitz's was a more purposeful style. Very Johnny Depp.

"I'm glad I finally get to see you all play. I've never actually been to a show." Noah avoided her gaze. Her stomach tightened.

"Then it's about damn time." Calvin exaggerated, rolling his eyes.

A face appeared in the doorway behind Noah. The Garage stage manager signaled them to go on and disappeared without saying a word.

Josh slapped Calvin on the knee and jumped up from the couch.

"Good luck! We'll see you after." He disappeared through the door. Noah waved and followed him.

Josh and Keith grabbed their instruments and headed for the wings. Fallon eased across the green room, super aware of Fitz's lingering presence. He hadn't moved in the time he'd been in the room. As she reached the doorway, she could smell his cologne—subtle but familiar.

She paused as he tilted his head toward her, now only inches away.

"Have fun." Fitz's words were so innocent. So basic. But Fallon knew they were anything but.

Fun had always been their motto—the reason they did anything. They partied for fun. They played music for fun. They had sex for fun. Fitz saw life the way she did. She didn't know his damage, just like he never knew hers, but they agreed on that one very important thing.

What was the point of living if you weren't having any fun?

She met his gaze and smiled her most wicked smile before heading backstage to meet Calvin and Keith.

CHAPTER 22

"I've missed seeing you play classic rock," Josh yelled over the crowd. "I forgot how much fun you make it."

"You say that like classic rock can't hold its own." She drank from her beer.

"Classic rock is just fine, you know, for people too old for punk." Josh laughed, and she smacked his arm.

"I enjoy classic rock. Really. I just prefer the energy of punk." He finished off the rest of his beer.

To her relief, the gig had gone great, better than expected considering the rocky weeks of practice that she couldn't help but feel partially responsible for. Knowing she was being watched by Blue Streetlights had also thrown her off her game, like she was being judged. It was nice to prove herself again.

They'd celebrated by getting drinks with Blue Streetlights. Calvin had even convinced Noah to stay. He'd ordered water, but he'd stayed.

Now they all sat perched on stools at the end of the bar, buzzed and ready for anything. Dangling lights glowed dimly around them, and the current band was loud enough they had to yell to hear each other. Her idea of a perfect night.

Even so, she couldn't quite relax. Despite the gig being over and a beer in her system, something itched at her.

Not something. Someone.

Noah.

Every time Fallon glanced his way, her chest ached. She was probably just wound up from the gig.

Keith downed the remainder of his beer and slammed it on the counter.

"I'm calling it." He threw a few bucks on the counter. "I got stuff to do."

Meaning he was probably meeting up with a dealer or getting high with buddies.

"Am I too late for the party?" A melodic female voice approached from behind Fallon as Keith slipped into the crowd. She turned in time to see a girl she'd never met plant her lips on Josh's.

Her stomach twisted into a knot. She'd forgotten Josh was bringing his girlfriend tonight. It shouldn't bother her, but apparently no one told her body that. Tension tore at her shoulders, and her fingers gripped the bottle in her hands.

The girl greeted Fitz and Noah, and Fallon used the opportunity to size her up. She was pretty with wavy black hair that reached a few inches past her shoulders, warm brown skin, and a petite frame. Thick brows were the perfect balance for her plump lips and sharp cheekbones.

"Let me introduce you." Josh pulled her against

him. "This is Calvin."

"Nice to meet you." Calvin waved.

"And this is Fallon." Josh motioned to her.

Fallon raised her drink. She didn't trust herself to say anything quite yet.

"This is Priya." Josh beamed at the girl in his lap. Fallon looked away. She hadn't ever seen Josh look at anyone else that way, and it stung.

"I'm so glad to finally meet you." Priya smiled at her. "Josh has told me all about you. You knew each other in Arizona, right?"

Her other bandmates all looked at her in surprise— all but Noah—but her gaze shot to Josh. She raised a brow. How much had he told her about their past?

His lips formed a line, and he gave her a small nod.

Priya knew everything.

The tension in her body multiplied. "Yeah, we knew each other."

Priya smiled brightly at Fallon, like this knowledge somehow made them friends. Fallon gulped from her beer.

Fitz eyed her carefully. He had said very little since the show, but he'd been there, always just a breath away from her. Not too close, but she couldn't say she wasn't extremely aware of his presence.

"I better get home." Calvin threw a few bucks on the counter.

"I'll drive you," Noah offered. His gaze darted between her and Josh, but he didn't say another word before leaving.

Between her twisted feelings toward Noah, the

anxiety about the couple sitting next to her, and the alcohol in her system, she should probably be halfway to the door too.

Instead, she let the alcohol feed her bitterness and turned to face Priya.

"So, you and Josh, huh?"

"Yep. I'm the luckiest girl in the world." Her eyes twinkled as Josh offered her his seat and she slid onto it.

Fallon hummed an acknowledgement. She knew Josh was an incredible boyfriend, but she didn't care at that moment.

"And how long have you two been together?" she pried.

"Four months," Josh answered.

"I'm sorry I missed the show tonight. I got stuck at work." Priya sounded genuinely disappointed. "I'll catch the next one."

"Where do you work?" Fitz's voice made Fallon jump. She still hadn't forgotten he was sitting around the corner of the bar on her other side, but he'd been so quiet, she hadn't expected him to jump in.

"I wait tables. It's not the most glamorous, but the tips are good. On a night like tonight, though, if there's a rush, I end up working late." She sighed. Josh's hand moved in circles on her back.

Fallon hated that they were actually cute together. She tried to summon the bitterness she felt toward their relationship, but it would have been easier if Priya was less likeable or if Josh was truly being disloyal. Unfortunately, neither was true, and Fallon was just going to have to come to terms with that.

She hopped off her stool. "I'm going to run to the ladies' room. Watch my drink for creeps."

Fitz picked up her bottle and downed the last of her beer.

"When I get back, there better be a fresh drink waiting for me."

"Or what?" Fitz smirked.

"Or I'll tell these two all about the time you watched *Sleepless in Seattle* and cried."

She spun on her heel before Fitz could respond. Of course, she was lying through her teeth. She'd never seen Fitz cry. But that wasn't the point of the game. He knew she'd never tell his secrets, and she knew he'd have a drink waiting for her.

She made her way through the crowd of people to the back hall where the bathrooms were when she heard her name being called. She turned and found Josh trailing after her.

"I don't need your help in there." She flicked her chin at the bathroom door a few feet away.

"I'm sorry." Josh's breathing seemed heavier. Weighed down. "I shouldn't have made you meet Priya."

"That's stupid. She's...nice." It sounded forced, even though it was true.

"It's weird for you. I hoped it wouldn't be, but it is." He scratched at the back of his head, a nervous habit she'd forgotten he had.

"I'm just not used to seeing you with someone else. I'll adjust."

He nodded but hesitated. She waited for him to say whatever it was he was working through, hoping it wouldn't be what she very much expected.

"Listen," he finally said, "I know you don't want to talk about her, but I need to say something. Then we can never discuss it again." He sighed heavily. "I loved Annora. I think I will always love her."

A tremble echoed in his voice, and Fallon swallowed the lump forming in her own throat.

"And I will always think of you as my sister, regardless of everything else," he continued, "but it's been years. I can't hold on forever, and neither should you. We have to find ways to live our lives without her here."

He reached for her hand, squeezed it once, and walked back toward the bar.

Fallon pushed the swinging door into the bathroom and was grateful to find it empty. She walked to the mirror and fought off the tears that pooled as she wiped at a bit of runny black eyeliner. Blue and purple smudges of shadow reached nearly to her eyebrows, and her lips were still painted a deep purple, even after the drinks. Her hair was ratted and messy, as it always was after she drummed. It fell around her collarbone, covering a few inches of skin past her sports bra. She looked hammered. Hopefully it was just the dim bathroom lights.

A deep breath rattled in her chest.

Josh wasn't wrong. Annora had been gone for years. She hadn't expected him to never date anyone else, but Fallon still thought of Annora every day. Did he? She couldn't imagine him being with someone else if he still thought of her sister that way.

He loved Annora so much. He'd even told Fallon once that he wanted to marry her. Looked at rings and everything. He would have been her brother. But they were both really young. He'd wanted to wait until they were a little older to propose.

He never got the chance.

Now Josh was moving on, living his life to the fullest—just like her. She should be glad. She breathed deeply and decided she'd support it. No wasted days.

She washed her hands and yanked a few paper towels out of the dispenser before returning to the bar. Josh and Priya were nowhere around, but Fitz hadn't moved.

"As promised." He nodded to the fresh beer dripping condensation on the napkin beside him.

"Where'd Josh and Priya go?"

"They left. Priya works in the morning." Fitz slid the drink toward her.

"So do we. But here we are." She lifted her bottle in mock cheers and took a sip.

"Everything alright with you and Josh?"

"Fine."

He nodded once but didn't ask for more. Fitz was one of the few people she knew that understood that some things weren't any of his business.

"You enjoying the guesthouse?" he asked, surprising her with the sudden shift in subject.

"It does the job." She took another drink and wished she'd had Fitz order her something much stronger.

He looked her up and down. "What's next?"

"Depends on how Twisted Fest goes. I've got a few options."

"Is staying with Cooper one of them?"

"Guess we'll have to wait and see." She wasn't sure why she was playing this game with Fitz, but it was a nice distraction.

He chuckled, and she knew he was thinking the same thing. She watched him twist his bottle with his long fingers.

"And what if you win?" she asked.

"You mean if *we* win."

"I'm temporary."

"Fair enough." Fitz shifted in his seat. "If Blue Streetlights wins, then we record. Maybe go on tour."

"Tour, huh?"

"We've talked about it a couple times. Just a few cities up the coast."

"That would be incredible." She meant it. A tour would be unreal, possibly better than a record. Moving from audience to audience, night after night. Edge of September had never discussed a tour. They'd never even talked about what winning Twisted Fest would mean for them as a band besides *not* breaking up. "It's nice that you three are so close."

"Feeling jealous, Boots?" Fitz's mouth turned up in one corner.

"Of Josh and Noah?" She chuckled. "Sure."

"Of Josh and me."

A laugh burst from her chest. "Noah's a roommate.

That's it."

"I was with him in the crowd tonight. The look he had watching you?" Fitz shook his head. "Not the look I'd give a roommate."

"You have no idea what you're talking about."

She'd spent an hour with Noah after Edge played, and he'd barely looked in her direction. If he was looking at her differently while she played, it was likely his relief at escaping the awkward tension between them.

He was obviously attracted to her, as she was him. It's why he'd almost kissed her the other night and why she'd almost let him.

But chemistry wasn't love.

Fallon's phone dinged in her boot, and the vibration thrummed against her ankle.

Noah: *Can we please talk?*

Her stomach turned. Whatever Noah needed to say to her, she was absolutely sure she didn't want to hear it. In fact, she didn't want to even think about Noah the rest of the night.

And she knew exactly how to make sure she didn't.

She shoved her phone back into her boot without responding.

"What if we got out of here?" She shouted over the band at the other end of the room.

"We going somewhere?" Fitz signaled for the check.

"Your apartment?"

His eyebrows raised.

"Unless you don't want to." Maybe he didn't want her going home with him. Last she knew, he had a girl he was into and wasn't looking for anything else. She didn't actually know if that was still the case.

"You're asking if I want the crazy sexy drummer from tonight's hottest band to come home with me?"

"Bike outside?" She flipped her hair over her shoulder.

"You sure you're ready?" He raised a brow, and she knew his question was about more than just leaving the bar.

"You taking me home, or what?"

Fitz draped an arm over her shoulder, and they left the bar.

CHAPTER 23

Fitz's place was exactly what anyone who knew him would expect. Tidy but not spotless. Simple but not boring.

The one-bedroom apartment had a small kitchen just inside the door with a tall bar and a living space on the other side. A worn leather couch was the only seating outside the stools by the counter. He had no TV, but an incredible sound system was strung through the whole apartment. The only door led to his bedroom. A dark gray throw draped over the edges of his king bed matched the gray dresser across the room. Two doors, one to the bathroom and one to a closet, took up another wall. But the last wall, the one directly behind Fitz's bed, was the one worth noticing. The entire wall, likely twelve feet long, was a mural of Los Angeles, hand-painted and absolutely stunning. Fallon could barely take her eyes off it the first few times she had been there. Fitz didn't say much about it, but she knew he'd painted it himself. She doubted many people knew.

She accepted the water Fitz offered and lowered herself onto his couch. He stayed a few feet away, leaning on the edge of the bar.

They hadn't spoken much on the way here, which wasn't completely unheard of on a motorcycle but still unlike them. Fitz watched her as she glanced around his space, a small crease between his brows.

"You want to tell me what's going on?" he finally asked, swirling his own water.

"Not especially." She avoided his glance until he sauntered over to the couch and landed beside her.

"What happened with Cooper? You couldn't change the subject fast enough when I mentioned him, and he keeps texting me looking for you." He leaned forward, bracing his forearms on his knees and interlacing his fingers.

"Did you tell him I was here?" Panic gripped her. Noah could never know she went home with Fitz.

Except... *why not?* He already believed she and Fitz had been in a relationship. Maybe if he thought they'd started things up again, it would help keep him away.

But the panic didn't subside. She didn't want Noah to know.

"No." Fitz shrugged. "It's none of his business."

"No, it's not." She sighed heavily, relief loosening the knot in her stomach.

"So, what happened?"

"It's nothing." She flopped against the back of the couch, and he had to look over his shoulder to see her.

"Nothing?" The corner of his lips lifted.

"Nothing."

He turned toward her and braced an arm on the back of the cushion, leaning almost directly above her.

"Then why did you come home with me?" His jaw clenched, and she traced the movement in his throat as he swallowed.

"I thought it was pretty obvious why I was here." She snaked a finger down his firm chest.

"I'm going to be very blunt with you, Boots." He slid his leather jacket off his shoulders and tossed it onto a chair. "If all you want is a good time, then I'm in. But if you don't actually want to do this, I'll get a blanket right now and set up on the couch for the night. Bed's all yours."

"Why wouldn't I want to?"

"Cooper."

She twisted away from him. "God! I would love to not discuss him for another second tonight."

"Fine by me." He shrugged. "But you didn't answer my question."

His cologne fogged her senses. She focused on the sharp lines of his face, his dark eyes, and smooth lips. Fitz was good-looking—like, insanely good-looking. And she knew he was good in bed. He was everything she looked for in guys: mysterious, guarded, and unattached. He didn't ask personal questions or get emotionally involved. Ever.

The exact opposite of Noah and exactly what she needed tonight.

But as she waited for heat to spread through her body and that magnetism to draw her lips to his, it didn't come. Butterflies didn't ambush her stomach.

No breath was stolen. No limbs were paralyzed.

"Boots?" Fitz lifted a single brow. "What do you want?"

***

Sleep blurred Fallon's vision as morning light streamed through the window. Bedding that was not her own wrapped around her bare legs, and it took her a moment to place herself.

Her gaze cleared, and Fitz's bedroom walls surrounded her.

She was in Fitz's bed.

Alone.

She'd almost invited him to join her last night, but something hadn't sat right with her. Fitz had been cool about it. He'd taken a pillow and blanket to the couch without complaint.

But as she untangled herself from his white sheets, it wasn't thoughts of Fitz that filled her mind.

She swiped on her phone. It was still open to Noah's text from the night before. He hadn't texted again. He must have gotten the hint.

A weight settled in her chest. She'd see him at practice today. Knowing him, he'd stayed up 'til sunrise, and he'd realize she never came home last night.

He could never know she was with Fitz. With their history, Noah would never believe she'd slept alone. She still wasn't sure why it mattered—and she didn't really want to—but the dread filling her body had nothing to do with hurting Noah. That was ridiculous. It was about keeping up the lie and pushing him away.

That was all there was to it.

Her phone buzzed in her hand, and another text came through.

Calvin: *Keith's messed up from last night. No practice today.*

Lovely.

A noise came from the other side of the bedroom door, and she raced to the bathroom before Fitz could get there.

After a quick shower, she returned to the bedroom to find him awake and scrolling on his phone from the edge of his perfectly made bed. Gray sweats hung loose around his waist, and he had his bare back to the mural.

"Look who's finally awake." Fallon squeezed water from her hair with a towel.

"You beat me by about a second, you know."

"So, you've just been sitting here this whole time?"

"Someone was in my shower." Fitz winked at her. "Sleep alright?"

Fallon nodded and glanced at the mural behind him.

"Is this your only piece?"

"On this scale, there's only a few." He rubbed the back of his neck. "But I've been painting smaller pieces."

"Why don't you do more?"

He shrugged.

Fallon padded across the carpet, aiming for the

kitchen. "Coffee still in the same place?"

"Yep," Fitz called from his room. She heard footsteps as she pulled the door closed behind her.

He emerged a few minutes later, hair still dripping wet from his shower and soaking the collar of his deep red Henley. He held his phone out as if to show her a message.

"We need to talk." He lowered the phone. "You have to tell Cooper the truth about us."

"What are you talking about? Why?" About her going home with Fitz last night with every intention of hooking up? Absolutely not.

"You told him we dated?" He raised his brows, emphasizing just how ridiculous that idea was.

Oh. That.

"I never said we dated. You're the one that told him we had a history. I just didn't clarify what that history involved."

"I don't care what you tell people about you and me." Fitz opened a drawer brimming with Dum-Dums, grabbed a blue one, and shoved it in his mouth. "But you almost kissed him, Boots."

"He *told* you that?" She couldn't begin to guess why five days after the fact Noah would decide to share that information with Fitz. Her neck heated, not in embarrassment but in frustration. It was none of his business what they did outside of the band, and it was obnoxious that Noah had told him anyway.

"He *apologized* for it. Do you realize how messed up that is?"

"What did you say?" she asked.

"I tried to blow it off." He shrugged. "I told him our relationship was complicated, and everything is cool."

"Great. Problem solved."

"No. Not great. He's a wreck. He thinks he hit on his buddy's girl, and it's all a lie you've created for God knows what reason. It's *killing* him."

"Why?" Her stomach tightened, guilt coursing through her.

"Because he's obviously in love with you, and he can't do anything about it."

"He's not." But her voice shook.

"And I can't help but think you are just as hung up on him."

She couldn't answer. Her heart was beating out of her chest, singing the truth of every word Fitz said.

He pulled the sucker from his mouth and locked eyes with her.

"Boots, you and I hooked up regularly for three months, and you never looked at me the way you look at him. I don't know what your hang-up is or why you are playing with him like this, and it's none of my business what goes on between you two. But you need to tell him the truth about us." He paused. "Or I will."

Fallon huffed a breath and slumped onto his couch, arms crossed like a child.

Fitz had no right to bust into her personal life.

Except maybe he did...

Noah and Fitz had been bandmates, friends even, for longer than she had even known Noah by a long shot. Their non relationship relationship was affecting his relationship with Noah as much as it was affecting her own.

"Fine. I'll tell him."

"Thank you." Fitz's posture softened, and he relaxed onto the couch beside her.

She stared out the window and pushed out the words she knew he deserved to hear.

"I'm sorry I used you." It was a mumbled whisper, but she knew he could hear her.

"I wouldn't have cared if it had been anyone else, but Cooper deserves better."

She didn't know how to respond to that, so she stood up and walked back to the coffee maker on the kitchen counter.

"Coffee?" She filled two mugs. "Can I ask you something?"

Fitz shrugged and accepted the mug she offered him.

"Would you really have slept with me last night?"

He set the mug back on the counter and returned the sucker to his mouth.

"No." His dark eyes met hers, and she realized how little she knew about him regardless of the time they'd spent together. "I wouldn't have."

"Then why'd you bring me home?"

"Because you seemed like you needed me to."

"I needed to get blue-balled?"

"You needed a friend."

CHAPTER 24

He wouldn't look at her. Nearly three hours of practice and not a single glance. Noah had cheerfully spoken with both Fitz and Josh, but not even a look of disgust came her way. The few times he'd been forced to respond to her, he'd made himself busy with something else and kept his eyes locked on anything but her.

Something had changed. Things had been awkward and uncomfortable all week, but this was a whole new level.

Josh gave her a questioning look, but a quick shake of her head and a scowl had told him to back off. Fitz hadn't acknowledged it at all.

But as practice ended and the band cleaned up their stuff, she knew one of them was going to have to break their silence. They lived together, and there was no way around that.

She circled her kit and moved toward where Noah was coiling a cord, but Fitz stepped directly in her way, close enough they were almost touching. He leaned in, and his breath brushed her ear.

"Fix this. We can't play Twisted Fest with tension in the band." He pulled back just enough to meet her eyes.

She nodded. "I'll deal with it."

Two of his fingers linked with hers and squeezed. "My bed is yours whenever you need it." He winked.

He stepped away, leaving Fallon with a direct line of sight to Noah who'd chosen that very moment to look at her for the first time that day. His face darkened in a way she'd never seen before. His jaw clenched, and his eyes narrowed.

"You riding home with Noah?" Fitz called across the room, motorcycle helmet in one hand.

She genuinely didn't know how to answer.

"Noah?" She hated the shame in her voice.

"I can take her home," he responded. She didn't miss that he had responded to Fitz—not her.

Fitz gave her one last, meaningful look and walked out the door. Josh sent her a smile that looked more like a grimace and followed him.

"Let's go." Noah's voice was hard and cold.

She followed him to his car and climbed into the passenger seat. Neither of them spoke on the ride home. He didn't even turn on music. It was like he wanted her to stew in silence.

This was so much more than awkward tension.

Noah was pissed.

He swung into the garage, threw the car in park, and slammed the door behind him. Fallon scrambled out and chased after him, needing almost two steps to each of his long strides.

"Noah!" she yelled across the yard.

He didn't turn.

"Will you at least talk to me?" she called again.

He stopped dead in his tracks. He whirled back in her direction, legs planted wide in the green grass. She could see the whites of his eyes even from across the yard.

"*Now* you want to talk?" he snapped.

"I don't want it to be like this between us." She inched toward him.

"It doesn't work like this." He motioned between them. "You can't decide you don't want to deal with stuff and shut me out until you feel bad, then suddenly decide you want to mend things."

"I didn't shut—"

"You did." He cut her off. "I've tried to talk to you all week, but I could never get you alone. I even texted you last night to ask if we could talk, and you ignored it. God, Fallon! You stayed at Fitz's last night just so you wouldn't have to come home and see me!" He ran both hands through his hair.

"Who told you I stayed at Fitz's?"

Noah's arms dropped dead at his sides.

"*That's* what you want to know? How I *found out?* Is that seriously your concern right now? Fine. No one told me. You were the last people at The Garage last night, and you showed up on the back of his motorcycle this morning. I solved the mystery myself."

"Nothing happened," she blurted and immediately

207

regretted it.

What was wrong with her? Her head was completely scrambled, and nothing she wanted to say to him was coming out right.

"I didn't think anything happened." His forehead scrunched.

"Oh…well…just sayin'." Was it possible to erase an entire conversation and start over? Because she was literally vomiting stupid.

"Is that it? That's all you've been dying to say? That you don't like that we're fighting and you didn't shag Fitz?" Anger radiated from him, and she didn't know how to deal with it. Usually when someone was mad at her it was Keith or Calvin or her parents, and she forced herself not to care.

But with Noah…

She cared. She cared badly enough she couldn't speak, couldn't stop Noah from turning his back to her and stomping away and into the guesthouse.

She ran after him and caught him on the stairs, no doubt headed for his room where he could shut her out, just as she'd been doing to him.

"Please wait. I'm sorry."

He stopped but didn't turn around.

"I'm sorry I shut you out. I'm sorry I avoided you and ignored your texts. I just didn't know how to deal with this."

"Deal with what?"

"You."

He finally faced her, but she immediately wished he hadn't. The hard lines and cold stare had softened, and the Noah she knew was now looking back at her, the power of his gaze weakening her knees.

"Me?" he asked gently.

"I'm not used to having friends, not real ones anyway."

"What about Calvin?"

"We aren't that close."

His eyes narrowed like he was confused by the idea.

She breathed deeply. "And I lied to you. Fitz and I were never actually together."

Noah stilled. Even his chest stopped rising and falling with each breath. He said nothing, so she continued, purging the truth while her courage remained.

"When I found out you would be both my roommate and bandmate and it was clear we could be more than friends, I knew I had to find a way to shut that down. Lying about Fitz was a way to stop you from asking me out without making things awkward in the band. We hooked up a few times last year, but that's it."

He studied her, brows drawn and forehead creased. His jaw clenched and unclenched as he read her face. Every second he didn't respond was agony.

"Why?" he finally asked. His voice was still soft, imploring.

"Aren't you mad? I lied to you," she deflected.

He shook his head.

"No, Fallon, I'm not." He dipped his chin. "Why did you push me away?"

"You are…I can't…" She pushed the words out,

fighting for each and every one. "I'm not good at having friends, but that's all we can ever be."

His face didn't change, but something flickered in his eyes, too fast to identify. His throat shifted as he swallowed hard.

"Okay."

"Okay? That's it?"

"Okay," he repeated and walked down a step. "I never meant to pressure you, and I want desperately to be friends." He sighed. "However, if you don't want that, if it's just too hard, I understand. I'll give you that space."

Her heart thundered in her chest. Her limbs grew heavy, and her senses dulled.

This was it—the moment in every friendship when she had to push them away, to guard herself above all else, no matter how badly it hurt her. She'd done it to her friends in Arizona. She'd done it to Calvin that night at Atlas.

But as she studied Noah, his heart bare before her, ready to be crushed, she couldn't do it.

She couldn't bring herself to hurt him and shatter what they had into bits. She could still never let herself love him, but he was right. If they couldn't be more, at least they could stay friends.

She knew she should come clean, tell him the truth about why they couldn't have what they both so obviously wanted, but it wasn't an option. Keeping his friendship was risky enough. If he knew how badly she wanted to be with him, she'd never be strong enough to lock him out.

He moved a few steps closer. She breathed deeply, but his vanilla scent only blurred her mind more.

"Fallon?" His mocha eyes cut straight through the fog. "What do you want?"

"I want to be friends." She forced strength into her voice.

"Me too." He reached for her hand and squeezed her fingers in his. Warmth spread up her arm and wrapped around her chest. Her heart was still racing, and she was certain her feet wouldn't move.

He released her hand, walked up to his room, and closed the door.

She didn't see him for the rest of the day.

CHAPTER 25

Noah was already awake and working on a bowl of Froot Loops when she came downstairs the next morning. She'd slept until nearly eleven, but judging by Noah's pajama pants and rumpled hair, he hadn't beaten her by much.

"Coffee?" he offered and filled a fresh mug for her.

"Please." She grabbed a bowl, slid onto a barstool beside him, and reached for the box of cereal and milk he'd left on the counter.

It was Sunday, and while that meant no Blue Streetlights practice, it also meant she had a video call with her parents. The previous weeks had been awkward at best, but at least they hadn't fought the whole time.

"Plans today?" Noah asked after swallowing a bite twice the size of hers.

"Call with my mom and dad." She clamped her mouth shut. She was getting way too comfortable sharing things with him. Was that good? She figured it was what friends did, but she was much too out of practice for it to feel anything but invasive, like showing up to a party severely underdressed—which she'd done many times and had never given a shit about.

This time she gave a shit.

"No Edge practice?" he asked and took another huge bite of cereal.

"Nope. Day off."

"Well, if you'd like to take your call in the sitting room today, I promise not to invade. I'm headed for the main house around then. The guesthouse is yours."

"It's fine," she said. "I can set up in my room."

Noah had been true to his word. He'd yet to set foot in her bedroom since she'd moved in. She'd never appreciated her personal space more.

"Please. Use the sitting room. I don't want your parents thinking you've been shut away because of me. Besides, it'll give me a chance to show you how fantastic I am at not being in the way. I need a do-over from last time."

"I don't think real life has do-overs."

"Says who?" He smiled.

"Alright, fine. I'll use the couch." She left her empty bowl in the sink and went in search of a shower.

When she returned just before noon, he was gone. She called out his name a few times to make sure he wasn't in his room, but he didn't answer.

She sank into a cushion and tucked her legs beneath her, opening the laptop to rest on her lap. She shoved out her breath and opened the video call that rang through right as the clock hit twelve.

"Reinita! Happy Sabbath!" Manuel called out much too loudly for how close he was to his laptop.

"Happy Sabbath, Dad."

"How's the band?"

"Doing great. Had a gig the other night." She chose not to mention the possible breakup. Her parents wouldn't care anyway.

"Less than two weeks until the festival, right? Can you believe it?"

She couldn't believe it. The last few weeks had flown by, and she knew the next two would go just as fast.

"How is the new house?" her mother asked.

"Very nice. I've earned my food privileges back, and soon they're going to let me use the bathrooms."

Her mother shot her a look that said she was not amused by Fallon's sense of humor.

"You are still living with that boy?" Her father's tone hardened.

"We both live here, yes." They'd asked the same question for the last two weeks, clearly still unhappy with her roommate situation.

"I thought so." Manuel puffed up his chest and folded his arms. "We've discussed it, and we would like to meet this boy you live with."

"Absolutely not."

"I wasn't asking."

"I can't make him do that, Dad. He isn't my boyfriend, and he doesn't know you."

"Exactly."

214

"He isn't even home right now." This shouldn't even be a discussion, but her parents had never been ones to back down from a fight.

"Find him."

"I don't know where he is," she lied.

"Fallon." His deep voice rumbled through her speakers.

Her body tensed.

He never used her name. Ever. He hadn't called her Fallon in years, maybe ever. Her mouth went dry, and suddenly she was six, and her father was the most powerful man in the word. He had never hurt her. That was not Manuel Rivera's way. But she'd known he was the boss, and suddenly, despite her not relying on them for rent, despite them being miles and miles away, her father was the boss again, and Fallon couldn't bring herself to tell him no.

"Hang on." She muted the call, turned off the camera, and set the laptop to the side. Dread filled the pit in her stomach as she removed her phone from her boot, scrolled through her contacts, and hit 'dial.'

Noah picked up on the first ring.

"Hello?"

"Can you come back?" She clutched a throw pillow and placed it on her lap.

"What's wrong?"

"They want to meet you."

He was silent for a moment. "Is that what *you* want?"

"It's just how it is on this one."

"I'll be right there."

She tossed her phone beside her and threw her head back onto the cushion. Her parents had never met any of her friends in California—not one. She figured if they were going to meet somebody, Noah was the best choice. He was the most PG of the group, or at least he gave that impression.

But the more she got to know him, the more he surprised her. That wicked grin he'd given her in Elliott's apartment had been on her mind ever since. What else was Noah Cooper hiding?

"Your parents want to meet me?" Noah closed the door behind him and circled the couch to sit beside her.

"They demanded to meet you." She picked up her laptop, her parents still on hold and muted. She scooted as close to Noah as she could without brushing against him.

"I'm going to introduce you. That's it."

"That's it," Noah confirmed.

She took a deep breath and unmuted.

"Mom and Dad, this is my roommate, Noah."

Noah's face appeared on the screen beside hers.

"Hello, Mr. and Mrs. Rivera. It's a pleasure." Noah's accent had become second nature to Fallon, but hearing it through her parents' ears made her appreciate its elegance once again.

Elegance. Sexiness. Whatever.

"It's nice to meet you, too," her mother smiled. Her father glared.

"How is Arizona?" Noah asked.

"Hot as ever."

"You ever been to Arizona?" Her father demanded.

Noah shook his head. "No, sir. Spent my whole life in England until I moved here last winter. Relocated with my family."

"You moved with your family? That's lovely." Lisa somehow pegged Fallon with a look through the screen.

"But you live with my daughter." Manuel's tone was serious but not angry. She stiffened, praying Noah could talk his way out of this one.

"She's renting a spare room in my parents' guesthouse. I do the same."

"And how do you know each other?" Her father's brows were still pulled together.

Noah bumped her so lightly with his knee she thought she may have imagined it until she saw him glance at her in the camera.

He wanted to know what she wanted him to say. She took the reins.

"I've been filling in as drummer in Noah's band."

"You're in a new band?" Her mother's brow creased. "What happened to Edge of September?"

"Still going strong. I'm just helping Blue Streetlights for a few weeks."

"And Blue Streetlights is your band, Noah?"

"Yes, ma'am." Noah smiled again. "I sing."

"Oh, that's lovely. Did Fallon tell you she—"

"Well, Noah's busy, so…" Fallon interrupted. Noah took the hint, waved, and scooted down the couch.

"Hold on there." Her father's frown had softened, but his usual happy demeanor hadn't yet returned. "I'd like to talk to Noah alone for a moment."

"No way." She started to close the laptop but froze at her father's voice.

"Por favor, Reinita." The demanding authoritarian had disappeared completely, and somehow the pleading, fatherly love in his voice now was so much worse.

She looked at Noah. His forehead creased, not in worry for himself, she realized, but with concern for her. He knew this was her version of torture. She'd introduced him, he'd been pleasant, and he'd left the conversation the second she asked him to.

This was more. And it felt so much bigger.

"Please," she mouthed, begging him not to dive any further than he knew she wanted. She handed him the laptop. His fingers brushed hers as he took it and placed it on his own lap.

"It'll be okay. I promise," Noah whispered back.

Fallon darted out the front door and closed it behind her.

She waited just outside to see if she could hear anything before realizing it was useless and walked into the yard.

The enormous chunk of land that housed Noah's family was gorgeous. It was a side of California many never saw. Grass covered most of the ground, but cement paths snaked through the green—one leading to the guest house, another to the main house, one to the pool and so on. Tall trees grew around most of the property, and it almost felt like they could be in the middle of a forest rather than on a suburban street in

Glendale.

She climbed to the loveseat she'd once shared with Noah in the shade of a tree and cut through the grass to take a seat. A cool breeze rustled her hair. It was a perfect day, the kind of day people moved to SoCal for.

Her mind spun trying to work through what everyone might be saying in the guesthouse. Her father might be laying into Noah for going near his daughter. Doubtful. Her father may not know the extent of her life here in LA, but she'd always been a little rebellious. Fallon was the reinita. Annora had been his ángel.

He might be asking questions about her life, using this opportunity to drill into all the details she'd kept hidden the last year. He'd finally gotten face time with someone that knew her, and he was capitalizing on it.

She just had to hope Noah would hold up. Not that he knew that much about her but it was more than she wanted to share with her parents.

Or what if they were the ones telling Noah all her secrets?

The thought jolted through her, and she shot from the loveseat ready to burst back into the guesthouse and rip the laptop from Noah's hands when the guesthouse door opened and he stepped out.

She stood frozen by her seat. Noah strolled casually in her direction. He didn't look shocked. Or broken. Or angry. All good signs.

"What did he say?" she blurted. He had a solid ten or so inches on her, and it had never felt like more.

"Not a lot." He shrugged and buried his hands in

the pockets of his plaid shorts. "Mostly just asked questions."

Fallon's stomach dropped. "What did you tell him?"

Noah's brows raised and a chuckle escaped. The corners of his mouth lifted.

"Look who thinks they're so important. We didn't talk about you."

She stilled. "You didn't?"

He shook his head slowly, teasing her.

"Then what did he ask you?" she demanded.

"He asked about my family, my music, growing up in England. Regular stuff." Noah blushed slightly. "He did actually ask one question about you."

This was it. He had been saving it.

"He asked if you were okay." His smile changed from teasing to sincere in less than a moment—that sincerity that had made him so dangerous from the start.

So dangerous but so addicting.

"If I was okay?" she repeated, trying to wrap her head around this exchange between her father and her roommate.

"He asked if you were okay and made me promise I'd look out for you."

"What did you say?"

"I told him you were well. That you didn't need anyone to look out for you but that I'd be around if you decided you needed anything."

Relief flooded her body. Noah had kept his promise. He'd had an entire conversation with her parents, even alone with her father, and not said anything to invade her privacy or spill her personal life.

Without thinking, she threw her arms around his waist.

Noah seemed shocked by her embrace at first but recovered and wrapped his arms around her shoulders, holding her against him. His vanilla scent clung to his shirt, and she let it calm her. She breathed in his steadiness, and it flowed through her. Her cheek rested against his firm chest, drifting in and out with every breath.

He pulled away, but his hands lingered on her shoulders.

"I do believe it is my turn to issue a dare. Could I interest you in a movie marathon this afternoon if I promise we'll only watch terrible movies and eat nothing but sugary cereal?"

"Hmmm…" She tapped on her chin, playing along. "On two conditions."

"Which are?" His smile grew.

"We're building a fort."

Noah let out a laugh of surprise, and any remaining anxiety she felt melted away.

"And the second?"

"We're inviting Amelia."

CHAPTER 26

Fallon had never really been a fan of kids, mostly because she'd never been around them. Annora had been her only sibling, and of her very few cousins, almost all were older than her. She didn't generally hang out places where it was socially acceptable to bring children, and it had all added up to her having no idea how to act around Amelia.

She wasn't even sure why she'd insisted he bring the little girl to their movie marathon. Something about his valiant—yes, Noah was nothing if not valiant—rescue of her train wreck of a video call had temporarily muddled her brain, and knowing he was giving up his Sunday with his sister to make Fallon feel better had caused her to act irrationally.

The Coopers had a projector that showed movies on the side of the house where Noah hung a large white sheet. He and Fallon pulled the cushions off their couch and carried them outside along with all the blankets they could find. They stacked cushions and pillows, with Amelia's help, until they had a soft, roofless fort.

She'd been awkward, maybe even a little uncomfortable, around Amelia at first. Absolutely nothing she said came out right, and at one point, Amelia asked her a question, and she responded by patting the kid on the head.

But as the movie went on, she relaxed. Amelia showed absolutely no hesitation and immediately cuddled up next to her. She even offered to share her blanket, but Fallon assured her there were plenty for them to each have their own. Noah reclined on the opposite side of his sister but didn't jump into their conversations unless invited.

They watched movie after movie in their makeshift theatre. Amelia helped choose the movie each time, and Fallon let Noah be the voice of reason on what a four-year-old was allowed to watch. He disappeared for a while during *Paddington,* and Fallon was pleasantly surprised when he returned with three melty grilled cheese sandwiches.

As the sky turned dark, she felt a weight against her right shoulder. She glanced down and found Amelia fast asleep. Her curls draped over her face, and her long lashes cast shadows across her cheeks.

"She's rather taken with you," Noah whispered.

"I guess so." She held as still as she could to not wake the little girl. "She's pretty cool, too."

Noah's phone lit up his face. "Hang on. Calling for backup."

A few minutes later, a shadowy figure approached their fort. Thomas stopped just outside and smiled as he took in their structure.

"You lot have been enjoying yourselves, haven't you?" His eyes caught on the little girl asleep on Fallon's shoulder. He sighed deeply. "You can't begin to understand how much it means to a father to see someone care for his little girl." Thomas met her eyes.

Fallon's chest heated, and her gut clenched. She nodded, unsure of what to say.

Noah helped shift Amelia into his dad's arms, and Thomas carried the little girl back to the house.

Noah sank back into the fort, legs bent and elbows propped on his knees.

"You didn't have to do that, you know." He clicked the projector off.

"Let her sleep on me? It was only a few minutes." Fallon reclined on a pile of pillows.

"Give up your day to watch movies with a little kid."

"It's no big deal. Besides, it was a dare." She winked at him teasingly.

"I'm grateful all the same." He tossed her another blanket.

"I'm not cold."

"I know." He shrugged and laid down, Amelia's cushions separating them. "When I was a kid, my father would take me outside on warm nights. We'd build a fort—not too different from this one—and sleep under the stars." He lifted an arm and tucked it behind his head. "I can't wait until Amelia is old enough to do the same."

She could hear the emotion in his voice, like he was

still there in that fort somewhere in England with his dad.

Fallon closed her eyes and listened to the sounds of LA. It wasn't as loud here in the neighborhoods, but the California buzz remained.

Arizona had a buzz too, but it was different. Her heart ached at the thought.

She let her mind drift back to her home, back to before she'd become the person she was now, back when she'd allowed herself to love someone.

A memory took shape in the darkness.

"When Annora and I were younger"—she swallowed the tightness in her throat and opened her eyes—"we'd sneak out after our parents were asleep and camp out on the trampoline in the backyard. We'd bring our blankets and pillows and stay up half the night listening to music and looking for meteors."

She hadn't planned on sharing any of this with Noah, but as the memory played out in her mind, she needed to voice it, as though it would disappear for good if it wasn't given words to cling to.

"Did you ever get caught?"

"Every time." She huffed a laugh. "One time, we woke up in the morning, and our dad was out there with us, fast asleep. He'd joined us some time in the night. I don't know how he climbed onto a trampoline without waking us up, but there he was." Her fingers tapped out a rhythm against the cushion.

Thomas's words replayed through Fallon's head.

You can't begin to understand how much it means to a father to see someone care for his little girl.

Did her father feel the same?

She loved her parents in the way that she figured everyone loved their parents, but she'd done her best to avoid them at all costs and minimize contact since she moved, even before that if she was being honest.

She'd lost her sister and best friend when Annora died, and since then, she'd pushed her parents away just as she had everyone else. Maybe that's why her father had asked to talk to Noah today. He really had just wanted to know she was okay.

She reached for her boot, pulled out her phone, and shot off a long overdue text.

Fallon: *Love you dad*

"There are no stars here," Noah spoke in the darkness.

"In your backyard?"

"In Los Angeles, smartass," he chuckled. "You can't see stars. Too much light from the city, I'm sure."

She tucked her phone away and stared into the night, eyes scanning the sky for a glimmer, but he was right. She'd never noticed, or cared, in the last year that there were no stars in LA, but suddenly it seemed an unforgivable deficit.

The stars back in Arizona were beautiful.

"Do you miss England?" she asked, desperate to get her mind off her own hometown.

"Every day." Longing coated his voice, but not sadness.

"I bet you're happy to be going back soon then."

Noah hadn't been specific about when he was moving back, but she imagined it had to be soon if Amelia was doing so well.

He didn't respond. It was dark enough she couldn't make out his expression, but she had no doubt he was listening. She waited.

"We'll see," he eventually said.

"Are you not going back?" She sat up. He did the same. She could tell from his movements that he was watching her.

"I haven't decided." He pushed his fingers through his hair. "Turns out California has a few things England does not."

"Like the band?" she asked.

"For starters."

Fallon laid back onto her cushions.

"We'll see what happens at the festival," he finished.

"Twisted Fest? Is that a factor?"

"It definitely could be."

Her mind spun. Twisted Fest would seal her own fate. In two weeks, she could be back in Arizona, and that thought alone sent panic shooting through her veins. Knowing that her performance could have that kind of impact on Noah's future too only added that much more pressure.

And what would that mean for *them*?

If he lost and returned to England, he'd leave her. If she lost and moved to Arizona, she'd leave him. Either way, one of them would leave the other behind.

Which also meant there was no chance of him

wanting a real relationship. If they both knew from the start that they couldn't last, there was no way they'd get their hearts broken. No commitment—guaranteed.

She'd been looking at everything the wrong way.

Noah wasn't a threat.

He was the safest possible option.

"Either way," he went on, voice lighter than before, "Twisted Fest will be incredible."

She gladly took his cue, still processing her new realization. "Hell yeah, it will."

"Is Edge feeling ready? Calvin seemed a little…unsure last time I spoke with him."

Her stomach turned again. Calvin was unsure, at least about the future of the band, but why was he having this conversation with Noah? She reached for her phone again but stopped.

It could wait for tomorrow.

She realized she hadn't responded to his question.

"We're ready."

Noah nodded and tucked back into his pillows and blanket.

"You up for another one?" He motioned to their temporary movie screen.

"Bring it on." She let out a heavy breath and forced herself to relax.

Noah pushed a few buttons and the next movie began, this time a comedy that would not have been cleared for Amelia's watching.

Fallon wrapped her blanket around her, but her mind darted in a thousand directions.

Twisted Fest. Arizona. Her parents. Annora. Amelia. England. Noah.

Everything had been so simple only four weeks ago. Go to Twisted Fest, get a record deal, stay in LA, and don't get too attached along the way.

Nothing was simple anymore.

She glanced over to where the light of the movie illuminated Noah sleeping soundly. Her stomach fluttered, and the river of panic coursing through her slowed.

One day at a time. She'd always lived in the moment, and that hadn't changed. She'd deal with the rest tomorrow.

An idea settled on her, and she smiled. These last few weeks she'd been picking challenges for Noah in the hopes that each might send him running. She'd been unsuccessful so far, but after all he'd done for her, it might be time to go a different direction.

A chilled breeze bit at her ears. She grabbed the extra blanket Noah had given her, pulled it around her shoulders, and sunk deeper into her cushions, still grinning in the darkness.

CHAPTER 27

Fallon had thought things were intense already, but as soon as the Twisted Fest countdown reached ten days, both bands turned up the heat, making her life a living hell.

Fitz made it perfectly clear Tuesday morning that they'd be adding extra practices and everyone should figure out how to make it work. Starting immediately, no more days off and a few evenings added on as well.

Unfortunately, Keith had had a similar idea.

"We'll never be ready in time if we don't amp it up," he explained from where he'd landed on the warehouse couch after a three-hour practice.

She didn't mention that that wouldn't have been a problem if he and Calvin hadn't cancelled so many practices the last few weeks. Instead, she crossed to the fridge and pulled out two waters. She handed one to Calvin who climbed onto the stool beside hers.

"I agree." He opened the water bottle and downed half of it.

"I have no problem with more practices, but Blue

Streetlights is adding more too. You might have a battle for the space." Her legs dangled a few inches off the ground, and she let her feet swing back and forth.

"It's our space. They can work around us," Keith shot back.

She shrugged. "Work it out with Fitz." She wasn't going to get in the middle of their pissing match. She'd have her hands full with two bands both pulling doubles. She'd be lucky if her arms didn't fall off before they even made it to Twisted Fest.

"One thing though"—Calvin swiveled on his stool—"I'm good to do doubles and extras and whatever, but I can't practice this Saturday. I've got stuff."

"What stuff?" Keith sounded more curious than upset.

Calvin shifted uncomfortably.

"Graduation," he mumbled but not badly enough for them to miss his answer.

"You're graduating this Saturday?" Keith's wide smile lit up his face. His curly brown hair and pointy chin gave him a cute, boyish look.

"It's not a big deal. I wouldn't even go, but my parents want me to do the whole cap-and-gown-diploma thing."

"Are you going to have the little hat dangle too?" Fallon teased. She bumped her knee against his, and he bumped her back.

"I have no idea. I didn't even know people walked for associate degrees." He was finally smiling about it. "But it means I can't practice that day."

"Can we come?" Keith asked. She wondered if he was joking, but he looked completely genuine.

"I guess," Calvin shrugged, "but it's a community college ceremony. It's not a big deal."

"It's a huge deal. I'll be there."

Calvin glanced sideways at her. She chose to keep her gaze on the water bottle she rolled between her hands.

"I know that's not your thing—personal events like that. It's okay. Really. You don't have to come." He smiled tightly.

She finally met his eyes. They were warm and kind, not at all full of the anger and resentment she'd expected.

She believed him. He was finally okay with her keeping her distance. She didn't feel the wave of relief she'd expected. Instead, there was a pit in her stomach and a burn in her throat.

"I'll think about it."

And she would.

***

Thanks to the insane demands of both bands, Fallon barely made it home all week. Aside from a brief stop she'd made for herself one evening on the way home, she'd practically been living at the warehouse. Luckily, Keith held off from adding a practice Friday night so Calvin could get ready for graduation the next day, and Fitz had called a night off for a "chance to rest up." He'd been watching her closely that morning before making the call, and obviously been worried about her when he'd made it.

232

She didn't care. A night off was a night off, and she owed Noah a dare.

"We have to go a little early." She punched the location into her phone and leaned it against Noah's dash so he could see it.

"But why?" Noah's hands gripped the wheel at their usual nine and three. She chuckled. She'd never met someone so polarizing. Eyes glued to the road and hands safely on the wheel, but he sang in a punk band and had broken into Elliott's apartment.

"Because it closes at ten." Since she'd been planning this dare for a few days, she'd done her homework. "Maybe you'll actually get to sleep tonight."

"Unlikely." He didn't sound bitter, just honest. "Does this still count as a dare if it's not in the middle of the night?"

"Yes. It's still night-ish and a going-out thing."

"Fair enough." He turned off the main road onto a narrow road leading into the hills. "So, do you have plans after Twisted Fest? I mean, you are welcome to stay as long as you want, but I'm just curious."

She stiffened. She'd considered telling him about her deal with her parents, but she wasn't ready for Noah to know. It didn't involve him, and he was already getting too attached.

She was getting too attached.

But she couldn't bring herself to push him away. Somehow in the last month, he'd completely invaded her life. Coffee waiting for her at breakfast each morning. Their rides to and from practice. Noah sprawled across the couch watching baking shows in the middle of the night. Their time together had become her favorite part of her day, and she found she missed him when she wasn't home.

Now that she knew one of them would be leaving Los Angeles after Twisted Fest, she'd decided she was no longer going to fight the ever present pull she felt toward Noah, but she also knew she'd have to be the one to instigate. She'd told Noah she didn't want to be more than friends, and as long as he believed that was the case, he'd never make a move.

Unfortunately, since then, she'd barely seen him. And if she was completely honest with herself, she was a little hesitant to try to kiss Noah.

Last time she'd tried had been the night they'd met, and that hadn't gone so great.

She didn't care that he'd rejected her. She hadn't cared enough about him to feel embarrassed or hurt, but there was still that inkling of memory that made her pause.

"Fallon?" Noah glanced at her, brows pulled together. She hadn't answered his question.

"I don't know yet. Depends on Twisted Fest." The truth—just not all of it.

"I think Amelia is rooting for Edge to win."

"Not Blue Streetlights?"

"She likes you more than me. And I'm pretty sure she's scared of Fitz."

Fallon bit back a smile. "She's got good instincts."

"I couldn't agree more."

Noah curved through the hills high above Los Angeles, following her GPS. As he reached the peak, he parked the car and studied the building in front of them.

"An observatory?"

She nodded and hopped out of the car. He circled to her side.

"This is tonight's dare? No high-rise? No beach party?" He gave her a sly smile and raised a brow, clearly expecting something edgier than an elementary school field trip hotspot.

"Don't question me."

"I wouldn't dare." He winked.

Did he know his teasing was setting her *entire body* on fire?

Together they weaved through the parking lot and toward the enormous structure. Triangles of grassy lawn separated by cement walkways led visitors to the white stone building, on top of which two black domes flanked a third, larger dome. Tiered decks, also made of white stone, circled the sides and back of the building overlooking the San Fernando Valley far below.

They moved through security and into the main entrance. Fallon reached for Noah's hand and dragged him down the hall, passing rooms displaying findings of different astronomers and huge science experiments. A wall with the periodic table flashed by followed by a room of pillars encircling pictures and diagrams of the sun, moon, and earth.

"Wait." Noah halted in front of the Tesla Coil. "Aren't we here to see all this?" People gathered as snaps of electricity shot from the ball atop a pedestal through the cage around it. It was like watching a miniature lightning storm. Any other day Fallon would be fascinated by the controlled chaos, but today she had one purpose, and if they weren't quick, it would be too late.

"Not quite." She tugged on his hand, and he followed without hesitation. They slipped out a door and onto one of the side decks.

He was silent as they approached the edge of the outer wall. He leaned a forearm against the stone, still holding her hand. His was warm, and her petite fingers looked even smaller against his long lean ones. His eyes scanned the valley sprawled before him, the sun disappearing behind the horizon.

The breeze whipped around them, rustling her hair. She pulled her hoodie sleeves lower over her hands, but Noah's olive-green chinos and fitted white Henley would be enough to keep him warm.

"This view might just beat Elliott's," he said.

"Don't tell him that." She used her free hand to point toward the mountain face to their right. "See the Hollywood sign?"

"I can't believe I've never seen this. It's incredible." Noah's lips curved upward, and her heart hiccupped.

"It is, but it's also not why we're here."

"No?" His brows lifted. The sun was completely gone now, but the glow from the city and the gleam of the lights around them lit his face.

"Not even close." She led him to the end of the deck to another set of stone stairs that looped around the building and spit them out on the roof. They weaved through the crowd to the other end of the building and a tower topped with one of the black domes they'd seen from the parking lot. Noah's footsteps were steady behind her, each one a soft beat against the cement.

They reached the door of the tower. Inside, they met a girl about Fallon's age standing beside a second door.

"No food or drink. Stay in the approved area." She held the door open for them.

Noah shot Fallon a questioning glance and stepped through the opening.

They entered a small, dimly lit room with machinery covering the walls. A metal staircase in the center led to a platform about ten feet off the ground. A railing bordered the platform, keeping them in what was likely the 'approved' area, but most of the dome was taken up with a telescope bigger than Fallon had thought possible before she'd seen it for herself. Knobs and levers were set to what she had to assume were the precise measurements and coordinates to make it function.

It was mostly dark, but she could feel Noah beside her. His steady breathing was the only sound as the door closed behind them, blocking the noise of the crowd outside.

"Why did you bring me here?" he whispered. She could hear the smile in his voice.

"Just take a look." The words were more breath than voice, and her heart thudded. Noah was so close she could feel his warmth through her hoodie, boiling her will not to kiss him right there.

He breathed out like he too was remembering they were only friends and turned toward the telescope. His hands gripped the railing, and he brought his eyes to the binocular-looking mechanism. A quiet gasp escaped his lips.

"Stars." He looked back at her. "You found stars in LA."

Her chest warmed at the obvious joy in his voice. She smiled widely, and he returned to the telescope.

She'd heard about the observatory when she'd first arrived in Cali, but she'd never actually visited. She'd known the other night in the fort, though, that she couldn't leave the state without showing Noah the only stars she could.

After a few minutes, he broke his gaze and motioned for her to look. During her reconnaissance visit the other night, she hadn't actually used the telescope. Something in her had wanted to share this moment with him.

She stepped to the telescope. Noah had had to bend slightly to meet the eyepiece, but Fallon needed the step stool provided. She took a step up and leaned into the mechanism.

The skies exploded.

Stars swirled through the mass of darkness, thousands and thousands of burning lights dancing and colliding. Her breath hitched. She'd never felt so small. Her mind shifted to Annora, and she couldn't breathe.

Fallon had been raised by her father to be religious. She learned about God and heaven and life after death.

Since Annora's passing, she wasn't sure what she believed. But looking out into the forever, she hoped that Annora was out there somewhere, whether it was in Heaven or among the stars, still a part of her life.

What would Annora think of her?

Shame burned in Fallon's chest. Annora would want her to be brave. She'd always thought she was, but lately she wasn't so sure. She was fearless, but was that the same thing?

She backed away from the telescope and found Noah watching her. Her eyes had adjusted to the dark, and she could now make out the lines of his face, the intensity of his eyes, his brows pulling together ever so slightly as they studied her. Standing on the step stool, she was nearly eye to eye with him.

There, in the dark, surrounded by nothing but the universe, Fallon pressed her lips to Noah's.

She felt his surprise in the stiffness of his lips. Then, as quickly as she'd brought her lips to his, he pulled away.

Her stomach dropped. He stepped back and turned away from her, raking a hand through his hair.

He was rejecting her.

Again.

Only this time, he couldn't blame the band or Fitz.

Her face heated, and she pulled at the end of her hoodie sleeves cupped in her sweaty palms.

It was the damn stars. They'd made her reckless and stupid. She'd known from the beginning, from the day they'd met. He was everything she avoided, and this was why.

Noah braced his hands against the railing, head hung and his back still facing her, rising and falling with each breath. He pushed off the railing and turned to her.

"We better get home." His eyes met hers, and the distress in them made her wish the room was even darker so she couldn't see them. She did her best to erase all emotion from her own.

She nodded, and Noah followed her out the door, through the observatory, and back to the car.

Neither of them spoke a word the whole way home.

CHAPTER 28

They trekked into the guesthouse, tension thick between them. Fallon ripped her hoodie off over her head, turning her already messy hair into full chaos and exposing her yellow crop top. She tossed the hoodie over the couch. She'd deal with it later.

Noah followed a few steps behind her. She headed for the stairs, prepared to lock herself in their bathroom and never come out again.

"Fallon?"

She paused, one hand on the banister, and turned back to him.

"Don't you dare apologize to me right now." If he pitied her, she'd Boston Tea-Party every speck of Earl Grey in this house.

"Why did you kiss me?"

"Why do you think?" Her tone was sharper than she'd intended. She was stuck between wanting to rip his head off and wanting to rip his clothes off, and the battle was getting the better of her.

"You said last week we could only ever be friends."

"I know what I said."

"What changed?" He stood behind the island, keeping it between them like a shield. Her gaze landed on the chocolate cake displayed in the middle of the counter. He'd been making it the night before when she'd gotten home. It was gorgeous, if a cake could be described that way. Swirls of frosting and chocolate shavings covered the enormous dessert. It must have taken him hours.

"Nothing changed." She wasn't going to tell him the truth—that she'd only decided they could be together once they had an expiration date. She hadn't even told him she might be leaving yet.

"Something must have."

"Why does it matter?"

"Because I'm a little confused here! One day you tell me even being friends is a stretch and only a few days later you kiss me. What am I supposed to do?" He raked his hand through his hair, leaving it all kinds of messy and attractive.

"Just do whatever you want. That's what I do."

"Then why did you push me away before?"

"I did it to protect us!" Her frustration was getting the better of her, and she clutched wildly at the control slipping away.

"From what?" He ground his palms into the countertop.

"Getting hurt." She couldn't stop the words.

"Hurt?" His forehead wrinkled, and his voice immediately settled. "Fallon, every second with you is excruciating."

His words collided with her heart, and her lungs contracted. The sting and humiliation of his rejection dissolved until all that was left was crushing heartache.

"You hate me that much?" She choked out. She should be thrilled. This is what she'd wanted from the beginning, and yet, the pain was unbearable. She slid away from the banister and moved to the island, bracing herself against the counter.

Noah shook his head slowly. The agony written across his face shredded her.

"I don't hate you. Honestly, it would be easier if I did. Because seeing you, talking to you, just being near you and knowing I can't be with you has been torture."

Her whole body froze.

"I've wanted you since the night we met, and every minute we spend together, every second I'm with you, I only fall more in love with you."

Time stopped. She couldn't breathe. Couldn't blink.

He finally stepped around the island. Only inches away, Noah reached for her hand and held it tenderly. His thumb brushed across the tops of her fingers. Her hand was so little in his.

"So, if protecting us from pain was your goal, you failed miserably." The corner of his mouth lifted, and that small smile cracked her heart wide open. He leaned in close.

"Please don't push me away, luv," he breathed against her cheek. His nose brushed along her jaw, and her boldness collapsed around her. She clawed for the determination and willpower to withstand him, but it was gone. She was empty.

"I can't—" She started and stopped. "I didn't—" Again, words failed her. Her thoughts were a jumble. Nothing made sense anymore.

Noah leaned away and studied her. The caring she'd seen in his eyes the night they met was amplified beyond what she could bear.

"I'm sorry." His voice was soft. Gentle. "If you aren't ready to talk to me, I understand."

"I'm not good at opening up to people."

"I've noticed." His smile was back, and he softly tucked her hair behind her ear. She studied his expression and found nothing but the sincerity and kindness that had once terrified her.

He loved her.

"You've really wanted to kiss me since the night we met?" She lifted one brow.

"Desperately."

"Then what the hell are you waiting for?"

His eyes widened in shock as her word sunk in, then, within a heartbeat, Noah's lips crashed into hers. He cupped her face firmly in one hand, the other gripping her waist.

Her hands flew over his chest. She gripped his shirt in her fists and pulled him against her. He responded immediately.

This was not a hesitant caress. This was heat and tongues and hunger and teeth.

His hands tore at her. Her fingers weaved through his hair. It was thick and soft, and it felt incredible.

His arms wrapped around her, and she arched into

his touch. Her entire body ignited. She'd never felt the intensity she felt now for him.

This was a terrible idea. They should not be doing this.

But she'd never been one for shoulds or shouldn'ts.

Their hearts raced as they fought for breath. His grip was possessive and firm. His tongue teased her, and she moaned involuntarily.

His hands drifted down her back and cupped her ass just as she jumped into his arms.

She knew she liked those back muscles.

He lifted her effortlessly onto the kitchen island, but when she threw a hand behind her to catch herself, her fist landed directly in his cake, launching chocolate all over the kitchen.

They broke apart. She looked around her at the mess of frosting and cake splattered across the counter, the floor, and both of them. Noah's eyes stayed on her, his chest rising and falling heavily.

"We ruined your cake," she breathed.

"I don't care," he rasped and captured her lips again. Frosting clung to Noah's hair as her hands wound through it.

He tasted like chocolate, and nothing had ever been more delicious. He braced a hand against the counter and trailed his lips down her throat. She tilted her head back and felt her hair drag through the smashed cake.

His kiss was explosive. She was wrecked for anyone else, no one else would ever compare. She could never want anyone else.

But this wasn't for forever. One of them was still

leaving California.

It was her insurance. If she knew he'd be leaving, it wouldn't hurt as bad when he did.

Noah's hand returned to her, cupping her head, tilting it to his desire, the other still gripping her hip like he'd never let go. His thumb brushed her exposed stomach, and she felt the frosting trail behind it.

He pulled back, and she instantly ached for his lips.

"We're not done talking." He heaved through racing breaths.

"Tomorrow." She wrapped her fist in his shirt, smearing chocolate across his chest, and pulled him back where he belonged.

CHAPTER 29

Fallon breathed in the scent of the pillow beneath her.

Sugar and vanilla.

And chocolate.

Not a pillow. Pillows weren't this firm. Pillows didn't move up and down. She opened her eyes and slowly pushed off Noah's chest, careful not to wake him.

They'd never made it to bed last night. They'd stayed up until nearly dawn talking. And making out. Sometimes Noah was playful and teasing. Other times he was all fire and passion.

Fallon adored both.

He'd held her close, trailing kisses up her neck and nipping at her ears, as they'd watched British baking contestants make sticky toffee pudding which looked nothing like the instant pudding that came in a box and more like a cake covered in caramel sauce and melted ice cream. Noah promised to make it for her.

He had still been awake when she'd drifted off.

She padded to the kitchen and fished coffee and tea

out of the cabinet. She filled the machine and kettle and plopped onto a stool, careful to avoid the crusty smears of frosting all over the counter and floor. The house was quiet besides the whirl of the coffee maker and an occasional soft exhale from the boy on the couch.

He had said he loved her.

Warmth spread through her chest, and her fingers tingled around her coffee mug.

She'd told him more than she'd meant to last night, but she couldn't bring herself to care, not when she could still feel his arms wrapped around her.

She spun on her stool and peeked over the couch. Noah slept soundly. His head rested on the throw pillow, sun-kissed hair streaked with chocolate frosting. He still wore his cake-smeared Henley and chinos, but he'd lost his shoes sometime in the night.

Her muffled ringtone sounded from the couch. She rushed to silence it before it woke Noah, but she wasn't quick enough. He stirred and lifted his head, squinting as he searched for the source of the noise. His hand disappeared into a crack between cushions and emerged holding her phone. He lifted it above his head.

She took it from his hand and swiped it open.

"Hello?" She pushed the phone to her ear. Noah sat up and rubbed his hands over his face.

"Geez, took you long enough," Josh teased. "Were you still asleep? It's almost noon."

"Screw you."

He laughed.

"Why are you calling me?" she asked. She returned to the cabinets, dug out a second mug, and filled it with hot water from the kettle. She unwrapped a tea bag and added it to the mug.

"I'm giving Fitz a ride to Calvin's graduation today. You and Noah want to ride with us?"

"You're going?" She circled the sectional and handed the tea to Noah. He took it gratefully. She lowered herself onto the couch beside him.

"Of course we are. Aren't you?"

Her gut sank. She definitely wasn't.

"Nope."

"I thought you might say that. How 'bout Noah?"

She held the phone away from her ear. "Josh wants to know if you want to ride with him and Fitz to Calvin's graduation."

"Are you going?" Noah rested an arm along the back of the sectional.

"No."

Noah nodded, understanding everything she didn't have to say.

"Tell him to pick me up here." He returned to steeping his tea.

She put the phone back to her ear. "He said—"

"I heard. Tell him I'll be there in two hours."

Fallon hung up and tossed her phone to the other end of the sectional.

"You okay?" Noah asked.

"Mm-hmm." She walked to the sink and rinsed out her now empty mug. Noah followed her, leaning sideways against the counter next to her.

"You sure you don't want to come today? We have a bet going on how many times Fitz is going to curse during the ceremony. Josh says he'll only hit nine, but I've got my money on at least eleven."

"And what if he ends up at ten?"

"You can claim ten if you'd like." He smiled and sipped his tea.

"Why do you care if I go?"

"Because I like being with you."

A terrible thought came to her.

"Wait, is this my next dare? Calvin's graduation?"

Noah's face became serious, and he set his tea on the counter.

"No. If you don't want to go to Calvin's graduation, you shouldn't go. Don't let the boys pressure you into it. If this would cross a line you don't want to cross, you don't have to justify that."

"It's not that I'm not proud of Cal."

"I know that, luv"—he brushed his fingers over her cheek—"but does he?"

She chose not to think about that.

"You should probably shower before Josh gets here." She changed the subject and tugged on his chocolate-smeared shirt.

"What about you?" He fisted a chunk of her hair and lifted it to show her the clumps of dried frosting clinging to it.

"Maybe I like it that way." She stuck out her tongue. Noah's eyes shot to her mouth and darkened.

"You okay there?" She winked and stepped away, her hair falling from his grasp.

He swallowed. "Fine."

She bit back a smile and turned away from him, enjoying their game.

"You can go first." She snatched a box of cereal.

"Tease." He wrapped an arm around her waist from behind, used the other to sweep her hair to the side, and placed a single kiss just below her ear. Electricity coursed through her.

She reached for him, but he slipped from her grasp and up the stairs.

"Now who's the tease?" she yelled after him.

She could hear his laugh from the hall above and thought it might be her favorite sound in the whole world.

***

By the time Josh got to the guesthouse, Fallon had showered and dressed and was headed back downstairs to the kitchen. Noah was sitting at the now spotless island below looking completely indecent in navy slacks, brown leather dress shoes, and a light blue button-up, sleeves rolled to the elbow.

Did someone tell guys how insanely sexy that sleeve-roll is, or did they figure it out on their own?

Her heels clicked against the wood floors as she rounded the bottom of the stairs. At the sound, Noah glanced up, back to his phone, and then up again. His eyes widened ever so slightly, and she'd swear his jaw dropped a little as his gaze explored her body from head to toe and back again.

"Cat got your tongue, England?" she smirked. He'd never seen her done up, and she knew this particular

251

little black dress did plenty for her figure. The black heels didn't hurt either.

He snapped his mouth shut and swallowed, finally dragging his gaze to meet hers.

"You look nice," he finally managed.

"Nice?" She circled the room and took the stool next to him. "This was way too much work for 'nice.'"

His eyes remained on hers, but he'd found his smile.

"Alright, you look unspeakably beautiful." He leaned in and brushed a soft kiss to her cheek. "And hot as hell."

He stood and tucked his phone away in his pocket.

"Much better." She flicked her chin at the door. "Is Josh here?"

"Yeah, he just texted me, but I was a tad distracted." Noah moved to leave, and she followed. He hesitated. "Are you coming?"

"Why else would I be dressed like this?" She swept her smooth hair behind her shoulder.

"When a woman looks as good as you do right now, I don't question it."

She stuck out her tongue and handed him her phone.

"Carry this for me?" She motioned to her heels. "No boots."

He took it from her outstretched hand and slid it into the pocket opposite his own, and together they headed for Josh's car.

Josh and Fitz were both surprised to see her but didn't say much about it. She noticed both their eyes lingering on her as she climbed in, Josh with the concerned gaze of an older brother and Fitz with an appreciative nod.

Noah winked at her.

When they arrived at the college, they parked and climbed the stairs to the bleachers along the large field where the graduation was taking place. The benches were filling up quickly, but the rows of white folding chairs on the field sat empty. If she remembered her high school graduation correctly, the graduates entered after the ceremony began. She assumed the chairs were for them. On the opposite side was a stage, complete with a huge screen blazing the Glendale Community College emblem, a podium, and flags from dozens of countries lining either side.

The sun shone high in the sky, making the air around them thick and hot. Fallon wondered how the guys could stand being in long pants when she was warm in only her dress, but none of them said anything. Even Fitz, in his maroon dress shirt, sleeves rolled and top two buttons undone, didn't complain about the heat.

They scanned the crowd and caught Eric's fiery red hair a few rows over and toward the front. Noah offered her his arm for stability. She took it gratefully, and together they descended to the row Eric had been saving.

"These taken?" Josh asked, motioning to the nearly empty bench in an otherwise crowded sea of people.

"I saved them for you! Have you all met Calvin's parents?" Eric motioned to the middle-aged couple on his other side. Mr. Graves stood and shook hands with Josh and Noah, but Mrs. Graves seemed hesitant to pull her gaze from the field, eyes scanning for graduates that were nowhere to be seen.

Everyone took their places on the uncomfortable metal benches, and the boys continued talking amongst themselves, Noah on her left and Josh on her right. Fallon joined Mrs. Graves in her useless efforts to spot Calvin.

Despite her cool, collected appearance, Fallon had been a jumble of nerves and anxiety since she'd decided to attend the graduation. In the shower, Noah's words had circled through her mind, over and over.

Did Calvin know she was proud of him?

It didn't really matter. They weren't anything more than bandmates. But graduating was a big deal, and even a bandmate could be proud of that. Even so, actually being there, meeting his parents, being part of such a personal accomplishment had fear eating away at her insides.

She tried to focus on the guys around her. If she could do that, she might be able to convince herself this was just another band thing.

But they were still missing one bandmate.

She glanced down the row one way and then the other before calling over Josh to Eric.

"Where's Keith?"

Eric's smile didn't fade, but something that looked a lot like anger flickered in his eyes.

"He's not going to make it. He wasn't feeling well

today." He gave her a knowing look.

So, Keith was hungover—at best. Anger of her own sent heat up the back of her neck. He'd said he'd be here. He'd told Calvin he'd be here.

She wasn't good about going to stuff, but at least she didn't lie about it.

Noah leaned toward her, sensing her tension.

"The rest of us are here," he whispered encouragingly.

She nodded and let her frustration roll off her back. She wouldn't let Keith's assholery ruin the day for Calvin.

A hush fell over the audience and a man in a black robe approached the microphone to welcome the friends and family of the graduates.

"How long do these things usually last?" Fitz whispered from Noah's other side.

Noah shrugged. "Not sure. In England they are only about an hour, but I've heard you lot in the States often double or triple that."

"Damn."

Noah looked back to her and mouthed, "One."

Much to Fitz's relief, the ceremony only lasted about an hour and a half. A few speakers said their piece about the "incredible future that lies ahead," and the graduates in their maroon robes, gold cords draped over their shoulders, had their names called one-by-one as they received their diplomas. Their whole bench stood when the woman called Calvin's name. Their shouting and screaming was loud enough Fallon swore she could see his blush from twenty yards away.

The crowd emptied onto the field afterward, and Calvin quickly found their cluster. He wrapped his mom in a hug, and his dad clapped him on the back. He and Eric embraced as well, and Eric placed a proud kiss on his cheek. Then Calvin turned to Blue Streetlights waiting patiently to the side. His smile stretched all the way across his face, and Fallon couldn't remember the last time she'd seen him look so happy.

"You came!" He'd obviously seen them there when he'd first entered the field, but he still seemed surprised at their presence. He shook each of the boys' hands and even hugged Noah before he reached her. He stilled, and his smile softened. "You came, too."

This time it was more of a question than an observation.

"Someone had to keep an eye on these tontos." She flicked her head at the band now talking to Eric a few feet away.

"It's really good to have you here." His smile grew, and the corners of her own lips curved to match.

"I'm glad I came." She wasn't sure what else to say. She was happy for Calvin and proud of him even, but being here was way more than she should allow herself, and talking about it was worse.

Luckily, Noah walked up at just that moment and saved her from any further conversation.

"You two want to grab some dinner?" Noah asked. "Josh is paying."

"Absolutely," Calvin said. "Why is Josh paying?"

"He lost a bet."

CHAPTER 30

Over the next week, Fallon burned through every emotion possible. She couldn't figure out if she was excited, nervous, or completely terrified. Twisted Fest was inching closer by the minute, and she had too much riding on it to tell herself she didn't care.

They would perform Friday afternoon, but the winner wouldn't be announced until Saturday. Then she'd find out if she was staying in Cali or getting a one-way ticket back to Arizona.

She tried to push the anxiety down and focus on the rush of performing at a festival like Twisted Fest. Luckily, she'd had very little time to spend worrying about it. Blue Streetlights and Edge of September had both practiced every day that week, so she was practically living at the warehouse again. Fitz and Keith had clashed over schedules, but in the end, Keith had pulled the "it's our space" card, and Blue Streetlights had had to work around that.

Due to her lack of any free time whatsoever, she had also spent almost zero time with Noah outside practice. He was always up when she got home from Edge practice well after dark, but no matter how much she wanted to stay up and play with him, she knew she had to get sleep if she had any chance of still being functional for the festival.

She awoke Friday with a buzzing in her bloodstream.

Today was Twisted Fest.

Despite her excitement for the festival, it had arrived way too fast. Every nerve in her body was on edge, and her stomach was doing somersaults. Her entire life would change this weekend, for good or bad.

She checked her phone and found a text from Noah to tell her he had left early and that Josh was on his way to get her. Her nerves settled. She was tackling today with her boys.

All of them.

"You ready to go?" Josh lounged at the door as Fallon finished her cereal. She sat at the kitchen island staring at a plate of fresh banana muffins.

"Yep." She shoved her phone into one boot and her house key in the other and followed Josh to his car in front of the house with a muffin between her teeth.

Energy pulsed in her veins. She wished Noah was here. His presence always calmed her.

Josh seemed to read her mind.

"What's going on with you and Noah?" he asked as he weaved through traffic.

She hadn't filled him in on anything, and they hadn't been touchy at practice, but he'd have to be an idiot not to sense something going on between his bandmates.

"Nothing." She swallowed the last bite of muffin and twirled a drumstick in her hand—a difficult feat in a car as small as Josh's, but it was the only thing keeping her from spiraling into her anxiety.

"Listen, I get it. You aren't a sharer." Josh parked in front of the warehouse and turned off the car. "But I know you, and I know him. He's a good guy and doesn't deserve to get ghosted." He pegged her with a serious stare.

"I'm aware." She rolled her eyes at his paranoia, but guilt curdled in her gut. "Now can we please go inside? Today is kind of a big deal."

In the warehouse, Elliott hovered as Keith and Fitz gathered gear. Noah and Calvin passed her at the door and headed to the cars with their arms full of instruments and accessories. Noah's face lit up when he saw her, and her tension eased. She went to work before Josh could notice.

The plan was to fill Calvin's car with guitars and amps and use Noah's SUV to haul Fallon's kit. Everyone else could ride with Josh, and Elliott would meet them there.

It was only a twenty-minute drive to the LA State Historic Park where Twisted Fest was held each year. They followed the directions Elliott had given them and found band parking on the far side. Noah and Calvin were already waiting by their cars.

They spotted Elliott waving them over to the first of three giant white awnings. Inside, picnic tables were scattered over the grass along with coolers filled with cheap water bottles. Groups of people clumped around the tables—musicians from the looks of it. She had spent enough time around them to get a sense. Probably a few managers, like Elliott.

Edge of September and Blue Streetlights found an open table, and Fallon claimed a seat. She had two full sets to make it through today. She'd rest while she could.

"These three tents are reserved for the bands," Elliott explained. "You can stay here as long as you'd like. Or you can go watch the other bands, size up the competition."

He handed each of them a pass attached to a lime green lanyard.

"These will get you where you need to go." He looked at Fitz and Keith. "Blue Streetlights is set for two-thirty. Edge of September will follow at three-thirty."

He explained that each band would have an hour slot—fifteen minutes to set up, thirty to play, and another fifteen to break down. There were two stages, so as one band finished, another band would start on the other stage. Fifteen bands would play today, and another six would play tomorrow. They'd announce the winner tomorrow afternoon.

Fallon's gaze drifted to Noah, but his eyes were locked on Elliott, brows drawn. Calvin shifted uncomfortably beside her. The nervous tension was palpable. Today mattered for everyone.

Elliott excused himself, and the remaining six of them headed for the park. They'd be fools not to check out the competition—and the crowd.

A little way from the band tents, two identical stages formed an "L" shape. Speakers held up by black poles towered above the crowd on either side of the stages. A sheer backdrop with the Twisted Fest logo stretched thirty feet in the air behind each stage.

The one stage was empty, but the first band of the day was just finishing their setup on the other. Fallon spotted a small awning a little further from the crowd. Beneath it, five people in lime green T-shirts sat in tall chairs. From where she was, it looked like they were each holding something—a clipboard or tablet maybe.

Music erupted through the speakers. Post-hardcore with an emo vibe. One of the beautiful things about Twisted Fest was the variety of genres that showed up to compete. But as the singer joined and the song picked up, Fallon's stomach dropped.

They were good.

Like, *really* good.

If all their competition was at this level, they didn't stand a chance.

Her bandmates' faces told her they were thinking the same. She felt more than saw Fitz at her shoulder.

"We can take them." He smirked, all cockiness and arrogance, and her breathing steadied.

They listened as the band slayed song after song. It was hard not to get caught up in the music, but that wasn't why they were there. The band wrapped up, the crowd roared, and within seconds, the next one started on the second stage.

The crowd only grew as the time passed. Several

hundred people gathered to cheer on bands they loved and discover new favorites. It was a sea of sunhats, bikini tops, tie-dye, and lime green wristbands. The ground was damp from spilled drinks, and a sweet scent that could only be one thing floated through the air.

As Blue Streetlights' slot neared, they made their way around the back of the stage, hauling their instruments with them. Calvin, Keith, and Noah helped Fallon get her kit to the prep area. A guy in all black with a microphone headset motioned them up the stairs at almost exactly two-thirty. Three more guys with headsets appeared out of nowhere to help them get set up.

As they hauled her kit onto the stage and she began putting it together, she noticed one of the stage crew watching her from only a few feet away. He was arranging the mics to pick up her sound. A half smile appeared as he caught her eye.

He wasn't bad looking. His tall, thick frame looked almost entirely covered in tattoos based on what could be seen outside his black shorts and T-shirt. His hair was also black, but not naturally. The half smile remained as he stepped closer. Fallon continued assembling her drums. They were mostly built but needed to be tuned.

"Need any help?" he asked.

"I've got it." She tightened her floor tom.

"You sure? Sometimes tuning drums takes a little more strength."

Her eyes narrowed. She was used to pendejos like

this guy. Every girl she knew got shit, but in the music industry as a five-foot-two female, it was everywhere.

She locked eyes with the crew member and wielded the most wicked smile in her arsenal. "I've got it."

He shifted on his feet, probably deciding if his pride was worth the fight. He made the right call and walked away.

A shadow appeared across her drum set. She turned to find Noah, clearly tense and agitated.

"Jealous, England?"

"Should I be?" His shoulders relaxed, but his jaw was still tight.

"Of that guy?" She flicked a thumb toward the stage manager now plugging cords into Josh's amp. "Yes, I love nothing more than a misogynistic asshole."

She'd said the words sarcastically, but once they were out, she realized just how true they were—or had been before Noah.

She spun back to her kit and went to work on her toms.

Fifteen minutes were over and gone, and before they knew it, the stage manager was giving them the go-ahead.

"Let's win this thing." Josh grinned at them. He clapped Noah on the shoulder and stepped to the mic. "Los Angeles!"

The crowd screamed back. Energy surged through the air and into Fallon's limbs.

"We're Blue Streetlights!" Josh was practically screaming now. The crowd responded. He looked at her and winked.

That was all she needed.

She crashed her sticks into her kit, and they were off. They had thirty minutes to prove Blue Streetlights deserved a record deal. She would give it all she had.

CHAPTER 31

It was hard to tell from her position on the stage, but the cheering seemed louder than it had for any other band when they wrapped up their set. Thirty minutes went fast when so much was riding on it.

And it wasn't even really her band.

She wiped the sweat from her forehead with the back of her hand and waved her sticks at the crowd. The screams rose higher, and her heart pounded in her chest. Her cheeks hurt from smiling.

The next band started up on the opposite stage, and Blue Streetlights broke down their equipment as quickly as possible and made their way back toward the stairs they'd come up. Calvin and Keith were waiting at the bottom with shit-eating grins on their faces.

"That was amazing!" Calvin yelled over the music. "The best I've ever heard you!" He rushed at them and slung his arms around Noah in a huge hug. Noah returned it. His laugh danced along her skin.

With a clap on the back, Calvin released him and

moved on to Josh and then her. He squeezed her tight before letting go, and she exhaled a deep breath. She couldn't identify when, but somewhere along the way, something had changed between them. If he'd hugged her two months ago, she'd probably have kneed him in the balls purely out of reflex.

"Edge of September?" A fresh stage manager called from the top of the stairs.

"Here!" Calvin called and joined him on the stage.

Fallon followed. As she passed Blue Streetlights, Fitz nodded encouragingly, Josh squeezed her hand, and Noah locked eyes with her, stopping her dead in her tracks halfway up the stairs. The corners of his lips rose ever so slightly.

"You okay?" Keith asked from below her.

"Definitely." She broke their gaze and finished her climb to the stage.

Edge of September repeated the process Blue Streetlights had gone through only an hour before. Her kit was still set up, so she watched as Keith and Calvin tuned, working together to get it just right, and a lump formed in her throat. She blinked away the moisture in her eyes as her boys set up for what could be their last gig as a band.

Her smile returned when she caught a glimpse of three familiar faces. Fitz, Josh, and Noah had fought the crowd to get near the front of the stage to watch their set. She'd been playing with Calvin and Keith for over a year now, and yet, this summer, Blue Streetlights had become as much her band as Edge was.

Only they weren't.

After this weekend, she'd go back to one band—or none if Edge lost. The thought yanked on her heart, and she pushed it aside. She needed to focus. Getting distracted or sappy would only hurt their chances of winning.

"You ready?" the stage manager called from the side of the stage.

The three of them instinctively faced one another. Keith raised his brows. Calvin nodded, and Fallon grinned.

"We're ready," Keith responded.

She lifted her sticks and counted off for the most important gig of her life.

Keith worked the crowd like a pro, and song after song, they owned the stage. Seven songs made up their set, but even with as much adrenaline as she had coursing through her veins, her energy was fading by song five. Her arms and shoulders ached and a dull pain throbbed in her lower back. She pushed through the discomfort. Today was not the day to give out.

The crowd knew most of their songs and sang along loud enough they overpowered Keith once or twice—the upside of playing covers. Girls rode on their boyfriend's shoulders and hoisted cups to the sky. During their one slower song, cell phones waved back and forth through the air like lighters.

Fallon's gaze continually drifted to Josh, Noah, and Fitz. They seemed to be enjoying the show, and even though she knew they'd fake it in order to support her, their joy seemed genuine. It was dumb now that their set at Twisted Fest was done, but she still wanted to prove herself to them, convince them they'd made the right choice in her.

She gave it all she had, and by the time the set ended, her abs were on fire and she could barely lift her arms. But they'd nailed it.

The roar of the crowd rumbled in her bones, and she wished just for once that she could freeze time.

The downside to living in the moment was that moments don't last very long. So, when a moment like this one arrives, it's gone as quickly as it began.

The next band struck their first chord, and just like that, the cheering was no longer for them.

Edge of September was done.

Fallon shook her head. She couldn't think like that. Edge of September had as good of chance at winning as any other band there, and when they did win, everything would be fine. The record deal and the prize money would be enough to keep her in LA.

They tore down their setup and descended the stairs to find Blue Streetlights waiting for them.

The boys exchanged handshakes and slaps on the back, but Noah's eyes never left her. Pride lit his face, and suddenly her legs were as wobbly as her arms.

"Now what?" Josh asked.

"You going to bounce now that you're done?" Keith smirked.

"Not before we eat something."

"Oh, hell yes," Fitz said.

"I wouldn't mind a bite either." Noah motioned to an open clearing on the other side of the park. "Food trucks?"

"Let's go."

They stashed their instruments in the holding area near the white tents, and Josh led the way through the crowd and to the clearing where five food trucks formed a semi-circle. Each had a line, but it wasn't nearly as crowded at the stage areas. The guys recounted their sets, each talking over the last to point out some moment they hadn't.

Fallon skimmed over the trucks—Mexican, barbeque, Korean—until her gaze landed on the last truck: specialty waffles, the kind that could be sweet or savory. Noah's eyes had locked on the same truck.

She brushed her hand along his arm.

"You want the waffle place?"

"I think I might." Noah smiled as well and that same touch of sincerity bled through.

"Calvin? Josh? Waffles?"

"I'm in," Josh answered.

Calvin shook his head. "Nah, I'm getting barbeque with these two." He motioned to Fitz and Keith before running off to join them.

She crossed the clearing with Josh and Noah trailing behind her, still talking excitedly about their set. They stepped into the short line, and she scanned the menu board on the side of the truck.

Nutella Passion

Berries and Dreams

Grilled Cheese

Classic Chick'n and Waffles

"Oh my god! You are the guys from that band!" A

petite girl with a high blonde ponytail and an upturned nose, no taller than Fallon, got in line behind them and immediately started gushing. "You're my favorite so far!"

The girl's friend kept quiet but didn't stop the bubbly blonde from fangirling all over Josh and Noah. Her honey eyes snagged on Fallon, scanning her up and down.

"Thanks." Josh gave the blonde a wide smile. "I'm glad you enjoyed it."

"Sooooo much." Her grin stretched from dimple to dimple. "I'm Brooklin, and this is Macayle." She linked her arms through her friend's. Macayle waved shyly with her free hand.

"I'm Josh. This is Noah and Fallon." He motioned to each of them.

"Nice to meet you both," Noah said.

"Where's the other guy? Wasn't there one more?"

"He chose barbeque." Josh pointed across the clearing to where Fitz, Calvin, and Keith had disappeared.

"Next," a guy in his thirties with a mustache and a nose ring called from the truck.

Fallon turned away from the new Blue Streetlights fans and stepped up to the truck.

"Berries and Dreams. Extra whipped cream."

The guy nodded and hit a few buttons on a tablet. "That'll be $13.16."

She retrieved her card from her boot, paid him, and stepped aside. She caught Macayle eyeing her again as Josh and Noah ordered.

"So, are you guys local?" Brooklin asked Noah after placing her order.

"Glendale." Noah hooked his thumbs into the pockets of his black jeans.

"You're British though, right?" She batted her lashes. "Your accent is *amazing.*"

"I am. I just relocated last year."

Another waffle worker called out Fallon's name, and she returned to the window to get her food when she heard Brooklin continue.

"Do you have a girlfriend?"

Fallon tensed. What did she hope Noah would say? They hadn't established a status, and she had no intention of doing so.

She heard his reply as Josh approached the window, picking up his food in one hand and Noah's in the other.

"My heart is taken."

Josh shot her a sidelong glance, and she narrowed her eyes in warning. She was not going to talk about it.

They said goodbye to the now pouty girls and headed back to the band tents.

"They were nice," Josh commented innocently, balancing his grilled cheese in one hand and a water in the other. "Why didn't you get her number?"

She knew he was trying to get a rise out of her, so she kept walking and refused to give him the pleasure.

"I'm not interested," Noah answered, oblivious to Josh's efforts.

"What about you, Fallon?" Josh called to her a few

feet ahead. "Her friend couldn't take her eyes off you."

"Can you blame her? I'm stunning."

Josh snorted. "You weren't interested either, huh?"

"Guess not." She shrugged. Josh could poke and prod all he wanted. It wouldn't do him any good.

They made their way back to the band tent with their food and crashed at an open table. Fallon swiped a finger of whipped cream off her waffle and shoved it in her mouth. The sweetness coated her tongue, and she moaned in pleasure.

She glanced around at her bandmates. Calvin and Noah were deep in discussion. Keith was scrolling on his phone. Josh was licking melted cheese off his fingers, and Fitz twisted a fry in his.

A warmth built in her gut. She'd tried to keep the truth at arm's length, but she knew she'd miss this. Her boys and all their shit. Regardless of what happened tomorrow, this would never be the same. It was its own kind of loss.

They wasted away the afternoon until they'd all eaten their weight in barbeque and waffles, listening to band after band that were both steep competition and highly entertaining.

Noah's phone rang, and he stepped away to take the call. The rest of them got their stuff together and worked their way toward the cars. Fallon slammed the trunk closed after the last tom was tucked safely inside. Noah finally hung up. He rubbed the back of his neck.

"I know it's probably not what you all had in mind to celebrate, but my mum wants to throw a party for us tonight. My dad's obsessed with barbeques, and they're both just really excited. It shouldn't go late, and then everyone could go really party." His brows scrunched together and the corners of his mouth lifted in a reserved smile.

Josh didn't hesitate. "We'll be there."

Fitz and Calvin nodded in agreement.

"How do your parents feel about celebratory alcohol?" Keith chuckled, but Fallon didn't think he was joking. Apparently, neither did Noah.

"Where we're from, drinking age is eighteen. I'm sure they will have beer." He lowered his voice and mumbled, "and champagne."

She wondered if anyone who played Twisted Fest in the eight years it had been running had ever celebrated with champagne and laughed at the idea. It was more of a vodka-and-Diet-Dew kind of crowd.

"Wouldn't miss it."

CHAPTER 32

Noah had mentioned the barbeque and his parents and even the champagne. What he had not mentioned was the people.

A shit ton of people.

Apparently, Thomas and Sarah Cooper hadn't wasted any time making friends since they'd arrived in California and had invited pretty much everyone they knew to their party. At least fifty people, not including the members of either band, roamed the Cooper's yard. Plates overflowed with baked beans, macaroni salad, watermelon, and burgers. Tables covered with tablecloths and loaded with sides and desserts had been placed around the patio.

Fallon could easily spot the dessert Noah had made. Near the end of the last table stood a tower of macarons—a rainbow of cookies, stacked meticulously so anyone could choose any color or flavor without knocking down the entire structure.

Fallon grabbed a pale green cookie in each hand. She'd been wanting to try these since the night she and

Noah had watched the televised bakers make them. She bit into one, and lime flooded her mouth. Perfectly balanced—not too tart, but with a bite.

And a hint of chocolate in the center.

Little arms flung themselves around her waist, and she nearly spit the cookie out in surprise.

"Fallon!" Amelia squeezed her tight, and Fallon found herself returning the squeeze with her forearm since her hands were still loaded with desserts.

"Hi, Amelia. Have you tried any of your brother's cookies yet?" She offered the little girl her unbitten macaron. Amelia shook her head.

"No, thank you. I don't like the green ones. The pink ones are yummy though." She took a step back to look up to Fallon's face. "I told Noah to only make pink, but he said the green ones were important." She shrugged in defeat. "Whatever."

She'd never sounded so American.

"Would you like me to help you get a pink one?"

Amelia nodded excitedly, and together they circled back to the table in search of a raspberry macaron.

Noah was refilling his tower, brows drawn as he carefully added cookies without knocking any others off. Amelia tapped his back, and he turned to her.

"Can I pwease have a pink cookie?" Amelia's eyes widened noticeably, playing her brother for the sucker he was. He gave her his million-dollar smile and handed her a pink macaron. She giggled mischievously, took the cookie, and ran away without another word. He watched her cross the yard and disappear into the crowd.

"Did she tell you she hadn't had one yet?" Noah was still watching his sister, but the question was clearly directed at Fallon.

"Yeah, why?" The realization hit her. "She's already had one, hasn't she?"

"Five, I believe." He finally looked at her, and she didn't miss how he stepped just a few inches closer. "She played you. You're as big a sucker as the rest of us."

She responded by shoving the rest of her cookie in her mouth.

Two middle-aged women, likely friends of Sarah, took cookies from the tower and bit into them.

"Oh, my Lord, these macaroons are ungodly," the shorter of the two groaned as her eyes rolled back into her head.

Noah bit his lips, no doubt holding back the correction he wanted to blurt out but was too polite to actually do so.

Fallon wasn't.

"They're called macarons," she called across the table.

Noah's eyes widened, and his ears turned pink under his blond waves.

The women glanced at each other and then back to Fallon.

"Excuse me?" the older woman asked.

"The cookies. They're called *macarons*, not *macaroons*. It's a common mistake."

The women stared at her like she'd told them the cookies were make of frogs. Finally, the younger one said, "That's interesting," before they shrugged and walked away.

"I cannot believe you corrected them," Noah whisper-yelled once they were out of range.

"I'm raising awareness," she shot back. "It's the first step to change."

"Ever the activist."

"Changing the world one cookie at a time."

Noah rolled his eyes, but a smile tugged at his lips. "You want another?"

"Of course."

He handed her three more lime macarons, and together they crossed the yard to where their bandmates were lounging on patio chairs. Josh was talking with Calvin and Eric whose arms dangled between their seats, fingers loosely entwined. Fitz and Keith attacked plates of food and scanned the gathering. Every few seconds, one of them would point to whatever they were looking for and say something quietly enough no one else could hear.

Noah and Fallon claimed empty seats beside them.

"What are you doing?" Noah pushed a chip into his mouth.

"Playing a game." Keith pointed across the yard. "Trevor."

Noah squinted and followed Keith's finger. "Are you pointing at Martin?"

"Hey! Don't go ruining our fun!" Keith scowled at him.

"You are *naming* the guests?" Fallon asked.

Fitz nodded and pointed to another. "Margo."

"Nah." Keith spoke through a mouth full of burger. "Regina."

Fitz hummed his agreement.

"What about him?" Fallon pointed to a middle-aged man standing near the guesthouse. His cargo shorts hung two inches past his knees, and bleach blond hair flopped out of his white visor. His tan matched the deck.

Both narrowed their eyes. Then, at exactly the same moment, they blurted:

"Raymond."

"Peter. But he goes by Petey."

Noah snorted and choked on his drink.

"Petey?"

"Why not?" Keith shrugged.

"And her?" Fallon pointed to another guest, a woman with short dark hair, warm brown skin, and a leather purse that she'd bet was carrying a small animal. One could only hope it was a dog.

"We already named her." Fitz leaned back into his chair. "That's Blaire."

"Like the Golden Girl?"

"I think that's Blanche," Noah answered.

Fitz raised a brow. "I wouldn't know."

That was fair. Fitz didn't watch TV. He knew everything there was to know about music, but he likely hadn't seen a movie or binged a show in the last decade.

"Are you out of guests to name?" Calvin, Eric, and Josh joined the conversation.

"Almost." Keith polished off his burger and set his

empty plate on the ground by his chair. "What about her?"

He pointed to a beautiful woman with familiar blonde hair, bright blue eyes, and a dazzling smile.

"Nope." Noah cut in. "I don't want to know what you'd name her."

"Why not? Cuz she's hot?" Keith's eyes narrowed.

Noah groaned and squeezed his eyes shut. Fallon sucked in her lips to hide her amusement.

"Because that's his mom." Fitz smirked. Keith did not look embarrassed in the least. If anything, he looked more intrigued.

"Game over!" Noah called out before Keith could say anything worse.

"How's everyone feeling about today?" Josh rested his ankle on his opposite knee.

"Grateful it's out of my hands, and anxious for tomorrow's results." Calvin glanced at Eric out of the corner of his eye. "We have lot riding on it."

"What do you mean?" Josh's brow creased.

Fallon sank back into her chair and brushed the crumbs from her fingers. Apparently, they were doing this right now. She couldn't avoid the topic forever, but the results and consequences of Twisted Fest were things she could deal with tomorrow.

"If Edge of September finds itself on the losing end tomorrow," Calvin paused, fighting for the words Fallon wasn't sure she'd be able to vocalize, "the band is breaking up."

Reactions toppled over one another, each more painful than the last.

"Breaking up?" Josh blurted. "Why?"

"You're done?" Fitz leaned back in his seat, eyebrows furrowed in thought.

But it was Noah that Fallon was all too aware of. His head snapped to her. He said nothing, but his face screamed everything going through his mind. No anger. No confusion.

Hurt.

His eyes narrowed, studying her, waiting for her to deny it.

"I've been accepted to school in Oregon. And Fallon…" Calvin trailed off and looked to her to finish. It wasn't his to tell. She blew out a long breath.

"I'm going back." She shrugged.

"Back?" Josh sat forward on his chair. "Back where? To Arizona?"

"If Edge doesn't win Twisted Fest, I have to move back home. That was the deal."

Noah's gaze bore into her, and the weight of it was paralyzing. She stared into her lap.

"Deal with who?" Josh's voice was heated.

"My parents."

"Screw the deal."

"It's not that simple." She kept her eyes down. A lump formed in her throat.

"And what if you win?" Fitz's voice rumbled low and smooth in his chest.

"If we win, we stick around." Calvin motioned to her. "Fallon gets to stay, and I defer for a semester. See what comes of it." Eric rubbed his boyfriend's back.

"Why didn't you say anything before now?" Josh

asked.

"You're friends, but you were also competition," Keith answered. "Knowing what we have riding on this would have put you in a real weird place."

"You thought we'd throw it for you?"

"We didn't want you to feel like you had to make that choice."

The circle was quiet. Fallon couldn't tell what was going through each person's head, and she couldn't turn off the building pressure in her own.

She could be going home. No more band. No more drumming. No more California. She'd return to Arizona, to the pain and the hurt she'd outrun when she'd escaped. They'd be waiting for her in Phoenix—in the bedroom she'd shared with Annora. At the mall where they'd gotten their ears pierced together. At the church where their father had dragged them each week for sixteen years. Everywhere she'd go she'd be faced with memories of her sister.

She had to hold out hope that they'd win tomorrow. The alternative was unacceptable.

Her gaze drifted to Noah. He had finally stopped watching her and was staring into the cup of lemonade in his lap.

She studied him, the strong line of his clenched jaw, his smooth skin. She ached to touch him, to run her thumb across his palm, brush her lips against his cheek, run her hands through that messy hair, anything to let him know she hadn't meant to hurt him.

She told herself again that tomorrow Edge would win. She would stay. The band would go on.

Everything would be exactly the way it should be.

Except Noah would be headed back to England.

The crushing grip around her heart tightened.

The crowd thinned as the sun lowered itself behind the hills. The guys recovered from Calvin's news and quickly picked up their conversations. Well, most of them. Noah had never gotten back to his usual self. He'd smiled tightly at something Fitz said, but when she tried to butt in, he'd excused himself and slipped into the guesthouse a few minutes later.

She tossed her soda into a nearby trash bag and trailed after him. She found him standing over the kitchen sink, hands dripping as he reached for a towel. The muscles shifted in his back as he dried off and tossed the towel back on the counter. The lights were dim but bright enough to see his surprise at finding her when he turned around.

Surprise and then restraint.

"You're home."

"Is that surprising?"

"I thought you'd be headed to Atlas with everyone else."

"That does sound like me."

"So why aren't you?"

She shrugged and wandered to the back of the sectional, letting it prop her up. She watched as Noah noted her position and carefully leaned himself against the cabinets, matching her stance and putting the entire kitchen between them.

Interesting.

"You want to watch anything?" She motioned to

the TV behind her. His brows shot up in surprise, but he hid it quickly.

"I should probably get to bed." His smile was reserved. Tight. Very un-Noah-like.

"You haven't gone to bed before three since I moved in."

"It was a big day, Twisted Fest and all. Wore me out." But he didn't move. He was trying to send her away but was too polite to tell her to go.

She wouldn't cave that easily. Over the last month he'd become the closest thing she'd had to a best friend in years. Now it was like talking to a stranger—a stranger who didn't especially want to be around her.

"You're mad at me." She wasn't really asking, but she also wasn't entirely sure. He really didn't seem angry, just closed-off.

"I'm not."

"Then you are upset about something."

Noah scraped both hands down his face and planted his palms on the counter behind him. His triceps flexed as he grasped the edge.

"You didn't tell me."

"About moving back to Arizona?"

"That you'd be leaving California if Edge lost."

"I don't talk about personal stuff. You know that." She gripped the back of the sectional on either side of her, mirroring him.

"I do. I know you. I know you better than anyone, which is why I thought—" He clamped his mouth shut like he'd said too much, then decided to say it anyway, "I thought you and I were beyond that." He really wasn't angry. He was hurt. It was way worse.

"I didn't want to deal with it. It's not exactly something I'm thrilled about. And it's not like you could do anything about it."

"Were you ever going to tell me?" The edge in his voice sliced through her. She ignored the stinging.

"I told you tonight."

"Because Calvin brought it up. If he hadn't?" His eyes plead with her, begging her for any answer besides the honest one. Guilt swirled in her gut.

"We don't even know if it's happening." She circled the island, unable to keep herself from him any longer. "Can we just celebrate tonight and deal with it tomorrow?"

She smoothed her fingers along his jaw. Instantly, the feeling of him both calmed and electrified her. He shivered like he was experiencing the same paradox. They stood so close she had to tilt her head back to see his face. She brushed her thumb over his bottom lip, but he caught her hand in his, and she stilled.

"Just promise me, if tomorrow goes badly, and you do have to leave..." he trailed off as he pressed her palm gently to his lips. Her knees weakened, and sparks radiated from his kiss down her arm and through the rest of her. "Promise you won't leave without saying goodbye."

Her pulse beat in her ears, but her breath faltered.

That was exactly what she was going to do. Or it had been until this moment.

Noah skimmed his lips over her wrist, pleading eyes still locked on hers.

"I promise." It was more breath than voice, but it bound her all the same. She could break it—still disappear without a word if it came to that—but she knew she wouldn't. She was a lot of things, but not a liar. Not with him.

The tension in his shoulders eased, and he leaned down and placed a kiss on her lips, as soft as anything.

"So, I believe the guys really were headed to Atlas to celebrate. You going?" He was still standing so close to her she couldn't see his face without looking up.

Her instincts told her to head for the club. She'd just told Noah it was a night for celebrating after competing in Twisted Fest, and she meant it. But a stream of warmth spread through her, steadying her and keeping her in place.

Regardless of who won tomorrow, tonight would be her last with Noah. As soon as she had confirmation one of them was leaving, she'd have to cut all ties. As much as she wanted to party tonight, she knew that days, weeks, maybe even years from now, when she looked back on tonight, the biggest regret she could have would be not spending one last night with him.

And she didn't believe in having regrets.

Instead, she took a large step back, slid her hand into his, and guided him toward the stairs. He followed her willingly, and by the time they'd reached the landing, he'd weaved his fingers securely through hers. She paused outside her door and reached for the handle. Only then did she feel Noah tense beside her.

"Your room?" His forehead creased in confusion.

"My room." She led him inside.

CHAPTER 33

Fallon released Noah's hand and slipped into her closet long enough to throw on a pair of sweats and her most comfortable sweatshirt—an oversized Arizona Cardinals hoodie. She'd stolen the hoodie from Annora's closet years ago, but based on its size, she'd bet her sister had originally stolen it from Josh.

She found Noah standing exactly where she'd left him, looking around as though each stray shirt or discarded sock was a clue to a mystery he was trying to solve. At least she wasn't a total slob. Aside from the few clothing items on the floor and a rumpled pillow or two, her room could mostly be called clean.

"It smells like you," he said, gaze finding her again.

"What a creepy thing to say. Is that how you get all the other girls?" Fallon batted her lashes dramatically.

"I don't care about other girls."

Her mouth went dry. She grasped his hand and pulled him onto her bed with her.

"All I meant," he continued, "was that it smells nice in here." He scooted up so his back pressed against the headboard. She laid the other direction across the bed and rested her head on his thighs.

"Comfortable?" he teased, but his hands immediately tangled in her hair. He ran his fingers through the long black strands, and her snarky response somehow came out as a groan of pleasure instead.

Noah grinned widely at her. She loved how happy she made him. No one else was ever that happy around her.

"You were incredible today, you know."

"I do know." She turned her head to look up at him. "But you can tell me anyways."

He leaned down and placed a kiss on her head and then went back to playing with her hair. She closed her eyes and let her body relax into him. She should be exhausted after the day they'd had, but she wasn't. In fact, she wasn't sure she'd sleep at all knowing what was coming tomorrow.

She wondered if she'd said that last part out loud or if Noah was just that intuitive when she heard him say, "It's hard to believe that this time tomorrow Twisted Fest will be over. After all the time we spent this summer in preparation, it feels like it all happened too fast."

The squeezing in Fallon's chest returned instantly, and her breathing faltered. She forced the anxious knots roiling in her gut into submission.

"It did happen too fast."

"Are you really moving to Arizona if Edge doesn't win?" His accent when he said *Arizona* almost made the idea tolerable. Almost.

"And you're headed back to England if you don't."

Edge of September wins, Noah goes back to England.

Blue Streetlights wins, she's on a one-way flight to Arizona.

Neither win, they're both headed home.

She clung to the hope that Edge would come out on top, securing her stay in California, but guilt seeped in. Hoping for her win was also hoping for Noah's loss. But they were separating regardless of the outcome, and Noah would be a lot happier in England than she would be back in Arizona.

Mostly she just didn't want to think about not being with him.

"I told you that's still undecided," he said.

Because they didn't have the results yet.

"You don't have to talk about it"—he brushed her hair out of her face—"but you can."

She turned on her side, facing away from him. His fingers crept beneath her hair and wrapped around her neck, massaging circles at the base. Her eyes flitted closed, and she let go.

"I loved where I grew up. Our house was perfect. We shared a room on the second floor. The window opened up to the roof, and we could climb out there and watch the stars or fireworks or rain or whatever. And it was always hot. We could wear shorts year-round."

"You would like that." Noah's voice was soft, but she knew he was listening.

"I did."

"You don't anymore?"

"It's not the same."

"Because of Annora?" Not a demand. An understanding.

"Because of Annora."

His hand shifted lower as he massaged the muscles in her shoulders, sore from a week of drumming almost nonstop.

"What was she like?"

Fallon didn't respond for a long time. She wasn't sure how. She didn't talk about Annora with her bandmates—or anyone—but Noah wasn't just anyone anymore. And opening up to him before had been like lifting a weight off her chest, a weight that had been there for a very long time.

"She used to make me pancakes when our parents weren't home. If they both had work or something. She'd make me pancakes, and we'd eat them on our mom's special Christmas plates. Then we'd have to hurry and wash them before our parents got home."

Noah huffed a laughed. She went on.

"She loved lotus flowers. She'd take me to this place in Phoenix that had hundreds of lotus flowers all the time. She always said that one day she would have a yard with a whole pond covered in them."

His hand stilled on her back for a breath before it continued.

"Your tattoo."

"I wanted something for her that wouldn't bring up a million questions from everyone that saw it."

He hummed but said nothing.

"When I was eight, I decided to run away from home after a fight with my dad. She found me packing my backpack with underwear and peanut butter. Without any hesitation, she'd grabbed her own backpack, stuffed it with her own underwear, and together we headed for the park down the street. It wasn't until we'd spent an hour on the swings that she mentioned reconsidering my choice. We were back home in time for dinner.

"And when I was fourteen, I had my first kiss. I'd been at a party, and Marcus Broodimeyer kissed me in the kitchen when we'd both gone to get another soda. I found out later he'd done it on a dare and didn't actually like me. Annora got her friends to go with her to toilet paper his house that night after I cried myself to sleep."

"Sounds like Marcus Broodimeyer deserved a lot worse."

"Annora wouldn't have done worse." Fallon smiled through the tears that slid softly over her cheeks. "She didn't have a mean bone in her body. That was probably the most vicious thing she ever did."

"I wish I could have met her."

"Me too." She wiped her cheeks with her sleeve and blinked away the moisture before turning back to face Noah. "She would have liked you."

"Yeah?" His eyes sparkled.

"Yeah. But she would have *loved* Amelia."

His laugh sent shivers across her skin. She laced her fingers through his but glanced away. She wasn't sure she could say another word if she had to look at him while she did it.

She told him about growing up with a big sister—stealing her clothes, following her around, fighting over their bedroom. As the memories flooded her, she let them spill over, each taking just the tiniest ounce of grief with it. Noah listened to them all. He asked questions, but he never pushed her. He never had.

The night moved forward around stories of Arizona and eventually of England. Noah told her about growing up as an only child until he was nearly sixteen and his parents announced they were pregnant. How he'd been thrilled to have a little sister but had totally freaked out the first time he'd tried to babysit.

"There really should be laws against older brothers babysitting children under a certain age. Everything I tried just resulted in crying and throwing things."

"Knowing Amelia, she was messing with you on purpose."

"Even as a baby?"

"Oh, definitely."

It wasn't until the morning glow peeked through her window that they finally curled up beside each other—Noah's arms wrapped tightly around her—and fell asleep.

CHAPTER 34

"You sure you don't want to come with us today?" Noah met her at the base of the stairs, a cup of coffee in his outstretched hand.

Blue Streetlights was headed for Twisted Fest soon to watch the announcement of the winners. Of course they'd invited her to go with them, but as excited as she'd been to play the festival, she felt nothing but anxiety at hearing who won. She still held out hope that Edge would win, but it was hard not to be discouraged after hearing all the amazing bands they'd competed against yesterday—including Blue Streetlights.

But win or lose, she knew where she needed to be today.

She, Calvin, and Keith had talked about going to see the announcement at the festival, but with all they had riding on it, they'd decided to watch the live stream on social media from the privacy of the townhouse.

"Nah, I'm going to watch with the boys." She took the coffee and followed Noah into the kitchen. He'd changed into black jeans and a gray T-shirt that hugged the muscles in his shoulders. He picked up the cup he'd left on the counter and sipped from it. She hopped onto the stool beside him, and he softly kissed the top of her head.

"Josh will be here any minute to pick me up. Want a ride to Calvin's?"

When she and Noah had emerged from the guesthouse holding hands, Josh grinned so wide she'd thought his face would break. Fitz quirked an eyebrow and gave her a crooked *look-who-you-did* grin. She flipped him off, and he let out a breathy laugh.

Noah sat with her in the backseat and held her hand the whole way to the townhouse, rubbing his thumb over hers. It was soothing. The closer they got to the announcement of the winner, the more her insides twisted. Edge had to win. They just had to.

Noah didn't say anything as Josh slowed in front of the townhouse, but he gripped her hand tightly, like he didn't want to let go. He looked as anxious as she felt, so she gave his hand a soft squeeze before she climbed out of the car.

Calvin was flustered when she walked in despite him knowing she was coming over. She figured it was a result of his own anxieties.

"Eric here?" she asked, hoping his boyfriend might help him relax. The tension was doing nothing to calm her own racing adrenaline.

"No. He's coming over tonight."

"Which will be awkward as hell since we're going out tonight after we win." Keith passed by and clapped him on the shoulder. It seemed Keith's nerves were manifesting as confidence.

She followed them down the hall to the living room. She'd brought her laptop to watch the livestream and set it up on their secondhand coffee table. She perched in the middle of the couch and tucked her legs beneath her. Her neon pink leggings were especially bright next to Calvin's dark jeans, and what had seemed like a lucky choice an hour ago now felt irreverent.

As she navigated to the Twisted Fest social media channels, Calvin was dead silent, a rare occurrence for him. Calvin always had something to say about everything. This silence was eerie.

Keith was his normal self, other than that he kept pacing the apartment. He'd sit next to her on the couch for a minute or two and then stand up and do another lap. She gave him a dirty look the fifth time he plopped down next to her, and he grimaced.

"When do they go live?" he asked.

"Website said one o'clock," Calvin answered. It was only the second or third time he'd spoken in the last half an hour. "But we should check now in case they start early."

She was already opening their page and scanning for any livestreams.

Nothing yet.

"They won't be early. No one in music is ever early for anything." Keith resumed pacing.

Fallon's anxiety got the better of her, and she wandered into the kitchen for a bottle of water—

something to focus on besides Twisted Fest results.

The kitchen looked as it always did. Bare countertops circled the room beneath dull, brown cabinets. She was taken back to the night of the afterparty, the night she first met Noah. Her throat tightened.

She needed to not think about Noah right now.

She grabbed a water from the fridge and headed back to the living room, but as she passed Calvin's bedroom door, she spotted a stack of boxes against one wall. She peeked inside, and her stomach turned again.

The walls—normally covered in pictures and posters—were blank. The dresser in the corner had been cleared off. The closet door hung open, and the inside was completely empty.

Calvin was already packed.

"Cal!" she yelled, unable to move from where her feet had cemented themselves to the carpet.

Calvin jogged down the hall, but slowed when he saw where she was. Guilt crossed his features. He bit a lip and hung his head.

"You're packed." She motioned to his room. "Are you leaving for sure then? Even if we win?"

He sighed heavily. "Fallon, why are you here?"

"I just was passing by to get a water—"

"No," he interrupted, "I mean, why are you at the townhouse?"

"To watch the winner get announced." She rolled her eyes. She didn't have patience for stupid questions right now.

"So why didn't we go to the festival?" He raised his

eyebrows meaningfully.

"We talked about this. There's a lot riding on Twisted Fest. We didn't want to be there if we… if another band…" She trailed off.

"Exactly. You and I were both at that festival yesterday. We heard those other bands. Edge of September is good, but we both know what our chances are today." He sighed again. "I would rather be prepared for bad news and surprised by good news than count on good news and be blindsided by the bad." He gave her a sad smile and motioned for her to follow him back to the couch.

She did, but she couldn't shake the feeling that she was not nearly as ready for the news as he was. Calvin had come to terms with their situation. She definitely hadn't. Maybe it was because for him, this was a win-win. Either they win and he gets a record deal for his band or they lose and he gets to move to a new state with his boyfriend.

Fallon's own possibilities were not so evenly balanced.

She curled up on the couch again and lifted the laptop into her lap. She refreshed the page, and her heart skipped a beat as a livestream appeared at the top of the feed.

"It's on!" Calvin called to Keith who quit his pacing to squeeze in next to her on the couch. The three of them leaned in close around the laptop.

The stream showed the festival just as it had been the day before. Two stages. Big crowds. She tried to find Noah, Fitz, and Josh, but there were too many people, and the camera they were streaming from wasn't positioned to see most of them. Instead, it focused on a woman moving on the north stage. She was one of the women Fallon had seen under the awning yesterday. She was curvy with chestnut brown hair in a shag style. She wore shorts—but the nice ones with pleats—and a silky sea-green button-up shirt. She held one of the tablets now.

She reached the center of the stage where a microphone waited for her. She tested the sound, and her voice rang out over the stream. The crowd quieted.

Keith and Calvin both leaned in closer to her, and she could feel their hearts racing. Her own was nearly beating out of her chest.

"Welcome everyone! Those who are here and to those streaming from far away!" The woman waved to the camera. "Let's not waste any time. We all know what I'm doing up on this stage, so let's just get to it!"

Fallon's palms grew sweaty. Calvin's leg bounced up and down. Keith blew out his breath.

The woman continued.

"We had over twenty bands compete in this year's Twisted Fest, and I'm not alone when I say that in eight years, this was the top talent we've seen and the hardest decision we've had to make. However, we scored each band based on musical skill, showmanship, marketability, and wow-factor, and we have ourselves a winner!"

Fallon's muscles tensed. Her hands shook, and she set the laptop back on the coffee table before she could drop it. Calvin entwined his fingers through hers and squeezed. Keith did the same with her other hand. Neither looked away from the screen. No one blinked.

"The winner of the Eighth Annual Twisted Fest Battle of the Bands, and the recipient of a record contract from Taylor Records and $15,000 is…"

Fallon closed her eyes. This was it. The beginning of her career. Her way to make it in California. Tomorrow she'd tell her parents she was staying indefinitely. Edge of September would have their big break.

She held her breath.

"Blue Streetlights!"

CHAPTER 35

When Fallon was only eight or nine, she and Annora taught themselves how to do backflips on the gymnastics bar at the playground. The horizontal metal pole was about eye-level, so they had to boost each other to get their legs over it. They'd bend their knees over the bar, gripping it with a hand on either side, and swing back and forth until they had the momentum to drop their upper body and flip their lower body over it to land on their feet.

It didn't take long before they had mastered the backflip, and they got reckless. Fallon decided she'd try doing one without using her hands. With Annora's help, she climbed up to the pole, bent her knees around it, and rocked until she had the momentum she needed, all the while dangling her arms.

But when she released herself from the pole expecting to flip backwards, she was surprised to find that without her hands pushing off the bar, she couldn't make the landing. Instead, she fell flat on her back in the woodchips.

The wind was knocked from her body, and she couldn't breathe for what felt like an eternity. It was like someone had sucked all the air from her lungs, and all she could do was stare into Annora's face hovering above her and wait for her body to come back to life.

As the woman's words sank in, Fallon was back on those woodchips, gasping for air.

Blue Streetlights won Twisted Fest.

Edge of September lost.

The woman kept speaking, but Fallon couldn't hear her over the ringing in her ears. Her eyes shot open, but her vision was fuzzy. The couch swallowed the weight of her body.

She was going back to Arizona. She'd had one last chance to stay in Los Angeles, and she'd failed. It had been for nothing.

"Fallon?" Calvin's voice was foggy.

She blinked and forced herself to process.

Pressure somewhere.

Her hand. It was being squeezed.

A touch.

Someone was rubbing her back.

The fog thinned. Calvin's face appeared inches from hers. His brow wrinkled and his eyes scanned her.

"Are you okay?" He squeezed her hand again.

"I'm fine," she mumbled.

"You don't seem fine." She turned her head toward the voice and found Keith still on her other side. His was the hand rubbing her back.

She wasn't fine, but that wasn't their problem.

Especially not now.

"Just surprised." Her voice was more solid now, but her mouth was dry. "Can you see the guys?" She motioned toward the laptop, still livestreaming from the festival. She should try to focus on her ex-bandmates. She should be thrilled for them, but the emotion wasn't processing.

"Fitz and Josh are there, but I don't see Noah." Calvin tilted the laptop to look closer.

She forced herself to concentrate on the screen.

Calvin was right. Fitz and Josh were on the stage now, accepting a trophy that had appeared at some point, but Noah wasn't with them.

Keith leaned back onto the couch, and she did the same. The cushions pushed against her, and the pressure grounded her. Her limbs tingled, but her vision had cleared.

"So…" Keith glanced between her and Calvin. "Is that it, then? Are we done?"

Her throat tightened.

"I guess so." Calvin sighed. "Edge of September is officially broken up."

No one moved. No one spoke.

Fallon couldn't bring herself to head back to the guesthouse just yet. All that waited for her there was packing. She'd stayed in California for the band. Now that there was no band, there was no reason for her to even fight to stay. As much as she didn't want to face Phoenix, at least she had something there. A house. School. Something.

"When do you and Eric leave for Oregon?" Keith's

voice sounded hoarse.

Calvin cleared his throat. "Next weekend. School starts soon, and we want to get settled before we have to worry about classes."

"What about you?" Keith nudged her knee with his.

"I'll be shocked if my parents don't have me on a flight by tomorrow." They'd probably bought the ticket weeks ago, expecting her to fail. She was down to her last few days in LA. Possibly hours.

She'd likely never see Calvin or Keith again.

Her muscles tensed, and a lump formed in her throat.

Why was this hurting so much? So what if she left them behind for good? They were just bandmates.

Ex-bandmates.

Pain coursed through her chest. This was exactly why she never let anyone in. No one was permanent. Everyone had an expiration date. And now what she'd known would happen had come to pass. She was losing them both.

It wasn't the same as Annora, but it didn't matter. She'd thought she'd learned her lesson three years ago, but clearly not if she'd let herself get hurt again. Calvin and Keith both had weaseled their way into her life, and now she had to deal with the pain she'd known would come with that.

"Let's go out tonight. One last blowout."

"I'm in." Calvin smiled weakly.

But the last thing she wanted was to drag this out into a teary goodbye.

Clean break.

"I'll pass. Lots of packing, you know?" Suddenly she couldn't be there for another second. She snatched her laptop—now frozen on the blank screen at the end of the livestream—snapped it closed, and hugged it against her chest. "I better go."

She shot off the couch, and the boys did the same.

"Seriously?" Keith raised his brows.

"Leave it." Calvin's shoulders sagged. "It's not personal, remember?" He spoke to Keith, but his eyes were locked on her.

"Don't be like that—" she started, but Calvin interrupted her.

"It's fine. You've always been upfront about what this was." He motioned between the three of them and shrugged. "Maybe you were right all along."

While she agreed with him, the defeat in his eyes brought her no joy.

"Well then, I better get going." She moved to the door.

"Do you want a ride?" Calvin offered.

"No. Walking sounds good."

Keith left the room without even a glance her way. She told herself not to care.

Calvin saw her off with a nod and a reserved wave. He likely knew she'd stop him if he tried to get emotional. Instead, she returned his nod and wandered down the street in a daze.

Tomorrow was her video call with her parents, and she'd have to tell them she lost—if they didn't know already. It would be like Manuel and Lisa to have watched the announcement of the winners live. It was possible they'd have her on a flight by that evening.

Today could be her last day in California.

She could argue for more time, but for what? She didn't even have a band anymore. In the span of twenty-four hours, she'd gone from being in two bands to none. Even if she found a way to stay in Los Angeles, she'd be starting over, and there was no way she could afford a place on her own. She'd need roommates. And a job.

Music would take a backseat, possibly for months. Years.

At least in Arizona she had a place to live rent-free. She could try to find a band there, maybe take music classes this fall.

Her shoulders slumped, and she kicked a rock.

Even with her most positive spin, Arizona sounded awful. Not to mention the memories of Annora that would haunt her constantly.

Despite the disappointment and fear roiling through her, there was the smallest glimmer of happiness. Her boys had done it. Josh and Fitz and Noah had won, and she couldn't help but be proud of them.

Even so, as she continued walking, she was grateful she was alone and could have the guesthouse to herself for a while without running into Noah.

She thought back over the last weeks they'd lived together. She'd let him in in a way she hadn't let anyone in years. Maybe ever. And now one of them was leaving. She would lose him, just as she'd known from the day they met that she would. She'd spent the last month trying to avoid this very thing, but she'd been too weak. She'd let him get too close. She'd justified every conversation, every night out and evening in. She'd hung out with his family.

Oh, God. He'd met her parents.

She'd told herself that one of them leaving was insurance that she couldn't get attached, but it was too late. She'd been lying to herself, trying to prevent the inevitable.

But she couldn't avoid it any longer. It would only get worse.

She had to end things with Noah.

CHAPTER 36

Fallon made it to the guesthouse without processing anything around her, but she slid her key from her boot to find the door was already unlocked. She pushed it open slowly, suddenly feeling very aware that she was not alone.

Noah was off the couch before she'd gotten the door closed. He wrapped his arms around her and pulled her against him. She buried her face in his chest and breathed in his scent. She could no longer hold back her tears. Her breath rattled in her chest, and she felt the vibration of Noah's doing the same.

"I wanted it to be you." His voice was so soft and so broken she likely wouldn't have even heard him if his face hadn't been buried in her hair.

She pushed back from him and looked up into his face. The intensity was paralyzing as his eyes seared into hers.

"How did you get back here so fast?" she asked. He wiped a tear from her cheek with his thumb.

"I left the second they announced it. Josh loaned me

his car so I could get to you."

She stepped away from his touch. After the unexpected pain at leaving Calvin and Keith, she knew she had to break things off with Noah now.

He lifted a hand to reach for her again but dropped it, as though he could sense her pushing him away and knew it wasn't the time to try again.

"We need to talk. I'll be leaving in the next few days."

"Maybe you could talk to your parents. Convince them to let you stay." He looked hopeful.

"They'll never agree. I was lucky to stay as long as I have." She finally closed the door behind her and moved toward the couch. She was suddenly very tired.

"But you can't just leave." He followed her but didn't sit when she did.

"I don't have a choice." Her frustration was growing. She knew he was just trying to solve the problem, but it wasn't helping at all.

"You do have a choice. You're an adult. You can stay—"

"For what?" she finally snapped. "I have no reason to stay! I have no job, no band, and no place to live."

"You live here." He'd stopped pacing and was now glued to the floor.

"I was never supposed to stay after this summer. You know that."

He stayed quiet, like he knew as well as she did that she couldn't stay with him now that Twisted Fest was over.

"Maybe you could stay on with Blue Streetlights."

"There's already a replacement drummer lined up. I was never permanent." She didn't add that that option would never, ever be a possibility. If this afternoon had reminded her of anything, it was just how painful it was to lose people she cared about and that nothing was forever. Joining Blue Streetlights could destroy her completely.

"Listen." She softened her voice. He leaned against the island, never taking his eyes from her face. "I'm grateful for everything you and the guys have done for me, but I'm going back." Her throat tightened, and her chest felt like it would burst. "The last week has been fun, but it's over."

"You're ending things with me?" His eyebrows pulled together.

"There's nothing to end. We made out a little." She shrugged, hoping he'd buy her playing off how much this was killing her. But she knew Noah. He'd never let her go unless he truly believed it was what she wanted.

"But it doesn't have to just be that."

"That's all it ever was." The words were gross on her tongue.

"Then what have we been doing the last few weeks?" He pushed off the counter at his back and stepped toward the couch, toward her.

"Wasting time." It was blunt and cruel, but he'd have to hate her if this was going to work, and hate was not a feeling that came naturally to Noah Cooper.

His eyes widened in shock, but he recovered quickly. He was not so easily deterred. She knew he wouldn't be.

He took another step to the island and leaned on it, hands braced against the stone surface. His eyes narrowed.

"And what about last night?"

She clenched her jaw and buried the words that almost spilled out. Instead, she shrugged, faking indifference all the while her insides splintered and cracked.

It's better this way. She clung to the words with every ounce of willpower she had.

"Don't act like that was nothing." He took a step toward her. "You told me about your life, your real life, because you want me to be part of it, for *us* to be part of it." Another step. "So don't tell me that you've just been *wasting time.*"

She lifted her chin.

But those eyes.

For a moment, she faltered. The depth and force of his gaze stopped the words dead in her throat. Maybe Noah was the one person she could keep.

But that was wishful thinking at this point. She was losing him one way or another, and it would only hurt worse if she fought it. This couldn't last—nothing ever did. Noah wouldn't accept it unless she hurt him badly enough he'd let go. It's how it was always going to end.

Noah straightened, but his feet stayed planted. She broke her eyes away from his, rallying her strength. This was it. Her stomach clenched, and tears filled her eyes.

One last twist of the knife.

"You were a place to stay and something to do

when I got bored. I don't need either anymore."

Nausea flooded her. She prepared for Noah's anger, letting the couch hold her up. If she could withstand his yelling and whatever insults he flung at her, this would all be over.

But it wasn't anger and hatred that stared back at her.

Noah's face fell. His arms hung limp at his sides, and his shoulders drooped. The flames that had burned in his mocha eyes fizzled out, and a flood of pain rushed in.

She had braced herself for the worst, but she never could have prepared herself for the hurt in his face.

She'd never felt so small. She hated herself. If it was anyone else hurting him this way, she'd rip them to shreds. Tears threatened again, but she refused to let them in. She swallowed the tightness in her throat, beating it down into the same dark hole she'd carved inside herself three years ago, where pain could hide and she could pretend it didn't exist.

"Why aren't you saying anything?" she finally asked. His silence was excruciating.

He scanned her face, and she fought to keep it aloof and callous. Noah knew her better than anyone else, and he'd call her bluff if he sensed she was anything less than 100% detached.

His brows pulled together, and he stood taller. Her neck heated.

"If you don't want to be with me," his voice rumbled, "then I'll deal with that. But I don't think that's true." He hadn't moved, but he felt so much nearer. She could smell his vanilla scent, but that was likely in her head. She knew his scent like it was part of her.

"I'm not doing this. Yell at me. Fight with me."

"No." A muscle flickered in his jaw.

She felt dizzy. He should hate her, but she could feel him, sense him. He didn't hate her. He wasn't fighting *with* her.

He was fighting *for* her.

She heaved a sigh and broke her gaze from Noah. Instead, she studied the guesthouse. Her eyes caught on the island where he'd taught her to make cookies, the stools where they'd sat together almost every morning sharing a box of cereal, the TV where they'd stayed up late watching baking shows, and finally, the sectional, where they'd slept that night, covered in chocolate frosting. It was the happiest she'd been in years.

In only a few weeks, Noah's guesthouse had become more of a home to her than her apartment had ever been.

But was it the guesthouse that felt like home...

Or Noah?

"I can't have you," she whispered.

"You already have me, luv." He gripped her chin with his thumb and lifted her gaze to him. "You always have."

CHAPTER 37

Noah respected her wishes to be alone that evening. She locked herself in her room, and a few hours later, she heard him leave. He didn't come back even after the sky turned dark. Her whole body ached like she'd been hollowed out inside. She missed him already. Him and Fitz and Calvin and Josh and Keith. They'd been carved from her life, and there was nothing she could do about it.

Eventually she left her room to wander the empty house and found the island littered with plates of cookies, scones, and muffins that hadn't been there hours ago. It looked like a bakery blew up in their kitchen. But Noah was still nowhere to be seen.

It's better this way.

She found her phone where she'd left it on the couch that afternoon and swiped it open to find a text from Josh and two missed calls from Elliott.

She tapped open the text first.

Josh: *I talked to Noah. You doing okay?*

She flopped onto the cushions and draped her legs over the back of the couch.

Fallon: *I'm fine. What did he tell you?*

She closed her messenger, but a response came through almost immediately.

Josh: *Nothing but he sounded terrible. Did you dump him?*

Fallon: *We weren't together.*

Josh: *Call it what you want.*

She had no interest in discussing Noah. Honestly, she didn't want to talk at all, but she was feeling more alone than she'd felt in years, and somehow that was no longer a good thing. She wasn't ready to be alone again quite yet.

Fallon: *Congrats btw*

He took her cue to change the subject.

Josh: *You too. I know it's not the same but you get your cut too.*

She'd forgotten about that. Fitz had promised her an equal cut of the prize money. She tucked the thought away to think on later.

Fallon: *Thx. What're you going to do with yours?*

Dots appeared and disappeared a few times as he typed and erased whatever he was saying. After a minute, his message finally came through.

Josh: *Blue Streetlights is going to go in on a place. If we pool our winnings, we can pay for most of a year's rent and focus more on the band. Hoping the record deal will lead to something.*

Her gut twisted. It was a good idea. They'd make the most of this momentum, and it'd probably pay off.

Another text notification bubbled at the top of her screen.

Elliott: *Call me asap*

Elliott was one of the last people she wanted to talk to right now, but he never called her. He always went through Keith, or even Calvin, if he needed to talk to them but never her. It had to be important.

She shot off one last text to Josh before scrolling through her short list of contacts and dialing her manager. He answered immediately.

"Hey, Fallon."

"What's up?"

"I spoke with Keith today." He paused and she could picture the exact face he was making—like he was testing her. She didn't cave, and he went on. "He told me Edge of September is coming to an end. Calvin's leaving the state?"

"Sounds like it."

"And you?"

"Yes." She really didn't want to get into it. Her heart throbbed painfully even thinking about Arizona.

"Well, Keith and I are working things out on our end, but I've got a proposal for you. Remember that weekend a few weeks back that I flew to Sacramento?"

A spark of electricity skittered down her spine. The weekend she and Noah had broken into his apartment.

"Well, I was visiting one of my bands up there," he continued. "There's been some moving pieces and some drama. I won't get into it, but they were at Twisted Fest this weekend." He paused again, and her patience ran out.

"It's been a long day. What do you want?"

"They were there to scope out a new drummer. Events like that are crawling with musicians, not just the bands that are playing. And they found a couple that might work. But when I found out you were no longer tied up with Edge of September, I knew immediately you'd be the drummer for them. They agreed. They saw you play. It was one hell of a show."

"Are you offering me a spot in another band?" Her mind raced. Ice tore through her, and her fingers tingled as they gripped her phone.

Another band. Another shot at music.

"I am. It's an all-girl band stationed up in Sacramento. You'd have to move up there but sounds like you're ditching LA anyway. They're indie punk. Your kind of thing. Pretty good, too. Currently in label negotiations. That's why they're so rushed to get the spot filled."

Fallon tried to speak but her mind couldn't process fast enough. Elliott was saving her. She wouldn't have to go back to Arizona. She could stay in California and play music. Record with a band.

"I don't need your answer this minute, but probably tomorrow. Take the night to think on it." He hung up without another word.

Fallon's phone dropped from her hand and bounced off the pillow beside her. She slouched deeper into the couch.

Six weeks. Six weeks had changed everything. She'd been perfectly happy in her private studio apartment, knowing nothing about anyone and living for nothing but the moment, playing for Edge and partying every night.

Now her band was shattered, her heart was mangled, and she might have gotten the greatest offer ever.

She could say yes. Playing with Blue Streetlights had taken her back to her punk roots. She hadn't realized how much she'd missed it. Not to mention she'd be playing with all girls in a town hours from here where no one knew her and no one could hurt her.

She threw her arm over her eyes. She'd let Noah down in a way she'd never planned. He was never supposed to get this close. No one was. She'd only agreed to be friends because he'd planned to go back to England. Somehow that had built into whatever they had become.

She wasn't willing to put a name to it. Especially not now.

When she'd agreed to drum for Blue Streetlights, she'd been sure she could keep the boys at bay, maintain that wall that kept regret and pain out.

Elliott was giving her an escape from all of it. Leave the boys behind and drum for a new band. A band that was about to record with a label. With her cut of the Twisted Fest prize money, she could get settled in Sacramento. She'd find a part-time job to cover the rest. She'd never have to live on someone else's couch—or in their guest room—again, and she'd be even further from Phoenix. She could keep the painful memories hundreds of miles away.

It was the perfect out.

CHAPTER 38

She wasn't sure when she fell asleep, but when she woke on the couch the next morning, it was obvious Noah still hadn't been home. The plates of treats were still on the counter, and there was no sign of his keys or shoes.

Fallon hopped from the couch and yanked open the cupboard. She'd barely eaten last night. After the loss of Twisted Fest, she'd been so distracted she hadn't even realized how hungry she'd probably been.

She scanned the shelves, snatched the box of Cocoa Puffs, and headed outside. She needed air. She needed space.

She needed to be somewhere that didn't feel like Noah at every turn.

But finding that somewhere was harder than she'd expected. Eventually she returned to the guesthouse, loaded her laptop into her backpack, and took off for the warehouse. It would still remind her of Noah, but at least it wasn't *his*.

Nothing had been touched since they'd dropped all

their stuff off after Twisted Fest. Amps were stacked carefully but haphazardly behind the couch, and guitars in their cases leaned against the bar. Only her kit was where it belonged, but it hadn't even been reassembled.

She had some time to kill before her video call, so she decided to put her kit together. She'd be breaking it down again soon, maybe even today, but she couldn't bring herself to care. Despite deciding to take Elliott's offer in Sacramento, she still felt hollow. Every time she thought of Edge breaking up or leaving Noah and the rest of the boys behind, pain suffocated her.

It was her own fault. She let herself get comfortable. She had been the one to lower the wall and get attached knowing exactly how bad it was going to suck when it ended.

She'd learned nothing from Annora's death.

Noon arrived, and Fallon situated herself on the couch with her laptop. As much as she didn't want to talk to her parents, maybe getting it over with would help her move on. She had a new life and a new band to look forward to, and the first step was finally finishing these bargains with her parents. From now on, she'd do what she wanted. No deadlines, no deals.

"Hola, Reinita." Her father's usual excitement at seeing her was muted today. They already knew Edge had lost. No surprise.

"Hi, Dad. Hi, Mom." She smiled against her instincts. She should be thrilled. She had great news for them.

Her mother smiled weakly in return.

"We watched the announcement yesterday." She looked like she was about to cry. "We're really sorry, sweetheart."

"We were rooting for you," her father added. And she believed them.

"Thanks, but it's all okay actually. The guys that won are incredible musicians." Had that made losing to them any easier? She'd never actually thought about it until now. She'd never been upset about losing, only about the breakup. "I actually have some really exciting news."

Her parents both perked up at her tone, eyes fixed on her. She took a deep breath.

"I've been invited to join another band."

The reserved excitement she'd expected looked a lot more like reserved confusion. Her mother's lips pursed, and her father's eyebrows drew together. Neither of them said anything.

"My manager has another band in need of a drummer," she went on. "I'll be moving to Sacramento as soon as possible."

The reserved confusion morphed into open concern. No one spoke. Her mother opened her mouth but closed it again without a word. Her father was studying her. His deep brown eyes bore into the screen.

Her mother found her voice, but it was anything but confident.

"We thought you'd be moving home."

"I thought so too, but then I got this offer. That was the deal, right? I had the summer to find a way to support myself. You won't have to pay for my new life. I can work it out now."

Lisa nodded slowly. "What about visiting Annora? You promised to visit."

Shit. She had.

"I will. After I get things settled in Sacramento." She'd figure that one out later. Maybe she could still find a way out of it or at least figure out how to make it as painless and fast as possible.

Her mother bit her lip. Her father still hadn't said anything. The three of them bathed in the tension until she couldn't stand it.

"Aren't you happy for me? This is what I've been working for." It was no secret her parents had wanted her to move home, but she'd always thought they'd at least wanted her success. Didn't parents want their kids to be happy?

Manuel looked away from Fallon for the first time since they'd called to face his wife. "I'd like to speak with Fallon for a minute, my love."

Lisa nodded and walked away without another word, leaving Fallon alone with her father.

She squirmed uncomfortably on the scratchy couch. Even hundreds of miles away through a video chat, her father's presence was intimidating. She'd never seen him in the courtroom, but she'd always pictured him simply staring down his opponents until they admitted defeat.

"Reinita, why are you going to Sacramento?" Despite the sternness in his gaze, his question was gentle. Pleading.

"For my new band. I told you."

"And what about Edge of September?"

"There is no more Edge of September. I'm leaving Los Angeles. Calvin is moving to Oregon for school. It's done."

"And what about the other band, Blue Streetlights?"

"I was only filling in. They're—" How did she describe what they were? How did she put into words what Noah, Josh, and Fitz were to her?

"—nothing."

"And Noah?"

"What about him?" She didn't mean to sound defensive, but that's how it came out.

"How does he fit into all this?"

"He doesn't."

Manuel hummed and nodded. He folded his large arms across his chest and rubbed a hand over his scruffy salt-and-pepper beard.

"Reinita, when I graduated high school, I knew I wanted to study law. I'd worked hard and earned a scholarship so I could do just that. But when I got to college and took my first law classes, I failed them. They were much harder than I'd expected." He huffed a laugh. "Meanwhile I was excelling in my science courses. So I decided law wasn't for me. I dropped my pre-law program and joined pre-med."

This was all news to Fallon. Her father had told her stories of college before, but he'd never mentioned studying pre-med. All she knew was Manuel Rivera got a scholarship to college, graduated *summa cum laude*, and eventually went to law school.

"School went great after that," he went on. "I was getting excellent grades and maintaining my scholarship without any hassle. But I wasn't happy. Even though I was doing well in my courses, they weren't what I wanted. I told myself I was choosing to focus on my strengths, chasing success. It wasn't until your mother came along and called me out that I realized what I was actually doing." A smile teased at the corners of his mouth. "I wasn't chasing success. I was running from failure. I was so afraid I'd fail as a lawyer that I wasn't even trying."

"That's not what I'm doing," Fallon replied. "I'm not running from failure. The band broke up. I have another opportunity."

"I know you aren't." He waved off the idea. "You've never been one to run from a challenge."

"Then what are you saying?" She tapped her fingers anxiously.

"Do you remember what you said to me when you moved to Los Angeles? You were so anxious to move as soon as graduation was over, and I asked you why. Do you remember what you said?"

She shook her head. There had been a million conversations that year that had led to her moving. She'd said whatever it took to make it happen.

"You told me you couldn't wait another day to get away. Not to get *to* California, to get *away* from home."

"I wasn't trying to get away from you or Mom," she said.

"I know, Reinita. I know. But leaving was never

about chasing what you wanted. It was about running away. That's why your mom and I made you that deal. We wanted you to have that time to heal or grieve or whatever you needed to finally move forward, but we also hoped you'd be able to come back and face your demons when that year was over." He looked away and cleared his throat before going on.

"After Annora passed, you were different. We all were, but you could never move forward. You moved all the way to another state to outrun the hurt of missing her.

"Your mother and I love you. We are so proud of you, and we want you to be happy. And if moving to Sacramento to chase your dream is what will make you happy, then we'll support you. We'll load up the moving van ourselves. But I have to ask, are you chasing your dream or are you running away again?"

"Annora isn't in Los Angeles, Dad."

"I know that. But my gut tells me there's something else you're running from. The possibility of some other hurt you can't wait another day to get away from."

Fallon's skin prickled. She'd never spoken like this with her father. They always kept things on the surface. If he ever brought up anything too deep— usually Annora—she'd immediately cut it off. Or change the subject.

Or run away.

Her stomach plummeted.

He was right.

All her rules for keeping people at a distance, all the

one-night stands and meaningless parties. She thought she was protecting herself. She'd thought she'd learned her lesson with Annora, but that wasn't true. She'd been hiding from life. She'd been running from the possibility of someone else leaving a scar deep inside her where the pain of losing Annora had never healed.

She hadn't let it heal.

"I miss her too," Manuel whispered. Fallon met his eyes to find them glistening. Her own cheeks were damp. "But we cannot stop living because she did. I know it's scary—terrifying—to love again after you've lost someone. But it is worth it."

"I don't know if I can." Her voice wavered.

Her father smiled knowingly. "I think you may find that you already do."

The faces of her boys filled her vision.

Josh. Calvin. Keith. Fitz.

Noah.

Her heart raced, and her hands shook uncontrollably. Fear gripped her throat strangling any attempt at words. Not fear of letting them in—fear of letting them go.

She didn't want to. She wanted them in her life. All of them. It was worth the risk. *They* were worth the risk. She would let her heart shatter a thousand times over if it meant she could keep them for whatever time they had.

She fought through the panic and forced her voice to work.

"It's too late. There's nothing left for me here. Either I go to Sacramento or Phoenix. I lose them either way."

"You know, Reinita, sometimes the obvious solution is the right one."

CHAPTER 39

Noah was gone for longer than she'd expected. He was likely giving her space since she'd asked to be alone, but when he still hadn't come home by that evening, she'd given up and texted Fitz. He'd mentioned that afternoon that he and Noah were hanging out later on. So, by nightfall, she'd demanded Fitz make him go home. Fitz had been surprisingly cooperative.

She sat at the kitchen counter scrolling through drum videos on her phone when she heard the front door open. Even now, seeing Noah still stole the air from her lungs. His messy hair had only gotten longer since she'd met him, and strands now reached past his brows. His eyes still burned beneath them—a fire and passion Fallon now recognized and lived for.

He froze mid-step when he saw the kitchen. Dirty dishes scattered the counters in addition to the ones piled high in the sink. Eggshells dripped onto the counter, and flour coated literally everything. Chocolate frosting smeared handles and puddled on the floor.

Noah's eyes drifted across the disaster zone and to Fallon, now standing beside the stool. He scanned her slowly, taking in the white streaks of flour in her hair, the chocolate stains on her clothes, and her bare feet on the flour-coated floor.

"What happened in here?" His forehead creased, and a single brow lifted.

She wanted to kiss it, but instead, she walked to the fridge and removed a round chocolate cake. It was smaller than it had been when she'd put it in there an hour ago, and the middle had sunk to form a chocolate frosting pool, but she didn't care. She carefully slid the plate onto the counter.

"I made you a cake."

"You made me a cake?" Noah eyed her creation suspiciously.

"I made you a cake," she repeated. "To replace the one we… ruined. And I need to talk to you." She'd never had so much trouble getting words out. All her smoothness and confidence had disappeared, likely into her monstrosity of a cake. She swallowed hard and planted her feet. "Can we sit?"

"Where?" He teased as he took in the messy kitchen again. "You know, it's been rumored that one can bake without creating a hazard area."

She stuck out her tongue, and Noah's grin made his eyes sparkle. She pushed down the butterflies trying to fly up her throat.

"Fine, we won't sit. But listen." He folded his arms across his chest, and she went on. "Elliott called me last night. He offered me a spot in a band he manages in

328

Sacramento."

Noah inhaled sharply, but she pressed forward. He had to know everything.

"It's an all-girl indie punk band. They're finalizing contracts with a label. I'd need to move up there pretty much immediately."

"Congratulations."

"I turned it down."

His arms dropped to his sides. Maybe she should have made him sit, mess and all.

"What do you mean you turned it down? Isn't that exactly what you want?"

She shook her head. "No. It isn't what I want."

"Then you want to move to Phoenix?" His forehead scrunched in concern. "I thought you'd give anything not to go back."

"So did I. But I've been thinking a lot, and while I think I'm ready to start facing that part of my past, living in Pheonix isn't what I want either. I'm not moving back to Arizona."

"So, what is it you want? Where are you going?"

She sighed heavily and reached for his hand. He didn't pull away.

"I'm not going anywhere. I'm staying here in LA."

"What about the band? Isn't Edge breaking up? And my parents will be headed back to England in a few weeks. The guesthouse won't be ours anymore." His words toppled over one another as his concern took control. She squeezed his hand.

"I'll be joining a different band, one stationed out of Los Angeles. And this particular band happens to be renting a house together, so I'll be rooming with all of them from now on. Maybe you've heard of them—Blue Streetlights? They just won Twisted Fest, so they're kind of a big deal."

Noah sank onto the messy stool, flour poofing around him as he landed.

"You're joining Blue Streetlights? For good?" he finally got out.

"I asked Fitz to let me join today. We spent the whole afternoon talking it out. The pendejo said he'd count Twisted Fest as a formal audition. It's official as soon as you and Josh give your okay."

"The other drummer?"

"On her way to San Francisco."

Noah blinked quickly, his forehead scrunched in confusion.

"I thought you had to go back to Arizona if Edge lost. Was this an option from the beginning? Why wasn't this the plan all along?"

She sat on the stool beside him, gaze never leaving his.

"Because I couldn't imagine a life with you in it."

"With me?"

"You. And Josh and Fitz. And Cal and Keith for that matter." She smiled but it fell again almost instantly. Her every instinct shouted at her to shut up, to push him away instead of letting him further in. But she wasn't going to let that instinct win out any longer.

"I've spent the last three years doing everything I could to protect myself from getting hurt again, and keeping you away was my first priority. I never even considered the possibility that I could join Blue Streetlights permanently. Six weeks ago, the idea of living with the three of you would have been my worst nightmare."

"And now?" he breathed.

"And now, I want it more than anything." Her voice faltered. "I want *you* more than anything."

He said nothing. His eyes were locked on her face, filled with pure intensity and passion, but his hand, still holding her fingers, was gentle. His chest rose and fell like each breath was labored. She closed her eyes and confessed the truth she'd been hiding from even herself. Her words were barely a whisper, but in the heavy silence, she felt like she was shouting.

"I knew the second I met you that if I let you in, if I let you get too close, you'd become the person I couldn't live without"—she opened her eyes—"and I was right. I can't... I don't *want* to live without you. Even if it all blows up in the end. Even if you leave me or break my heart, I want to be with you." Her chin wobbled, and her arms were numb.

She loved him. She'd fought it and resisted it, but she could no longer deny it. He'd become her best friend, but even she knew that what they had was more than that.

Noah said nothing. He studied her, studied the kitchen around them, and finally landed on the cake she'd almost forgotten she'd made for him.

"Can we eat it?" he asked, solidly not responding to her declaration.

"Of course." She circled the island and retrieved

two forks from the drawer. She handed one to him but didn't return to her seat.

Noah stuck his fork directly into the chocolate cake, scooping up an enormous forkful and eating it in one bite. She watched him lick his fork clean. Her skin heated.

"Why did you make me a cake?" he asked.

She shrugged, but Noah waited. He was pushing her, challenging her like he always did. She loved him even more for it. Finally, she caved.

"Because that's what *you* do, isn't it? You bake for your family. For your friends. You bake for the people you love."

"For you."

"For me." She swallowed the dryness in her mouth.

He set his fork down on the counter, stood, and moved slowly toward her, leaning on the counter for support. He gripped her chin between his fingers and tilted it up to him.

"I want to be very clear about something, luv. Going back to England was never about the band. It was about you. It was always about you."

He closed the gap between their lips. Every nerve in her body erupted. If it was possible to die of happiness, she was sure today would be her last day on earth. He cupped her face tenderly, weaving his other hand through her hair. She kissed him back with everything she had.

Noah had been right. The rush, the thrill, the adventure of the life she'd been living could never hold up to this.

A throat cleared behind them. Their lips broke apart, but Noah didn't immediately step away. His face remained only inches from hers, his hands cradling her face, his chest heaving.

"Don't think we're done here." He growled low enough only she could hear him. Fire shot through her once more, and she nearly pulled him back against her.

The throat cleared again.

"You two animals think you could save it or do we need to come back later?" Josh asked from the doorway. Fitz leaned against the wall behind him, a look of arrogant satisfaction on his face.

Noah took a purposeful step back before ripping his gaze from her to look at Josh.

"The two of you have excellent timing." Noah smirked at Josh. The look was so unlike him that Fallon actually laughed.

"The three of us." Fitz motioned behind him with his head. "Elliott's in the car."

"We figured he better wait out there. We were afraid Fallon would kill him if he set foot in her house." Josh looked at her, and then his eyes widened as he took in the mess that she'd created in what was normally a very clean kitchen.

"Looks like Fallon told you the news?" Fitz asked. His leather jacket was nowhere to be seen. Instead, he wore a fitted maroon T-shirt that was doing him all kinds of favors. "She's in. The house will be ours by the end of the month."

"She told me. We had cake to celebrate." Noah winked at her.

"Did you save us some?" Josh grabbed one of the forgotten forks from the counter and dove into the cake.

"I wouldn't recommend that," Noah answered as Josh shoved the bite into his mouth. He immediately grimaced. "I tried to warn you. It's terrible."

"Hey!" Fallon smacked his arm. "It was not! I tried some of the frosting!"

"It tasted fine, luv." Noah wove his fingers through hers and kissed the back of her hand. "But it was the texture of paste."

Fitz chuckled quietly to himself.

"Alright, that's enough out of the two of you." Josh swallowed dramatically and rolled his eyes. "Is this what it's going to be like when we're all living together?"

"One can only hope," Noah said against her lips before he kissed her again.

EPILOGUE

"You sure you want me here?" Noah squeezed her hand as they walked together over the thick green grass.

"I'm sure."

They caught sight of her parents a few rows over walking toward them. Lisa and Manuel Rivera approached and hugged them both.

Noah kept her hand in his but shook Manuel's with his other.

"Nice to finally meet you in person, sir." Noah had hit it off immediately with her parents, and after all the Sunday video calls he'd been a part of over the last few weeks, they knew him as well as if he lived down the street.

"You as well. How was your flight?" her father asked him.

"Smooth as can be. We'll head to the house after this, but Fallon wanted to come here first."

It was true. Noah had recommended dropping their stuff off on the way, but she wouldn't hear of it.

"We'll see you soon, then." Her father nodded once to Noah before locking eyes with her. The love she found gazing back at her strengthened her resolution to see this through.

"Good to see you," Lisa smiled at them, eyes glistening. Her parents linked arms and strolled casually down the row of headstones toward the parking lot.

"Keep going?" Noah asked once they were alone again.

"Keep going."

They crested a small hill, and Fallon froze. The air rushed from her lungs and her throat tightened as she gazed over a small lake, lotus flowers blanketing the surface. Pinks and yellows glowed in the Phoenix sun, and her heart felt as though it might burst.

She led Noah down the hill toward the edge of the water. Only a few feet away, she found what she had come for.

A clean, smooth stone shimmered in the grass.

Annora Lisa Rivera

Fallon smiled.
"Hey, Sis."

ACKNOWLEDGEMENTS

I first met Fallon when I was writing my debut novel, *Chasing California.* She's only around for a few pages, but that's all it took for her to convince me she needed to tell her story. Since then, this novel has been my passion project, but it wouldn't have made it to the page without the help and support of many people.

Above all, I must thank my husband, Philip, and our children for their endless support of my dreams. I love you.

Thank you to my magnificent editor, Julia Allen. Your notes and feedback are invaluable.

Thank you to my critique partner, Caitlin, for responding to the many, many video messages I left along the way and for being the voice of reason when I wasn't so sure I would ever find the right words to tell Fallon's story.

And thank you to my wonderful friends and family. Your excitement for my work keeps me motivated when the going gets tough.

ABOUT THE AUTHOR

Born and raised in northern Utah, Annie has spent her whole life surrounded by books. She began writing her first novel in third grade and eventually earned a Masters in English. Now she teaches high school English and loves it.

Annie is obsessed with musical theatre, snowy days, her hubby and kiddos, and diet soda.

You can find Annie online:
www.anniejakes.com
Instagram: anniejakesauthor